PANIC!

The snow was cold and deep. And there was no one to meet her at the station. Tasha stumbled blindly through the drifts.

A fear gripped her! Snow killed people sometimes. They froze to death in it. She caught her breath and called desperately for help.

"Here—" She stopped suddenly. A tall dark figure loomed above her and one bright eye stared into her face, a great burning eye that seemed to be looking down into her very soul...

Bantam Books by Grace Livingston Hill
Ask your bookseller for the books you have missed

Grace Livingston Hill

THE
GOLD
SHOE

This low-priced Bantam Book
has been completely reset in a type face
designed for easy reading, and was printed
from new plates. It contains the complete
text of the original hard-cover edition.
NOT ONE WORD HAS BEEN OMITTED.

THE GOLD SHOE
*A Bantam Book / published by arrangement with
J. B. Lippincott Company*

PRINTING HISTORY
Lippincott edition published 1930
Bantam edition / June 1976

ISBN 0-553-02515-5

Published simultaneously in the United States and Canada

Bantam Books are published by Bantam Books, Inc. Its trade-
mark, consisting of the words "Bantam Books" and the por-
trayal of a bantam, is registered in the United States Patent
Office and in other countries. Marca Registrada. Bantam
Books, Inc., 666 Fifth Avenue, New York, New York 10019.

PRINTED IN THE UNITED STATES OF AMERICA

Chapter I

Anastasia Endicott shivered and drew her velvet evening wrap closer about her shoulders, as she sat forward in the Pullman chair and tried to look through the snow-blotched window at her side.

The train seemed to be crawling, like a baffled invalid that gained a few inches and then stopped to cough. It had been going on that way for an hour, and did not seem to be getting anywhere. It was outrageous, such service! A ride of only thirty-five miles taking all this time! What would her friends think of her? They would be waiting in their car at the station, and in such a storm!

But surely the train must be almost there!

She glanced down anxiously at the little trifle of platinum and diamonds on her wrist that stood for a time piece, and then out the baffling window again; but no friendly light outside illumined the blanket of snow that covered the glass, and she shivered again.

How cold it was!

She leaned down and touched the heat pipes that ran along under the window, and drew back with a shudder. They were cold as stone. The heat had gone out! How unpardonable in the railroad company to let a thing like that happen on such a cold stormy night!

She leaned forward and summoned the official who was passing rapidly through the car, speaking in a tone of accusation as if the fault belonged to him personally.

"Yes, Miss," he said, "fire's out. She's broke. We're trying to patch her up, but we can't make much headway. Something wrong with her connections. This ain't the only car is cold, Miss; the whole train is in the same fix."

She felt the lack of sympathy in his cold blue eyes as he started on again. She resented his suggestion that others were suffering. What had that to do with her?

"When are we going to get to Stonington?" she asked sharply. "We've been an hour and a quarter already from the city and this train is scheduled to do it in fifty-five minutes."

"Not on a night like this, Miss," said the brakeman. "Schedules ain't in it. The snow plow is ahead of us, and it's stuck in a drift high as a house. We got twelve men out there shoveling an' the wind blowin' forty knots a minute."

"But I'm going to a dance!" said the girl stupidly. "I shall be late!" Her voice was most impatient. "And I'm freezing!" she added and shivered again visibly.

The brakeman grinned.

"Better have yer dance in here then an' keep warm!" he advised. "There's a man in the next car goin' to his dyin' child!" His tone was significant, and he passed out of the car and slammed the door.

She was alone in the parlor car. The only other occupant had gone out to help with the shoveling. She drew her velvets closer and shuddered back into the plush of the chair, drawing her feet up and tucking one under her to get it warm. Then she remembered her delicate dance frock and put it quickly down again.

Dying child! What did he want to tell her that for? How horrid of him when he knew she was going to a dance. A dance and a dying child did not fit together. Oh, how cold it was! Why had she not brought her fur coat? But she had counted on driving back in the Lymans' limousine with her friend Adrienne, and there were always plenty of fur robes in the Lymans' car. She had not dreamed of being cold. She had come to the station in a taxi from her overheated home; there had been heat in the taxi.

The parlor car was always warm enough in her experience and she felt ill-used that it had suddenly failed her. She was expecting to be met at her journey's end by a heated limousine and conveyed to the country house some five miles from the station, where the dance was to be held. There really had been no need for a fur coat, for her evening wrap was lined with rich silk and warmly interlined.

She glanced helplessly about her. She had no hand baggage save a delicate beaded bag containing her compact, handkerchief, and gloves.

She had arrived home from a trip to Washington but that afternoon, to find awaiting her this invitation to a dance at a friend's magnificent country estate; had telephoned her friend Adrienne Lyman who was also an invited guest and arranged to return with her, and her friends; had dressed hurriedly, been driven to this train just in time, and here she was! Shivering! Snow banks on every side!

It began to occur to her that the return trip might not be so easy even in Adrienne's big limousine. Why, if a great iron train on a railroad track found it difficult going, how could an automobile manage? But then, railroads were different of course. Railroads had drifts on them. They went out in the country through queer places where there were winds that blew a lot and made a very little snow seem much. Of course a track got clogged up sooner than just a road where cars were going back and forth all the time. And the road between Stonington and the city was a main highway, with a great deal of traffic. Of course there wouldn't be any trouble in getting home.

She took her delicate handkerchief and mopped away at the window pane, breathing on the glass, trying to melt the clogging feathers and see through to the storm, but everything seemed a blot of impenetrable whiteness.

She settled back disconsolately into her cold chair and felt more like crying than she had since she was a child and broke her doll. To think that she, Tasha Endicott, should be caught in a fix like this! And then, just as she was in despair the brakeman came back through the car, slamming the door after him and stamping off snow from his feet. He gave her a familiar grin as he passed her, and lurched on out at the other end, slamming that door too. She felt a helpless fury rise within her. The impertinence! For a man like that to presume to grin at her in that leering triumphant way! He ought to be reported and discharged. She would tell her father about it. He should be discharged!

She got up and tried to walk up and down the aisle, stamping her gold slippered feet impatiently, trying to bring back life into them. It would be awful if she got her feet frost bitten. How could she dance? It was very painful to have frost bitten feet!

Then, without warning, the train gave a great lurch which sent her in a little rustling heap of rose color and gold in the aisle.

Angry and dishevelled she arose quickly, for a sudden draft of air told her that someone had opened the door; and looking anxiously she saw the grinning brakeman with a lantern in his hand, standing in the open door, a twinkle of merriment in his eyes.

More furious than ever she essayed to be seated, with dignity, but just at that instant the train gave another tremendous lurch that precipitated her into her chair in a hurry and completely robbed the act of all dignity. In fact one gold slipper flew off in the aisle and she had to catch herself with inglorious haste to keep from sliding back onto the floor again.

She did not look up at the brakeman again, but when she had rescued and donned her slipper she felt that the door was closed and she was alone. Also, she realized that the train was moving once more slowly, creakingly, but steadily with a pause now and then, and a lurch, but moving.

They had gone perhaps a hundred yards or more when the train slowed down and stopped with something of its old decision, and the door opened and the brakeman called out:

"Stonington! Stoooooo-ning-toooon! All out for Stonington!"

Tasha arose hastily, excitedly, and made her shaky way down the aisle. She seemed somehow weak in the knees, and trembling. Perhaps it was the fall, or her anger. She came to the platform, and the obnoxious brakeman with his lantern stood on the bottom step looking as if he meant to assist her.

She stiffened and threw her shoulders back.

"Is this really Stonington?" she asked sharply, trying to peer into the blear of blanket whiteness that constituted the air. It had not been snowing like this in town when she started. At least she had not noticed that it was so thick.

"Yep!" answered the brakeman. "Jump, an' I'll put you over where the snow ain't so deep."

Tasha drew back.

"Where is the porter?" she asked haughtily.

"Out shovelin'!" said the brakeman. "Better jump quick ef you wanta git off. We ain't stoppin' long!"

Tasha advanced to the steps and looked down into the sea of whiteness, then drew back again:

"Why, this is outrageous!" she said crisply. "The railroad company has no right to stop in a place like this. Where is the platform? I'd rather go to the other end of the car."

"Say, Miss, ef you don't git off here you git carried to Elkins station. We're only 'commodation this far, and then we're 'xpress. You sure you wanta git off at Stonington?"

"I certainly do!" she said freezingly. "But I want you to go and get the porter for me!"

A snort from the engine and a slight lurch of the train broke upon the conversation.

"Nothin' doin'!" said the brakeman. "Either you git off ur you don't!"

He gave a quick glance around, peering beyond the station into the white darkness.

"Say, Miss, is anyone meeting you? Because this station is closed for the night."

"There certainly is someone meeting me," said Tasha, still haughtily.

The brakeman cast another uncertain glance about, and saw a tiny spark of light wavering toward them several rods away.

"Oh, all right then!" he said with a relieved tone, "here you go! We ain't got any more time for fooling!" and to her horror he caught her in his burly arm like a bundle of baggage and swung her across the steps and far out over the billows of whiteness, setting her down under what seemed like a great shadow, in comparative shelter, where only a few of the stinging snowflakes cut into her unprotected face, and bit her lips and her eyes. And then he was gone, clinging to the lower step of the car, his lantern swinging out into the white storm, signaling to some force in the impenetrable whiteness beyond. She saw him moving slowly away from her, leaving her in sudden awful loneliness.

It had all happened so quickly that she had not realized. The chill of the snow on her silken ankles seemed to enfold her as if she were in the grasp of a new and awful power. She realized that she was standing almost knee deep in snow, and she tried to take a step out of it, but nowhere was there a shallower place to put her foot.

In new horror she cried out and tried to run toward the train that was slipping past her now with its lighted windows, the very window where her breath a few minutes before had melted a black circle on the pane, was leering mockingly down upon her now like a bright eye, and her soul suddenly knew how safe and warm she had been inside and how fearfully perilous was her present position. She cried again and waved her arms toward the brakeman whose lantern was giving its final swing, as he jerked himself in out of the storm, but her voice was flung back upon the blanket stillness and frightened her the more.

The tears were running down her cheeks and freezing as they fell, but she did not know it. She was stung to sudden panic and began to run after the train, but she fell in the first attempt and lay there helpless for a moment, her bare hands plunging elbow deep into the heavy snow, her face even going down into its smothering chill. Snow inside her flimsy inadequate garments, snow round her throat like icy fingers, snow in her eyes and her mouth and her hair, smothering, icy snow!

One of her little gold slippers, the loose one that had come off before, came off again and was lost in the whiteness. The snow bit into the little gold silk foot that felt in vain for its covering.

Tasha cried aloud and knew not what she said as she sobbed, but it seemed to come to her dimly through it all that there was no one by to help her and she must help herself. She had never had to help herself in any trying situation before, but now she must. There had always been servants, or persons whose business it was to care for her, close at hand, in any predicament before. Now she was alone! It was somebody's fault of course that she was, and they should suffer for it when she got home, but now she must take care of herself. Home! Would she ever be home again? A fear gripped her! Snow killed people sometimes. They froze to death in it. Even now she could feel it would be easier to lie still and sink, sink, and forget it all. She was so cold! Oh, how her feet hurt! She wouldn't be able to dance to-night! But that didn't matter! Oh, why didn't the chauffeur come after her? He must have seen her get off. Was he waiting around the other side of the station?

She looked up and the dark shadow of a snow draped building loomed above her. She must get up and find that slipper. She must get around to the other side of the station quickly before the chauffeur decided she hadn't come and went home without her. She must! She must!

She called as she struggled to her feet:

"Hello! Hello! I'm here! Wait! Wait! I'm coming!" But the wind caught her voice and flung it back into her own ears, and the snow flung a blanket over the echo too so that she knew she had not been heard.

At last she got to her feet again, her poor insensate feet, and then with a mighty resolve, she clutched around in the snow with her bare hands until she came upon the little slipper. She drew it to her breast and hugged it with her bead purse as if it were something precious, and turned stumbling, cautious, moving slowly, with difficulty, toward the station till she almost fell against the stone wall, and her feet came unexpectedly upon shallower going. She stood for an instant to get her breath, leaning against the wall, and finding that the wind here did not swoop and search her quite so violently, as out by the tracks. Perhaps if she could get around to the other side it might be even more sheltered. Oh, why did they close stations in places like this! If she could only get inside the door!

But when she reached the other side of the building and came unexpectedly in contact with a latch she found it would not open. She stood within the doorway, braced against it, one little gold slipper and her bead bag still pressed against her breast, one little icy foot drawn up against her cold cold knee. The other icy foot was trying to balance on a tiny gold spike of a heel, and one slender arm was frantically clutching the big bronze knob of the closed door for support as she tried to peer into the blank whiteness beyond.

But nowhere could she see a sign of a car! It was all a level whiteness, earth and air and sky, all full of whirling whiteness, stinging and snatching and biting at her, and how long could she hold out?

Suddenly out of the terrible white darkness before her a light danced, glared and danced away again, like a new menace. Was it the headlight of a car? It did not seem large enough for that and yet as she looked, there it was again, still larger, glaring into her eyes like some beast of prey. She shook off the new fear that took hold of her. Of course it was the car which was to have come for her, and she must make them know where she was.

She lifted up her voice and shouted:

"Here! Here! Here I am!"

The wind flung her words down her throat. They

could not get by the blanket that hung between her and all human kind. It was silly! It was nightmare! She must rouse herself and make them hear or they would go away again and leave her here all night. She doubted not she was in the first stages of freezing, else why could she not get her words across to that stupid chauffeur? She must!

Down went the little cold gold chiffon-stockinged foot, into the feathery snow, almost comforted from the bitter cold above, and she caught her breath and called again:

"Heeee-rrrr!—"

But she stopped suddenly as a tall dark figure loomed above her and one bright eye stared into her face, a great burning eye that seemed to be looking down into her very soul.

Chapter II

"Why, what's all this?" said a great voice just above her. It wasn't the brakeman come back— Or was it? A great gust of wind came hurricaning round the corner of the station and filled her mouth and her eyes with stifling flakes, and she was almost strangled. Then the hurricane and the snow seemed suddenly shut out. It grew more luminous about her, and the big voice was shouting through the storm over her head.

"Are you waiting for the train? How ever did you get here? It's outrageous to close the station on a night like this!"

She was aware of a pair of kindly eyes shrouded in snow, bushy white eyebrows, cheeks plastered with flakes; eyelashes, too, fringed white. The rest was covered with a woolen scarf bound firmly about head and neck. But the sight of another human being suddenly broke her down. Even if it had been the impertinent brakeman she couldn't have helped it.

"Oh, I'm soooo-ccc-ooo-llldddd!" she chattered, more tears flowing over the icicles on her face, "I can't find the ca-ca-ca-rrrr-r!" she babbled feebly.

"What car?" asked the apparition, glancing keenly about the white distance.

"The Framstead c-c-arrrr!" answered Tasha trying to keep her teeth from chattering. "They promised to be here when the train came in!" There was a wail in the end of her words.

"Framstead!" said the man in a startled tone. "They can't get down from Framstead's to-night! The bridge is down and the other road is impassable! It is drifted twelve feet at least!"

"Oh! What shall I do-o-o-o-oo!" cried Tasha in terror. "I'm freezing! My feet are dead now. I ca-ca-can't feel them any more at all. How l-l-l-long does it t-ake to fr-f-f-reeze?"

"You poor kid!" said the man stooping to lift her in his snowy arms, and feeling with one hand for her feet. "You poor little kid! No wonder! Why—you haven't but one shoe—! Well that settles it! We'll have to get inside here somehow at once. Just wait a minute and I'll get this door open!"

He set her down again in the snow, but she was not conscious of feeling any colder. It seemed that she was numb all over except for the sharp point of hurt where the cold was still aching and stinging.

She felt as if she were come to the end of life in a terrible way. She gave a pitiful thought back to the gayety that had been hers but a few short hours before, and wondered that her butterfly existence had been so short. But it didn't seem to matter any more; the cold was so terrible, as if it had her by the throat and were putting her out like a candle flame being snuffed.

She heard a crash of glass in the dark, and then saw the imp of light go flashing again and presently she was picked up and carried inside the little box of a station.

She felt the cessation of the storm, and the dry warm air of a room that had at least recently known fire, and then she was put down in the darkness on a wooden seat.

"Now," said the man, as he seemed to be moving about a few feet from her, "we've got to get you warm first. Whoever let you out a night like this with so few clothes on?"

Tasha giggled hysterically. She had forgotten her haughtiness. In this warm darkness with the roar of the storm shut away, she could no longer hold her pride.

"Haven't you any baggage with you?" asked the man's voice. He seemed to be shaking some heavy garment on the other side of the room. A spatter of snow reached viciously and hit her cheek. The room was a very small one.

"No," she said in answer to his question. "No," almost stupidly, "I am going to a dance!"

"Oh!" said the man almost shortly. "Some dance!"

Then he came over to where she was sitting in the dark, and almost roughly lifted her to wrap a great rough garment about her. "It must be his overcoat," she thought to herself, and tried to protest.

"You'll nnnn-eee-ddd it!" she chattered.

"Not as much as you do!" he said shortly. "Now, what can we do about these feet?"

"They are dead!" she said, and shivered in the roughness of the overcoat. "It won't matter."

The man stepped out the door and brought in a bag. He set it down on the floor and flashed his torch into it, searching for something. She watched him apathetically. The snow had melted from his features now, though they were still well swathed in brown woolen scarf.

"Not entirely dead yet," he answered as he laid the flash down on the floor and came toward her with something dark in his hand. He reached for her unslippered foot and began to rub it, finally tearing away the little rag of a gold silk chiffon stocking and chafing the foot with his big warm hands from which he had taken the heavy woolen mittens that now lay on the floor beside the flash light.

She watched him as if it were a sort of moving picture in which she had no part, but most surprisingly the foot began to feel alive again, and to prickle under the chafing. And when he had it quite dry and warm again he drew on a long thick woolen stocking, that came well up to her little cold knee.

"My mother insisted on my taking these golf stockings with me to-night," he meditated, "and now I'm glad I brought them."

Tasha did not say anything. She was wondering how she would look going through life with only one foot. One foot had come alive but the other was stone dead. And she was so cold all over in spite of the great rough overcoat that she felt as if she were made of ice with a hot hot fire inside of it.

"Now!" said the man, "that's better. Do you begin to feel a little more comfortable?" and he began his ministrations toward the other foot.

She did not see the look on his face as he unbuttoned and laid down the other little gold slipper, a mixture of awe and contempt upon him. He went on silently chafing the cold little foot till it too responded to treatment and came alive.

"Now," said he, "I suppose you'd like me to telephone to Framstead's. They'll be wondering what has become of you. We'll see whether I can pick the lock of the inner office and get at the telephone. What name shall I say?"

"Endicott," said Tasha stupidly, "Miss Endicott." Somehow the dance no longer seemed real. She was getting a little warm again in spots, and longed only to get somewhere and lie down to rest. She felt as if she had been battling against wild beasts.

There was a sound of some little metal instrument trying to force a lock. An interval of silence and the dancing flash light; more metal grinding against resisting locks, then the shudder of a thick door against a great forceful shoulder. Presently the man returned to her.

"Well, it's no use. I think there is a big bolt or bar to that door. Anyhow I can't budge it. I suppose they have to be extra careful for they keep a safe in there I think, and it is rather lonely around here."

"Oh, what shall I do? Shall I have to stay in this awful place all night? Are you going away?" she asked in sudden fright.

"No, you can't stay here," he said decidedly. "I'll have to take you home to Mother. There's no other house nearer where you could stay. I'll have time to take you back before my train gets here." He turned the flash light on his wrist watch now, and she could see his face studying the dial anxiously, then he lifted his wrist and listened.

"What train did you come on?" he asked suddenly. "Did you come up from the city?"

"Yes, on the six-five. But my train was late. We just got in. I had not been here but a few minutes when you came, though it seemed like hours it was so cold."

She shuddered at the memory, and realized that a slight sense of warmth was really stealing over her.

"Why?" she asked suddenly. "Is there a train back now? Oh, are you going to the city? I must go too. I can't stay here alone, since there is no way to get to Framstead's."

"No," he said gravely, "I'm not going to the city; I'm going up the road about fifty miles where I'm supposed to preach to-morrow. There is no train back to the city that stops at this station to-night. The only down train is an express and you have to go five miles up the road to get it. But I was thinking. If your train was as late as that, the next train will be still later. I shall have plenty of time to get back, but we can't lose a minute talking about it. I'll take you to Mother, but you'll have to do just as I say and be quick about it!"

Tasha had no time to resent this dictatorial

speech, for he came over, picked her up summarily, and slung her over his shoulder as if she had been a bag of meal.

"Excuse me," he said as she gasped. "It isn't very pleasant but it's the only way, and I simply must get that train."

She tried to struggle, to protest, to say she could not let him take so much trouble, but he strode to the door, and was out before she had finished a sentence.

"Your bag!" she called. "Stop! You must not leave your bag!"

"It's all right till I get back!" he shouted over his shoulder. "Lie still, can't you, and put your arm around my neck, that way. Now, keep your face down and you won't get the worst of the blast."

He plunged off the platform, and wallowed for a moment till he found the solid path, dancing the flash light ahead of him weirdly through the storm.

The girl gasped, and hid her face perforce on the broad shoulder that held her. The touch of the rough wool made her conscious that she was wearing this man's overcoat, and that he was unprotected himself. She tried to say something about this, but her words were flung back into the soft plush cold of the storm, and caught away into space. She made a feeble effort to reach the top button of the coat and show him that she wished to take it off, but he shouted back, "Lie still, can't you?" and struggled on.

And it was a struggle, she could see. Slender though she was and lightly clothed, yet wrapped in that great heavy overcoat she made a burden that was by no means easily carried through such going.

As her eyes became accustomed to the strange white darkness, she could peer out occasionally, and catch a glimpse of the depth of the drifts through which he had to wade. Up to his knees, above his knees sometimes. Once when he almost lost his footing and very nearly went down with her, she saw he had to lift her high above his head to keep her above the snow.

And the way seemed interminable.

He had said it was the nearest house, but how far away it seemed! Occasionally she thought of his train, and thought she heard the roar of its coming. But the darkness kept on being thick and white and impenetrable, and the little firefly of light danced on and made no impression except to illumine a step at a time.

It strangely did not enter her head to be afraid, even though she could not see the man who was carrying her, had never really got a view of his face, yet she knew she could trust him. It occurred to her that perhaps she was being kidnapped. Perhaps he might have seen the flash of her jewels at throat and wrist. But she dismissed that as foolish. If he had wanted her jewels it would have been easy to overpower her and take them, even to have killed her. There was no one by to see, and the snow would have covered all tracks by morning. No, she was strangely at peace, almost even interested, as she hung there over his shoulder, her arms clasped around his neck, trying to help all she could in the struggle he was having to take her to safety and warmth.

She was by no means warm even now, for the wind swooped around and roared down the neck of the overcoat, and even the thick golf stockings seemed but flimsy protection. But the feeling of the strength that bore her, helped her to bear the deadly cold that swirled all about her and chilled her to the heart; and when it grew too awful she could hide her face entirely and breathe through the thick rough wool of his coat, to gain a moment's respite from the agony of breathing in the cold.

It seemed a space set apart in her lifetime never to be forgotten, that journey through the storm on the shoulder of an unknown man. She was growing drowsy with the cold and excitement, and had ceased to wonder if it would never end, when she felt him turn sharply from the road, a pace or two, then up some snow-muffled steps to a porch, and stamp, and knock at the door.

"It's I, Mother, open the door please! I can't get at my key!" he called. She roused and noticed that he

was panting. How hard it must have been for him! And
he was in a hurry. It came to her that the minister of
their fashionable church in the city, which they attended semi-occasionally, would never have at-
tempted a thing like this, would not have been able
physically to carry it out if he had. Then hurrying
footsteps interrupted her thoughts and a flood of light
broke over the little porch, and blinded her eyes.

"Oh, my laddie!" she heard a sweet voice ex-
claim, "and what have you got? Did you lose your
train?"

"No, Mother, the train is late But I found this
alone in the snow at the station, and brought her to
you. Take care of her please, till the storm is over or I
get back, for now I must hurry."

He turned to the girl and began unbuttoning the
great coat, blinking his eyes that still were blinded
from coming into the light.

"I'll have to have my coat now, if you please,"
he said pleasantly, "and I hope I wasn't over rough
with you. I hope you'll not suffer from the exposure."

The coat fell away and she looked up and tried
to say the conventional thing—what was the conventional thing for such a time as this?—but she could
only blink and give a sorry little smile. Then her velvet
wrap slipped back, and fell away around her feet, and
she stood there in the bright little cottage room in her
rosy silk and tulle dance frock, like some lovely draggled flower plucked out of its garden.

The young man stepped back and looked at her
for an instant with a drawing in of his breath, for she
was lovely. Her delicate make-up was a wreck, with
the storm and her crying, her wisps of coral tulle were
trailing limply about her feet, her hair was tousled and
falling about her face, yet she was lovely, and he
looked.

His mother too, looked, and was filled with dismay.

"But—Thurly!—" she gasped, and the word
brought him to his senses.

He turned, picked up the coat from the floor, and swung into it with a single motion, buttoning it high around his chin which was still swathed in the brown woolen scarf.

"But Mother, I must go!" he said, "I've not an instant to waste. The lady will explain!" and he stooped and kissed his mother's forehead. "I'm all right, Mother! There's nothing to worry about."

"But, Thurly! The storm! It's so terrible! Just give it up and telegraph them it's impossible!" she pleaded, following him to the door. "Do, Thurly, do! For my sake!"

"But, Mother, you know we had all that out on our knees awhile back. You know I must go, dearest. Now away to the lady, for she's well nigh frozen and needs a hot drink at once, and warm blankets or she'll be ill!"

He smiled and was gone, and the mother stood for an instant watching him down the white path vanishing into the white darkness, till even the little twinkle of the flash light was invisible. Then the mother turned and shut the door and came back to her strange and unexpected guest.

Chapter III

Thurly Macdonald's mother was small and frail and gentle. Her sweet old face had grown lovely with age, like a well bred rose, with nevertheless a ruggedness about it that spoke of autumn frosts, and weathered winds, and a strong green vital stem.

She stood and faced this exotic girl that her son had suddenly thrust upon her, and her keen, far-seeing eyes read much in the one glance with which she swept her very soul, before she set to work to care for her.

The glance gave due tribute to the visitor's loveliness, to the exquisite texture and vivid coloring of her attire, but it went farther and seemed to analyze her character in one brief flash. Tasha felt suddenly unduly clothed. She shivered and tried to draw her cloak up from the floor.

"But we must get you warm at once!" said her hostess, flinging open a closet door, and drawing out a thick warm plaid shawl, so old and soft that it gave pleasure to the touch.

She wrapped it around the girl and tucked her up on the couch:

"Why, you poor little lassie," she said in a sudden tenderness. "You're all of a tremble! Wait, I'll get some blankets and a hot water bag. We'll soon have you warm."

She hurried into the kitchen and set the hot water running, then upstairs and came down with her arms full of big soft blankets. It was incredible how fast a little old lady could move, and how much she could accomplish in a brief moment.

"We'll just lift this off!" she said crisply as she came back to the girl who was struggling to control the shaking chill which had seized her as the warmth of the room began to penetrate her senses.

She seemed to know just how to get off the wisp of rose silk and tulle, even though its intricacies must have been strange to her, and she did not gasp at the brief silk trifles that were revealed beneath, though their brevity must have shocked her. With just a few motions she had the girl arrayed in a long, warm flannelette nightgown, one of the old fashioned kind with long sleeves and a high neck. It was probably the first of its kind the girl had ever seen, and certainly the first she had ever worn; but she shuddered into its folds gratefully, and was glad of the big blankets that were tucked close about her. With a hot water bag at her feet and another against her back she presently began to feel a sense of delicious warmth, and the great shudders which had shaken her began to relax. But it was not until the cup of hot tea was given her that she really began to feel comfortably warm once more.

"Now," said Mrs. Macdonald eyeing her keenly, "you'll be wanting something more substantial. When did you eat last?"

"Oh," said the girl remembering, "why, I was going to dinner, a dinner dance it was. It was to have been at eight thirty. It must be more than that now." She dropped her head back wearily and snuggled into the blankets. "But don't bother. I'm not the least bit hungry. I had lunch on the train coming up from the South. I'd rather have another cup of that nice tea."

Mrs. Macdonald gave her another searching look and vanished into the kitchen, whence she returned in an incredibly short space of time with a tempting tray.

"Thurly and I had an oyster stew for supper tonight, just for a treat," she said as she drew a small table to the side of the couch and put the tray upon it. "This hot broth will keep you from taking cold."

The girl saw a sprigged china bowl the steaming fragrance of whose contents made her know suddenly that she was hungry. There was a plate of delicately browned buttered toast, a tiny mound of ruby jelly, some crisp hearts of celery, and the cup of tea. She sat up almost briskly and did full justice to it, still enveloped in her blankets.

"I didn't know I was so hungry," she said gratefully. "But I'm sorry I have made you so much trouble. I really ought to get in touch with my home and have the chauffeur come for me—"

"But, my dear!" said Mrs. Macdonald glancing significantly toward the window. "No chauffeur could get through the drifts to-night. This is a blizzard, you know. I have sore anxiety over my son going out in this terrible storm. I tried hard to keep him from attempting it, but now I see it was the Lord's will, for he tells me you would have perished if someone had not helped you."

"Oh!" said the girl, a kind of gray horror filling

her face. "Yes, it was awful!" and she shivered at the memory. "Yes, I really didn't know what to do. The snow went inside my clothes, and my slipper came off—"

"You poor little dear—!"

But Anastasia Endicott was not accustomed to pity from anyone, not since her long gone baby days, and the sound of this gentle voice calling her a poor little dear brought a rush of quite involuntary tears. She could not understand such weakness in herself. She considered herself to be quite "hard boiled."

"I don't know why I'm doing this," she said, trying to pass it off with a laugh, and mopping her eyes like a little girl with her pink flannelette sleeve.

"There, there, little dear," said Mrs. Macdonald, "you're all fagged out with the storm. Thurly said it was terrible! Here, let me get you a nice warm wash rag and wash your face. Then you'll feel better!"

She came with the soft wet cloth and a towel that smelled of lavender, and washed the girl's face and wiped it as if she had been a little child. A soothed sense of love and care swept over the young thing that filled her with a strange yearning for something she had never known.

"Now, finish your soup, darling, and we'll get you to bed," said the elder woman comfortably.

And Tasha obediently did as she was told.

"It's a great pity we can't telephone your folks. Our telephone seems to be out of order," said her hostess. "Will your mother worry about you? Will the Framstead people send her word you have not arrived?"

The girl laughed, a hard, sharp little laugh full of a bitter mirth that did not belong in the elder woman's world. She looked at the girl startled, with the same doubt and trouble in her eyes that had been there when she first viewed the lovely little made-up face, and the drabbled rosy finery.

"Lucia worry about me?" she mocked. "Not so you'd know it. She never concerns herself in the least about me!"

Then she saw the shocked sadness in the face of her hostess and explained:

"I haven't any real mother you know. Lucia's only a step. At least I guess that's what you'd call her. Dad's been divorced twice, and Lucia's the second mistake, though she's not quite so bad as Clarice was. She was impossible. My first mother married an army officer and she's stationed in India. I haven't seen her since I was four years old. Dad hated her so for the way she went away that he got the court to fix it so I couldn't go to her till I'm of age. But I'm not keen about her. I doubt if she remembers me any more. I'll be of age next summer, but I don't think I shall bother with her. Why should I? She went off and left me, didn't she? And India really never attracted me much. I'd rather stick to Dad."

Mrs. Macdonald had lowered her eyes as at something indecent and began slowly going about the room dusting the furniture with her best pocket handkerchief in an absent-minded, careful way, not realizing what she was doing.

"Oh, my dear!" said Mrs. Macdonald, brushing away something like a tear from the corner of her eye, as Tasha wound up her tale. "Oh, my little lost lamb!"

The girl looked at her half perplexed. Here seemed to be something sweet offered her which she did not quite understand.

"Oh, it's all right," she said carelessly. "Lucia isn't half bad. She lets me alone and I let her alone. We get on finely. The only thing I can't stand is when she borrows my car without asking me, but Dad has stopped that now. He told her he'd get her a new town car if she'd let mine alone."

There was silence in the room while the girl finished the last bite of toast and jelly, and drank her tea. Thurly's mother was working thoughtfully with the books between the book ends on the little mahogany center table, changing them elaborately, the blue one next the gold and brown, the red leather cover against the green leather; and then back again, studying them, as if their arrangement mattered. At last she lifted her sweet eyes to the girl and smiled.

"I wonder?" she said. But she did not say what she wondered. The girl felt as if she would like to know, as if it might be something that mattered.

Then the elder woman turned briskly, sweeping all other considerations aside.

"We must get you to bed!" she said. "You've been through a great strain, and got a terrible chill. You must get tucked up all nice and warm and sleep it off. We'll talk about it in the morning."

A great-blast of wind swept round the house, and a little visible drift of snow peppered in around the edges of the front window. The girl saw the mother glance toward the front windows, with a quick anxious frown. Suddenly she realized that her rescuer was out there in the storm again, and there came a pull at her heart at the thought of breathing that cold cold air, and breasting those drifts that long way back to the station. Where was he now? Had he reached the train in time, and was he riding safely to some other place? For what?

She voiced her thought.

"Why did your son go out again? He ought not to have gone!" She drew her own brows and looked anxiously toward the window.

"He had to go, lassie. He was on the Lord's errand. The Father will care for him."

There was something beautiful and trustful in the woman's face, a kind of silver radiance. The girl looked at her wonderingly, and said:

"Oh, is his father out there? What is he doing? What can anybody do in such a storm as this?"

"He rides upon the wings of the storm," was the astonishing answer. The girl looked and the silver radiance was still there. The woman was not crazy for she had a lovely smile in her eyes, like one who talks in tender enigmas.

"If his father is out there why doesn't he come in?" persisted the girl impatiently. She did not like enigmas. They baffled her.

The woman turned from the window and gave her a sweet full look, the silver radiance changing to a golden smile.

"He *is* here, my child. I mean the Father, God!"

The girl stared. She did not sneer as she might have done at another time. She did not mock and say there was no God, as she had often felt in her heart. There was something in the woman's look that prevented any such thought. It was a great bright assurance. She had spoken with the conviction of one who has seen with her own eyes.

"Now, we will go up to the little room upstairs, dearie. Can you walk? I should have made Thurly carry you aloft before he left, only he had so little time, poor laddie."

"Oh, I can walk!" cried Tasha and essayed to spring up, but found her knees strangely weak, and a great inertia upon her.

"It's queer!" she said, catching hold of a chair shakily. "I feel as if I hadn't any power to move! I shouldn't have made much of a show at that dance, even if I'd got there. I didn't imagine just getting cold could make a person feel this way."

"There's a mighty power in cold," said Mrs. Macdonald, slipping her arm around the girl and helping her up the stairs. "You know the Bible says: 'Who can stand against His cold?' "

"Does it?" asked the girl coldly. "How queer! I never read the Bible. It's such a big book. I never thought it would be interesting."

"Oh, but it is, dearie. It has a many hidden treasures. You ought to take a dip into it and see. After you've had a good sleep I'll show you a few."

Tasha yawned and dropped down upon the bed gratefully. It had seemed quite a journey up those stairs.

The little white room was cheery with a border of roses at the top of the wall, and roses on the little white painted set of furniture. The bed had a white starched valance clean and crisp, and a gay patchwork quilt dimpled with infinitesimal stitches in intricate pat-

tern, and when it was turned back there were soft
white blankets with pink bindings. There was a little
rocking chair with a pink flannel cushion, and a small
lamp on the dressing bureau with a pink crêpe-paper
shade, that shed a rosy light on the white linen cover.
There were quaint hooked and braided rugs on the
floor, soft and warm, and a few pictures about the
walls. One was merely a text beautifully lettered and
framed: "WITH GOD ALL THINGS ARE POSSIBLE." What
a strange thing to put on a wall! But there was a
lovely painting of a sunset on a summer evening, and
a water color of a shepherd on a hillside with his
sheep; and across the room over the white painted
desk was a photograph of a young giant in football
regalia. There was a haunting familiarity in the eyes
that looked out laughing from the picture that caught
her gaze.

Tasha wondered at the little room, so simple,
with its white ruffled curtains against the white snow
covered windows, yet so restful. Then she lay down
on the soft bed, let her hostess tuck the pink and white
blankets around her, and pull up the patchwork quilt,
and somehow she felt more like sleeping than she had
felt for months. What a quaint sweet place she had
fallen upon! How did it come to be hidden away so
near to the rushing world of excitement.

"Now, lassie, we'll just have a bit of a prayer,"
said Mrs. Macdonald, as simply as she had brought
the cup of tea, and kneeling down beside the astonished girl she spoke as to One close beside her:

"Now Father we thank Thee that Thou hast
brought this stray lamb safe in out of the storm, and
we commend her to Thy care and keeping. Give her
sweet refreshing sleep, grant new strength for the morrow, and may she know what it is to be a child of the
Heavenly Father. We ask it for Christ's sake. Amen."

Gentle lips pressed a kiss lightly on the girl's forehead, and then the light was snapped off.

"Now, lassie, I'll be in the next room and I'll hear
you in case you call. I'll just close the door to, but not
tight. Then you'll not be disturbed by the light in the

the wildness of the storm. One could hear nothing but the roar of the wind. He must be ready to signal them to stop, for it might be that on such a night the engineer would not think it worth while to stop at a little station like Stonington, unless he carried passengers who wanted to get off there. Things were not going by schedule of course. But he must husband his flash light, for he might have a long wait and it would be his only means of signaling to the train.

As he stooped to snap his grip shut his light fell upon a small gleaming object that gave back the light in a hundred delicate facets. Startled, he went over to it, and picked it up. A little gold slipper, with a gleaming slide of flashing white stones on the strap! The girl's lost slipper!

He had almost forgotten the girl in his own struggle with the elements, and his anxiety to get to his appointment in time. Now the memory of it all rushed back upon him with a thrill of wonder as he stood and held that frail gold foot covering, and studied it carefully, forgetful of his wasting battery. How curious it was, how intricately, yet fragilely formed! A bright spike of a heel, a tiny pointed shelter for a lovely foot, a few gilded straps and a cluster of sparkling stones! That was called a shoe! And that girl had stepped out into this awful storm shod in a trifle like this!

His face grew stern as he stood in the shadowed station, the flash light in one hand and the little gold slipper in the other.

The wind swooped down upon the solid little building and boomed along its trig tight roof in vain, but the sound startled the young man, and reminded him that he must save his flash light.

He snapped it off quickly and put it in his pocket where he could reach it instantly. But the little gold shoe he held in his bare hand as he paced to and fro, thinking about the girl, and how cold she must have been. Thinking of the chill of those little frozen feet in their silken covering when he rubbed them into life again and swathed them in his heavy golf stockings.

He was glad he had had them with him, glad his mother put them into his bag. He would be grateful for them now himself, for his feet were getting numb. He sat down to rest himself, and kept on thinking about those little cold feet, and his own grew colder. He got up and began to pace the floor again, and became aware that his hands were bare and cold. He had forgotten to put on his gloves again.

The little slipper was in his way and he stuffed it into the breast of his coat while he dived into his big coat pocket and got out his warm woolen gloves. He laughed to himself about that slipper as he drew on his gloves. Suppose the train should suddenly come, and he have to run for it, with the slipper inside his coat, nd suppose the slipper fell out in the train! What a l gh the conductor would have on him! And the other assengers if there were any on a night like this! A gol n slipper in the breast of a young minister's coat! Suppose some of his fellow classmates should hear of it! He of all fellows in the class, to carry a golden slipper in his breast! He who had always fought shy of girls! Who had no use for the modern girl! Who had never had time nor money to hunt up a girl who was not modern. Who had scarcely any faith that there were any left that were worth hunting for! Carrying around a gold slipper in his coat! He laughed aloud at himself, and then hushed again. It was as if he had been rude to the girl who so short an hour ago had sat in this very room with him; whom he had rescued from what might have been an awful death of a bright young thing that God had made.

Awe came upon him. After all, these girls that he had despised and shunned were living souls for whom Christ had died. And probably not for nothing had he been left to meet this special one in the storm and carry her home to his mother.

Ah! His mother! A satisfaction filled his heart. His mother would know what to do. His mother would help the pretty child if she needed help. She had started to a dance, but God had turned her aside by a few snow flakes and sent her to his mother! Well, all would be well. He thought of her as he had seen her with the coats slipped off and the rose petal frock billowing about her, a lovely child! A strange thrill filled his breast. The touch of the little gold shoe became magnetic. For an instant a beautiful fleeting vision filled his mind. Ah! She was lovely! He was glad that she was with his mother! She was a child of the world, and not for his admiration, of course, but he was glad that such a lovely young soul could come into contact with his mother even for an hour.

He would probably never see her again, but mayhap some day she would come home to God, led by his mother's touch, his mother's prayers. And he would have been the humble instrument to bring her to such leading! A strange gladness filled his soul, and grew as he thought about it! It would be a great thing to lead a lovely soul like that to God!

But what should he do with the shoe? Keep it of course somehow, and take it back home. The girl would be gone Monday morning when he got back, but his mother would have found out her address, and anyhow, if she had not he could send it up to Framstead and say he had found it in the station, and that it belonged to the young woman who had come on the evening train in the storm.

Yet he walked several times back and forth in the station with that little gold shoe in the breast of his coat, as if he hated to put it out in the cold again; as if keeping it warm were somehow keeping the girl warm too, and undoing some of the cold she had suffered.

Then his clear mind got the upper hand.

"Fool!" he said. "What are you dreaming about? Fool!" He turned on the light, went to his bag and thrust that little warm gold slipper down beneath his heavy flannelette pajamas at the very bottom of the bag, put his Scofield Bible on the very top, and snapped the bag shut with a click.

"There!" said he aloud. "That's the end of that incident. Now, I'll think of my sermon. This is a splendid place to preach!" and so he went walking up and down, preaching aloud to the storm, shouting out thunderous sentences against worldliness, uttering tender pleadings for repentance, growing eloquent at times. Till suddenly he realized that he was really preaching to that girl, calling to her from the side of God's children, to give up her frivolous life as typified by those trifling dance slippers, and come where joy and peace and safety abounded. His voice was yearning and tender, and he seemed to be looking into her blue eyes. He stopped, astounded.

"This is most extraordinary!" he said to himself sternly. "My mind must have been affected by the storm. I must have hit my head on that tree harder than I knew! I never had such a foolish obsession before!"

So he buttoned his coat to the chin and went out in the storm to investigate the tracks once more, but the snow was coming with just as driving a force, and the wind was slanting the drifts on the road bed, till one never would have known there had been a track there, or that a train had ever gone through that part of the country. He soon came back to his refuge, and began his pacing again, and this time he fortified his mind with repeating scripture. Chapter after chapter, verse after verse, but somehow he always seemed to be repeating it to that little girl. The memory of her shivering form upon his shoulder, and the feel of her small arms about his neck seemed wonderfully sweet and dependent to him. Till suddenly he came to a stand still, and lifted his eyes up.

"God!" said he aloud, "what do you want me to do about this?"

Then straightway he fell upon his knees beside the bench where Tasha had sat while he ministered to her, and began to pray. For a burden seemed to be laid upon his soul for this girl, and he must not be afraid of it.

If Tasha in her warm pink blankets could have heard that prayer for her young straying soul, what would she have thought! Tasha, millions of miles away from this young man's world, Tasha, an utter stranger, strayed into his home for the night! And Thurly Macdonald was upon his knees in a lonely cold station, praying for her as if his very life depended upon the answer to that prayer.

It was after one o'clock when Thurly finally rose from his knees and went out to view the storm, and this time he decided there would be no train any more that night and he would go home. He had prayed till the burden had left his soul, and he was suddenly weary with a great heaviness.

The road to his home was almost impassable, but he managed it, though it took him a good hour, and the little flash had spent itself down to a mere pale wisp when he finally stumbled up the steps of the cottage and fumbled for his latch key.

But he did not need the key. His mother was at the door before he could unbutton his coat with his stiff fingers. There was light and warmth and a glad welcome.

Marget Macdonald was fully dressed, and there was coffee hot on the back of the stove.

"I watched and I listened for the train," she explained when her son reproved her for having sat up. "I hied me up to the little loft where I can always see the light of the evening train when you go, and I was sure it would at least show a bit luminous through the storm, even if I could not hear the rush of it. But no train went by. I said I would not undress till I heard the train go by."

"Mother! Mother!" he said as he kissed her tenderly. "There's never such a mother as you are the world over, I'm sure!"

She helped him unwind the woolen scarf that was frozen round his chin; she helped him unbuckle the great galoshes, for his fingers were still stiff with the cold. She lugged his wet overcoat out to the shed, chafed his hands, passed her rose-petal soft little fingers over his cold face, till it glowed, and she kissed him and murmured, "Ah, my laddie! God has brought ye safe through the storm!"

And then while he was drinking the coffee, and

eating the bit of hot toast she had made he asked her quite casually:

"How's your guest?"

Marget had been waiting for the question. It would have seemed significant to her whether it came or not. Such bits of lovely flesh and blood do not drop down upon a quiet household like theirs without making a notable stir. For years Marget had been dreading and waiting for the time when the first girl should take hold upon the notice of her son. And now it had come! It could not help but come. She had been casting the thought of it upon her Burden Bearer during the long hours of her waiting. She had waited anxiously for the moment when the recognition of this should come between them.

Yet she took it calmly and answered with a smile:

"Oh, she's sleeping quite sweetly, and seemingly no bit the worse for her chilling."

"That's good!" he answered with a relieved ring to his voice. "Mother, I've been thinking. Perhaps God sent her—" his voice trailed off perplexedly—"for—something—you know—" he finished lamely.

"No doubt in the least, laddie!" said his mother, trying to make her voice sound hearty. "But, laddie —she's a bit thing of the world, you know."

"She's all that!" agreed Thurly earnestly, looking deeply into the dregs of his coffee cup, and then, lifting serious eyes as if he were stating something quite new and original: "Yes, she's all that!" and there was something like a sigh in the end of his words.

Marget thought of it long after Thurly was asleep, that "bit sigh" as she called it to herself, "more like a sough in the summer trees! Ah! laddie! laddie! I knew it had tae come some time, but it's sore against my will that it comes this way. Nevertheless the Lord has ways, and it's not for me to question."

She thought of it again the next afternoon when she slipped up to "redd" up the rooms, and opened Thurly's bag to put away his things in the closet again.

Tasha had slept late, and the mother had let Thurly sleep as long as he would. They had merged breakfast into a midday meal about which they had lingered pleasantly, though it was but a "picked up" dinner. Just a meat pie out of some bits of meat of last week which Marget had thought plenty for herself when her boy was away over Sunday. But the bits of meat snuggled beneath the most delicate flaky crust that could be imagined, and the potatoes were baked to that perfection of turn that made even the skins a delicacy. There were stewed tomatoes and crisp coleslaw, with apple sauce and cookies for dessert, and it all tasted perfectly wonderful to Tasha who never in her life had eaten real "home" cooking before.

So, they had lingered around the table, and finally all helped with the dishes. At last while the two young people were looking over some college photographs of Thurly's, Marget slipped up to the rooms, for it was not her way to leave them untidy far into the evening.

It did not take long for the guest room to be put right. It meant only the making of the bed, which evidently it had never occurred to the guest to do, and the hanging up of the various garments which had been brought out for the girl to choose a dinner costume from.

Marget smiled as she hung up her various offerings to think how the girl had picked the unlikeliest one of her things she had brought, an old black silk wrapper. She had slipped it on, with a pin here and a pucker there, and strung an old Roman ribbon around her waist and made a frock of it. There she was downstairs now, sitting beside Thurly on the couch, looking over those foolish football pictures, and "havering" with Thurly as if she had known him always, just because she once met the sister of one of Thurly's fraternity brothers. It made her a bit uneasy to have them sitting so in friendly converse, the two heads together over the book, the gold one and the brown. She must hurry and get back to them. Nothing really alarming could happen with her right there in the room with them. Though of course falling in love was a strange thing and had ways of its own, and to have Thurly lose his heart to a girl of the world who would string his scalp to her pretty little waist and go her dancing way, was not to be prevented by just sitting in the room with him. Marget sighed as she went with swift steps to Thurly's room.

Thurly always made his own bed. She had taught him that when he was a little boy, and he had kept it up to save her work. There was not much to do save to unpack the bag, put the things away, and the bag on the shelf against the time when he had to go and preach again. Even that could wait until the next day. She hesitated and almost turned to go down, then her thrifty soul turned her back to the bag. It would take but a minute and be so much more tidy when Thurly came up at night.

She hung up the dressing gown as she called it, though Thurly had tried to teach her it was now called a bath robe, and she put away the comb and the brush, and the sermons on his desk. Then she reached in for the pajamas and came against something hard and sharp and lumpy. Turning the flannelette back, curious, she came upon the little gold slipper!

For a full minute she stood and looked at that slipper, lying on the bottom of the bag—*hidden* under the pajamas! What did it mean? That Thurly was treasuring it, and did not mean her to see it? She readily understood that he must have found it somewhere at the station when he went back, and had probably picked it up in the first place to restore it. But in that case why was it not on the top in plain sight, tumbled in anyway, and not put carefully down at the bottom, as if he were ashamed of it?

Ah, laddie, laddie! Was it too late? Had it happened then before she was aware, before even *he* was aware?

She put out her hand to take the little gaudy shoe, thumb and finger, as if it were something not nice to handle, something she hated that she would like to fling away, and then she drew back, and looked again. No, she could not do that. She could not ruthlessly pull out what Thurly had taken pains to cover. There had always been respect between them toward what each had done or wanted done, even when he was a mere baby. She had never thrown out even his toads and his pebbles from his pocket without asking his leave, or rather reasoning with him to show him that a pocket was not a proper place for mud and toads, and preparing a better place for them.

But this was something different. She could not go down and say, "Thurly, lad, perhaps you've forgotten it, but you've a lady's yellow slipper in under your night things, and that's not a suitable place for a lady's slipper. Won't you go up and bring it down to the lady? Perhaps she would rather wear her own than the flat-heeled black ones of mine she's wearing now."

No, she could not shame her son. She could not even call him out and tell him privately what she had found, because she must wait for her son to tell her about that slipper if he wanted her to know. She had come to the place where she must not go ahead of him. She must go behind. And she must not let him even know that she had found it.

Softly she laid back the pajamas over the slipper, giving a quick glance to the hook on the inside closet door to make sure he had worn his old ones without unpacking his bag last night, and not just put these clean ones back this morning to hide the slipper from her. Softly she tiptoed over to the bureau and the desk for the brush and comb, the black leather cover that held his sermons, and put them all back just as she had found them. Then she shut the bag quietly, and went out of her son's room without looking back.

But she did not go down to the little parlor where her son sat with the woman of the world. Instead she went into her own little bedroom, and shutting the door and locking it, she knelt beside her plump white bed. And there she poured out her heart to the One who knoweth all things, and seeth the end from the beginning.

Chapter V

The storm raged on, with no sign of letting up.

The two young people in Marget Macdonald's litt' getting acquainted without realizing it, over the book of college photographs which Tasha had found on the under part of the little stand. Idly she had reached from the low chair in which she had seated herself after the unusual task of wiping dishes, and pulled it toward her turning over the pages, with little idea of being amused, till she suddenly came upon a face which she knew.

"Why! Isn't that Jerry Fisher?" she exclaimed. "This one with the football in his hand? Do you know Jerry?"

"I sure do!" was the hearty response, as Thurly came over to her side and looked over her shoulder. "I roomed with Jerry for two semesters at college!"

That was the beginning. At once her respect for the young minister went up several degrees. He couldn't be such a prune if Jerry had him for a roommate. Jerry was a perfect scream.

"I had his sister down at the shore with me last summer all the season. She's some peach, Betty Fisher. Do you know her!"

"No," said Thurly with sudden reserve in his voice. "That is, I met her once I believe, she came down for the game. Jerry is some kid!"

He did not add that he had not cared to more than meet Betty Fisher, that she was not a type of girl he admired.

But Tasha did not notice the reserve in his voice!

She was only glad to find some common topic of conversation.

"He must be!" she said eagerly. "Betty used to be really nuts about him. She had her room at school all plastered over with his photographs, and she used to be always raving about him. I imagine he must have been pretty speedy!"

"Well, he wasn't exactly slow," said Thurly gravely, remembering several serious scrapes that Jerry had got into. Thurly had had to help him out of them or see him expelled.

Tasha turned over the pages and discovered more pictures.

"Why, that is yourself, isn't it? Really! Why, you were captain, weren't you?"

Thurly nodded gravely, watching her vivacious little face and trying to study her possible background. Betty Fisher and her ilk would be just about what this girl admired, likely. Oh, she was far from being his kind of a girl. Why had she dropped down upon them in this intimate way, when he could not get away, and must stay by and attempt to entertain her? His natural shy reserve that had been forgotten over the old college pictures, returned upon him, and he stepped back and glanced out of the window into the still fine whiteness of the blizzard.

"Yes, I was captain," he said coldly, and deliberately walked over to the couch on the opposite side of the room and sat down stiffly.

But Tasha was interested.

"Why, isn't that perfectly gorgeous! You captain! What year? You don't mean it! Why, that must have been the year they beat Yale! Macdonald! Why, surely, I remember! I was at that game myself. My friend Adrienne Lyman and I went up with Dad! And you were that Macdonald! Why, you were the whole team that day! I watched you with the greatest admiration, and rooted for you till I was hoarse, but I never dreamed you would some day save me from freezing to death! It's quite like a fairy tale to think I should have come upon you when I stepped out of that cold tomb of a train into the snow. No wonder you carried me off as easily as if I had been a feather. I heard a lot about how strong you were at that game. Simply everybody was raving about you on every side!"

Thurly was almost embarrassed. He watched her as she talked, her eyes all asparkle, her face vivid with interest, and felt a sudden warmth around his heart again, but almost immediately despised himself for it. Here he was falling for a girl merely because she admired his football of other days. She probably had no higher standards for any man than merely to see him play football better than the next one. Yet she was a lovely little thing. Even in his mother's old black silk wrapper, she had an innate grace and charm about her that made him want to watch her.

"And who is this man?" she asked suddenly as she turned another page, and springing up she brought the book with her and sat down beside him on the couch.

So, together, the brown head and the gold one, Marget found them bending over more pictures and talking like old friends, when an hour later she came down, a chastened look about her lips, a peace within her eyes.

The two looked up smiling and Marget summoned a smile. Her face was one that radiated love, and Tasha felt it like a sudden sunbeam. She looked around on the homely cozy room with almost wistful eyes and thought how happy those two seemed together. What was it they had that made them happy, with so seemingly little of all the things that other people had to have to make them happy?

"Thurly, I'm wondering if the young lady doesn't sing?" said Marget, in the sudden silence that followed her entrance, "it's about our hour for a little sing you know."

"Sing?" said Tasha graciously, "sure, let's sing! What do you know? Have you heard the prune song? Of course you have. It's on all the radios now. Let's sing that. It's been ringing in my head all the morning and I'd like to get it out of my system."

"I'm afraid I'm not acquainted with it," said Thurly, casting a startled look at his mother.

"It goes like this," said Tasha, trilling out:

"No matter how young a prune may be,
It's very often stewed—"

Her voice was young and fresh and the words rang out clearly.

Thurly smiled gravely.

"No, I don't think I've happened to hear it," he said. "I'm not up on those songs since I left college, I'm afraid, and perhaps you won't like our kind, but I'm thinking this little mother of mine will be disappointed if we don't give her two or three of her favorites. Would you mind trying some of ours? We've some books that will help. Mother, where have you put the hymn books?"

A great light came into Marget's eyes at that. Her boy knew a way to carry off a situation! "Wise as a serpent, harmless as a dove," her glad heart murmured to itself, as she went to the little book shelf and hunted out three books.

"Get your fiddle, Thurly, lad, and we'll have a fine sing. The young lady has a blithesome voice, and I'm thinking we can have real music the day!"

Tasha accepted the hymn book meekly and watched the young man as he opened the worn old violin case and took out his instrument lovingly. So he was a musician too, as well as football player—and preacher! What a combination! But then most of the college fellows could play something if it was only a mouth organ, and likely he didn't really play much!

But the first touch of the bow to the strings made her certain that he could. Such rich sweetness, such tender melody, wailed from the strings, that she sat and watched him in amazement.

"Is that the one you want first, Mother?" he asked stopping his bow suddenly. "It's number fifty-six, I think. Mother always likes to sing that when there's a storm."

The mother smiled tenderly at the gentle note in her boy's voice.

"It seems so cozy like and comforting when it's all noise and bluster outside," she explained apologetically to the visitor.

And then they sang, and Tasha, wondering, opened her book to the number and followed the words, humming along with the triumphant tenderness of the violin, the sweet quaver of the old lady's voice, and the splendid baritone of the young man:

> "From every stormy wind that blows,
> From every swelling tide of woes,
> There is a calm, a sure retreat,
> 'Tis found beneath the mercy seat."

Tasha had seldom gone to church in her young life, only occasionally to Sunday School; if she had ever heard this hymn before she had taken no note of it. She sat and read the strange mysterious words over while the other two sang them. She wondered what it was all about.

At the fourth verse she trilled in clearly:

> "Ah, whither could we flee for aid,
> When tempted, desolate, dismayed,
> Or how the hosts of hell defeat.
> Had suffering saints no mercy seat."

The words were still more puzzling. What could a mercy seat be, and why did saints have to suffer? It was all entirely out of her line, but she sang on:

> "There, there on eagle wings we soar,
> And sense and sin molest no more,
> And Heaven comes down our souls to greet,
> And glory crowns the mercy seat."

It was all mystic and beautiful, whatever it meant. Probably it was just like all religion, kind of sweet and mysterious and full of imagination. Tasha didn't see much in it, yet somehow as she sang that line "Heaven comes down our souls to meet" she got a curious kind of thrill of spirit from it, and wondered. Nothing like this had ever touched her life before. She had never believed anything because she was utterly ignorant of anything to believe. She knew of all religions only as a kind of cult that people affected, she had always supposed, because of some underlying fear or some weakness. Yet neither of these two people looked as if they had a fear or a weakness. Even the old mother wore a look of strength and character about her firm sweet chin that belied fears, or weaknesses, and the young man's record in football was enough to free him from any question in that line, even if she could not see the outline of his strong keen face, with its flashing eyes, and lips that yet could be stern upon occasion. No, there was no weakness here, no superstition or fear. Yet why, *why* did this sort of thing appeal to them? Was it merely tradition that they were living out?

But a glance at each of their faces as they sang the closing verse belied that. They meant it all with their whole souls, and they looked as if they could live it to the death.

"O may my hand forget her skill,
My tongue be silent, cold and still,
This throbbing heart forget to beat,
If I forget the mercy seat!"

The words had seemed too dreadful to the girl to take upon her own lips. Not that she was superstitious, but it sounded like a challenge to all the evil powers of the universe, and she shuddered involuntarily and turned her eyes toward the white window panes and remembered last night. It came to her that she might have been lying "silent cold and still" down under the snow by the railroad, if this young man had not found her and brought her to this retreat. And what was this mercy seat they talked about? She had no idea and she would not ask for anything, but she was glad when the song was ended and they fluttered the leaves on to another.

The night was fast closing in around them again, and the room was growing dusky. Thurly had made a fire of logs in the tiny fireplace and the flame gave a rosy tinge to the white shawl of the old lady, and glowed like sheen upon her silver hair.

They sang other songs:

> "Oh, God, our help in ages past,
>   Our hope in years to come,
> Our shelter from the stormy blast,
>   And our eternal home,
> Under the shadow of Thy wings,
>   Thy saints shall rest secure—"

There it was again, "saints." Well, as she watched these two in the gloaming, sitting there singing, they looked like saints. That is they looked as she should imagine saints might look, though she had never thought of strength in connection with sainthood before. Saints in her parlance were always spoken of with a sneer, as something too weak to be bad enough to have a good time.

It presently grew too dark to see any more hymns, and then Thurly played on, melody after melody. They were all unfamiliar to Tasha, but from the fact that his mother sometimes quavered out a few words to the accompaniment, she surmised that they were more hymn tunes, and she marvelled how they loved them! She had never known before that hymn tunes could be so tender and touching. She had supposed they were all gloomy and lugubrious.

But finally Thurly put down his violin, and the mother said:

"Put on the lights, laddie dear, and let's have our worship now, before we have our tea. It's so pleasant with the sound of the music still lingering in the room. It'll seem more like the Sabbath day. I hate to stay away from church on the Lord's day, but the Lord Himself has shut us in this time."

Thurly had turned on the lights before she finished speaking, and Tasha's eyes met those of the old lady as she spoke, and marvelled again at the strange things she was saying. It was as if she talked another language; the parlance of an entirely different world. How strange it was that people could all live on an earth together, and yet each one live a different life! How different for example was the life of these two, from any that she knew. Why, take Lucia, for example, or Dad, they would not know what it was all about! And they would laugh and mock! She knew they would! She would have laughed too, before she had come so close to this mother and son, but now she resented the thought that her friends would laugh at the two who had been so wonderful to her.

But what was this worship they were going to have? She was getting a little bit fed up on religion. Still they were so sweet about it, and it was interesting to see a young man like that, who had really been quite a notable character in the athletic world, just sit down and be interested in religion. It was queer—queer, but intriguing. He certainly was good-looking, too. There was no denying that.

They gave her a Bible, with soft old leather covers, the place all found for her, and she discovered they were about to read, and that she was to take her turn reading.

She had always boasted that she could be equal to any occasion that might arise, but somehow this performance was exceedingly embarrassing to her, and she stumbled over the simplest words as she read her first turn.

It was the story of the man born blind, and she found it interesting. She had not known that there were stories in the Bible. The mother made quaint remarks now and then about the "laddie" and his healing, and once or twice Thurly told what the Greek word was in a certain phrase, and just what significance it had in this particular setting.

Tasha listened and wondered, and felt that here was a third side to this versatile young man. He seemed to be a scholar. Moreover, and strangest of all, he seemed to take for honest fact the story he was reading, and talked about the Healer as if he were intimate with Him! It was all strange.

And then they did the oddest thing! The mother and son got up from their seats and knelt down, both of them, quite simply as if it were their common practice. Tasha sat there feeling dumb and foolish, till in self-defense she too slipped down, silently, and knelt beside the couch.

Thurly was praying for her, she discovered, earnestly, kindly; he called her "the young stranger whom Thou hast sent as our guest to-day." He asked strange mysterious blessings upon her which warmed her heart though she could not understand them, and they brought a great sense of loneliness to her, and of longing for something she did not have, though she did not know what it was.

And then quite as sharply there came to her the realization of how her friends would mock and scream with laughter if they could see her now, shut up in a little cottage home, arrayed in an old woman's black silk wrapper and flat-soled slippers, kneeling beside a hair cloth sofa being prayed for! And the revulsion almost set her giggling!

But there were tears in her eyes as she got to her feet at the close, and she went swiftly to the white blank window to hide them.

Thurly had gone at once down cellar to see to the furnace and the mother had bustled happily out to the kitchen. As Marget passed her she gave Tasha a smile and a little loving pat on her hand.

Tasha was almost afraid to go out to the dining room, though she was vigorously hungry, and the smell of hot coffee and something spicy and sweet drew her mightily.

But when she took her seat she found them both bright-faced and happy. The grace the young minister asked was so sincere that the girl forgot to be impatient over another dose of religion.

"They just live in it, like sunshine!" she thought to herself as she watched them. "It is not put on. It is real!"

It was a simple little supper, yet it tasted wonderfully good to this girl. A round bright pan of baked beans, piping hot from the oven where they had been all the afternoon. Delicate home made bread, brown and white, the like of which she had never eaten before, and sweet country butter. Sweet baked apples and cream, with little caraway cookies for dessert.

She would have laughed but a day before at such a menu, but she ate, and enjoyed it, and knew suddenly that she was having a good time. There was a half wish upon her that she might just stay here always and live this strange peaceful life with them, and get away from all the restlessness and fever of her own world. Only of course she couldn't. Of course it would bore her to death if she had to.

And even now she was feverish and restless from the lack of things to which she had been accustomed. She had not smoked a cigarette for more than twenty-four hours, nor tasted any stimulant stronger than coffee and tea, and her nerves were beginning to cry out against such treatment.

When at last the evening was over, Marget Macdonald went up with the girl, saw that her bed was turned down, and filled the hot water bag for her feet, for the wind was searching its way round the window cracks, swirling in at every crevice, and promised another wild night. Marget kissed her good night, called her "my dear," said she hoped she would sleep sweetly, and went down stairs.

Tasha opened the door after she had gone, and stood in the little hall listening. Thurly had gone down to the cellar again. She could hear him rattling the furnace.

With a quick stealthy step she crossed the hall into what she thought must be the young man's room. The desire for a cigarette had come over her so overwhelmingly that she was willing to go to any length to get one. There would be some in his room somewhere of course, and he would not notice if one or two were gone.

She listened for an instant at the door to make sure no one was coming up, and then snapped on the light from the button beside the door for it was scarcely light enough from the hall to find anything in a strange room.

She gave a quick glance about; at the bureau and table, not a sign of a pipe, nor a tobacco jar, nor a pack of cigarettes anywhere! Only a Bible open as if it had been read lately, and left reluctantly.

She turned impatiently to search on the closet shelf. Perhaps his mother was too neat to have anything like that around.

But she almost fell over the open-mouthed bag, standing in the middle of the floor where Marget Macdonald had left it.

Ah! There would be some in his bag, of course.

She could hear the cellar door being shut with a bang, and Thurly and his mother talking down stairs. She must hurry!

She stooped over the bag and looked in. The sermon case didn't mean a thing to her. She lifted the hair brush, and felt. There seemed to be something hard beneath the other things. She lifted the folded garment, and stared! There lay her own gold slipper, its gleaming slide of stones twinkling almost wickedly up at her! She dropped the things into the bag and started back, and turning met Thurly face to face!

Chapter VI

His face was stern! It frightened her. What right had he to look at her like that? It seemed to undo all the beauty of the day that they had spent together.

Her face was flaming, and for once her old pert self knew not how to explain. It suddenly seemed that she had committed some unpardonable offense. It made her angry to feel so. Who was he to look at her like that?

"I'm dying for a smoke!" she said, assuming her old hard-boiled attitude, and laughing with a sharpness that startled even herself. "I thought maybe you had left some cigarettes about, but I see you haven't!"

He just looked at her, opened his lips as if to speak, and looked again. That look went with her for many a day. She could not quite analyze it. It was stern, it was sorrowful, it even had a tinge of disgust in it; and yet there was an almost infinite yearning about it, as though he would, if he could, save her from the thing that had happened, and put her back in his estimation where she had been but a few moments before. Oh, there was no mistaking it, she had fallen in his estimation! She knew that from the minute she saw him standing there in the door.

It seemed eons that she stood there being looked through by those keen, tender, true eyes of his. Then he spoke, very quietly.

"I do not use them."

He stepped aside as if she had made a motion to pass, and she heard footsteps on the stairs. His mother was coming. She suddenly sensed that he would not want his mother to know she had been in his room. Would not want her to know she had been searching for a smoke.

Her cheeks flamed red, and her knees were trembling. For an instant she was tempted to defy him. To defy his mother. To stand there and laugh at them both! It was nothing she had done. She had been twice as indiscreet every day of her life without thinking of it. In her world no one would have dreamed of taking exception to her action. These people were a pair of old hypocrites!

Then suddenly his look upon her seemed like the eyes of the God they had been reading about and praying to, and she went swiftly past him into her room and closed the door, standing against it. She was trembling in every fiber, her eyes flashing, furious with the young man for his condemnation of her. Furious with his mother for the condemnation she would have given if she had known.

She flung herself upon the bed at last and cried silently in a fury of rage at her own situation; cried finally at herself for having caused that look in those pleasant eyes that had been so friendly all the afternoon. Cried out that she was she, and born into a world she could not understand, with always this great longing for something that could not be attained.

The other rooms were silent and dark a long time before Tasha roused herself to put out the light, undressing in the dark, and creeping in shivering to the grateful touch of the hot water bag, and the enfolding blankets.

Yet she did not sleep, even in the warm comfortable bed. She could not get away from the memory of those fine incredulous eyes as they looked her through. In vain did she turn over and tell herself that the young preacher was nothing to her. On the morrow she would be gone and never likely see him again. In vain did she call him a country boy, and a prig. The eyes looked steadily at her through the dark with that surprised contempt. And now she could not tell whether it was more for the fact that she wanted to smoke, or that she was willing to steal into a man's room to get his cigarettes, or whether it was because he had found her searching through his property.

Suddenly came the memory of the little gold slipper! In her confusion she had forgotten that he might have seen it, and known that she had found it. Then she turned back to the memory of his look again, but could find no answer to her question. If he disliked her finding him out, he disliked her still more for the smoking. The icy way in which he had said "I do not use them" told her that. Prig! Conceited ape! Coward! He was a sissy! Yes, a sissy, that he did not smoke as other men did. Even if he was a preacher, he needn't think he was better than all creation. It was sissy for a man not to smoke! Sissy! Sissy!

She said it over under the bedclothes, and set her

small white teeth in the blanket to emphasize the thought. Yet even as she said it she knew there was nothing sissy about that man. The man that had become famous by reason of his athletic prowess could never be called a sissy. She could see him now as she had seen him three years ago, running the length of the field, brushing aside all opponents, dodging, sliding, almost miraculously eluding his pursuers—no, he was no sissy. And the man who had carried her through that storm, taken off his own coat, and with her on his shoulder struggled through the snow in a blinding sleet to bring her to warmth and safety; and then struggled back again so unnecessarily just to fulfil some little appointment in a church somewhere, and waited far into the night in hope of a train before he came home to shelter! No, he was no coward.

Yes, and the man who could play such heavenly music, and then kneel down in front of a girl like herself and pray! No, she had to acknowledge that he was no hypocrite and no coward. Not any of the things she had tried to call him! She had a suspicion that perhaps the hardest for him to do of all those things she had named to herself, had been that prayer with her, an alien, present. For she sensed her own difference, and began to understand that the difference was not against him, but to her discredit. He was a strong man, a superman perhaps, and all the things she had thought herself before this night seemed to dwindle into nothing.

Tasha did not like to acknowledge this to herself. She fought against it. She loathed herself for letting such an idea pass through her mind. But it was there! And so were the eyes that had looked her through and scorned her. Yet he had protected her name in his mother's eyes by stepping aside and making her know that she must go quickly to her own room and shut the door. Oh, she loathed him for that! She would never forgive him for it! And yet she was glad somehow underneath it all that he had done so, that the sweet old mother had not seen anything by which to judge her ill.

Then the restless outcry of her nerves for sooth-
ing came upon her, and it seemed that she would sell
her very soul for some drug to quiet the anguish she
was in. Oh, for a good stiff drink from Barry's flask,
or one of the Framstead highballs! Oh, for anything to
still this fever and give her sleep! At one time she
thought with longing for the cold bitter sleet of the
outside world and wished she might plunge from the
window into the snow and never be seen again! Her
nerves were getting beyond her control, yet she could
not, or would not, cry out and call for help. Even a
cup of tea or coffee would have helped, if she only
could creep down stairs and get it, but of course she
would be heard. Even a drink of water would be wonderful. Was there any left in the glass Mrs. Macdonald
had brought to her last night?

She stole to the bureau and groped in the dark.
Yes, there was half a glass. She drank it eagerly and
crept shivering back to bed, but not to sleep. For now,
suddenly, the golden slipper took command and had
its innings. Should she demand that slipper in the morning? It was hers. He had no right to be carrying it in
his grip. How did it come there anyway? Its mate was
even now under the edge of the bed. It must have
dropped off in the snow. She remembered now, her
foot had been without one when he found her. All
after that was confusion. Had he rubbed her feet? Yes,
and put on warm soft woolen stockings that had
felt so wonderful! But how did he come to have that
slipper under his things in his bag? If it had been on
the top it would not have seemed strange, but to have
hidden it that way it almost looked as if he wanted
to keep it perhaps, just as the men were always trying
to get one's handkerchiefs and gloves for a collection.
But it did not seem as if he was like that. She found
she did not want to think he was. It would show a
weakness, it would show that after all he was human,
just like everybody else, and had his weak points. And
—she gasped at the truth as she began to see it. She
did not *want* to find him human. She wanted to think
there was one man on earth that was different; that

was strong, and fine and true and dependable; whose eye was clear, and whose heart was true. It was the kind of thing she had always mocked at, but she really wanted it, after all; one true fine man that one could adore, that one could really look up to and not despise.

Well, and if he was thinking to keep her slipper sentimentally and not let her know he had it, he would find he was mistaken. She was a woman of the world, whether he was a man of the world or not, and she would fling out upon him and ask for her slipper that he had hidden—and then her eyelids trailed down upon her cheeks, and she suddenly seemed to be caught in great strong arms and lifted over whirling, drifting snow banks, and carried miles and miles to safety, on a warm broad shoulder, held close, with a great sense of safety upon her.

She was asleep and the matter of the golden slipper had not been settled.

Sometime in the night the wind grew stronger, more steady, less turbulent, and the wild falling of sleet and hail against the window pane ceased. When the morning dawned the sun shone out in radiance over a new white world shining in startling unearthly beauty. It was so still and white and deep that it almost frightened one to look, as if this mortal had suddenly put on immortality unaware and were gazing through an unexpectedly open gate into another world.

Tasha slept late, after her vigil, and there were soft dark rings under her lovely eyes when she came down to breakfast.

The girl looked round half fearfully as she came into the pleasant breakfast room where the sun shone broad across one end of the table and caught the modest silver and glass, transforming it into prisms of beauty against the fine worn linen of the cloth.

There was no one in the room but the mother, however, and she need not have feared. It was plain the son had been a true knight and said nothing to his mother about her escapade of the night before. Well, she was grateful for that, but she dreaded his coming

down, and kept looking around nervously at the least
little sound.

Marget greeted her with a smile.

"Well, the storm's o'er at last, lassie," she said, as
she brought in a plate of hot biscuit, and a smoking
platter of ham omelette. "I'm thinking you'll soon be
leaving us, and we'll be sad to have you go. It's been a
cozy Sabbath with you here, and we've fitted very
well together. It will be pleasant if you can find time
from your friends to come visit us again sometime.
We'll be like old friends, now, I hope. Perhaps sometime when you have a spare day, you'll come and
bide with me when my laddie's away. He's preaching
hither and yon this winter, and not expecting to take a
regular charge till next summer, while he finishes the
course of study he's taking in the city. But there are
week ends when he has to go quite far to fill some
other body's place, and I'd be pleased for company if
you'd care to come."

The girl was deeply embarrassed over this invitation. She scarcely knew how to answer and found herself accepting almost eagerly, though it was the last
thing she wanted to do, and she had no intention whatever of keeping her engagement.

Marget passed her a china dish of delectably fried
potatoes, and smiled again at her. Marget too had spent
many wakeful hours that night. The gold slipper and
the girl's eyes had kept her awake. That and the look
in her lad's face. The lad was smitten at last, she
thought, and who was this lassie the Lord had let
come into their home in the storm? Was she a temptation to be dealt with, or a poor stray lamb to be comforted and shown the way home? Marget had laid her
burden down at the mercy seat, and come away with
a smile, and now she was calm enough, slipper or no
slipper, to note the faint blue lines under the beautiful tempestuous eyes, and reach out in sympathy.

She noted, too, the quick nervous glance now and
again toward the stair, and sought to set her guest at
rest on that point.

"Thurly's gone out at break of day to shovel,"

she said quite casually, and noted how the slender shoulders relaxed, and the girl began to eat as if she were really enjoying her breakfast and not just toying with her fork.

"Oh," said Tasha, blooming into a smile. "Shoveling? Does he have to do that?"

"Everybody will have to shovel, my dear. The snow has got the upper hand. It's been a big blizzard, and we're verra fortunate that it's o'er, and has done no great damage. There'll be some that will be suffering from the cold however, and even from hunger too, and perhaps some have perished in the storm. We'll not be knowing till the day is well up and the paper men have been able to gather the news."

"Oh!" said Tasha, quite stricken at the thought. "I would have perished, I'm quite sure I would, if it had not been for your son——"

"Well, dearie, the Lord was thinking on you, and brought him in good time, and we're all thankful for that. But, lassie, do you know you've not told us your name? And we can't have you going as you came and leaving nothing but your pretty memory behind."

The girl grew grave at once, as if she were suddenly confronted with her old self in the midst of these new surroundings.

"I'm Tasha Endicott," she said with a little shrug. "You've maybe seen my name in the papers, but I'm not much, really. Beside you people I'm absolutely the froth of the earth!" She laughed a little gay laugh without any merriment in it. A laugh that prepared her to slip away back to her own world again.

"Tasha!" exclaimed the older woman gravely, looking deep into the girl's eyes. "I've never heard the name——" and she looked almost troubled at the idea. "But that'll never be your right name I'm sure, dear! What was your baptismal name?"

"Oh, no," laughed the girl, "I'm really Anastasia, after a stuffy old grandmother years and years ago, but everybody calls me Tasha, and it really fits me much better than the other. I couldn't possibly live up to Anastasia."

"Did you ever look up its meaning?" asked Marget interestedly. "I like to look up names, don't you? Shall we look it up in Thurly's dictionary? There's often a great deal in a name."

Marget moved softly over to a little stand in the window where a worn dictionary lay beside a Bible. She turned the pages slowly, as if she were familiar with them, and Tasha watched her, wondering why she felt so drawn to this curious old woman, who was not beautiful nor yet nobly clad, but had the true grace of gentility in her every movement. Tasha did not really use the word gentility in her thoughts, because she had not been brought up to think in terms of real gentility. Her standards had been money and style rather than the finer virtues.

Marget looked up with a thoughtful light in her eyes:

"I don't find the name itself here," she said disappointedly, "not as a name; but the word is here, down in the small added words below the line. That'll mean that the word used that way is a bit antiquated, you know. But still the meaning will be there. 'Anastasia,' it says, and it has a bonny meaning, 'convalescence' it says, 'return to health.' That'll be a good thought to carry in a name, will it not?"

Tasha watched her thoughtfully, wonderingly, as she closed the book and laid it back beneath the Bible. Afterward this incident was to come back to her with a new meaning one day.

Chapter VII

It was nearly noon when the telephone tinkled at last showing that the line was open again. Thurly was on the wire to say he would not be back to lunch. They had found the Widow Frailey was entirely snowed under, and were still at work digging her out. They had been able to reach her door and found that she was all right, but there was still a lot of digging to make her place habitable, and not all the men could stay that afternoon.

Marget turned back to her guest, her heart at rest. She was not anxious that Thurly should return to the society of this attractive girl. She had put the matter of the gold slipper into the hands of her Father, but perhaps this was the way He was going to handle it.

As she hung up the receiver and turned around there was Tasha standing beside her.

"May I telephone home, please?" she said. "It is certainly high time I relieved you of my presence, though I have had a lovely time."

There was a wistfulness in her tone that pricked the soul of the good woman, and forgetting her fears she said impulsively:

"It's been nothing but pleasure, my dear, to have you with us. You made a bonnie spot in the storm, and I hope you'll soon come again."

And then she recalled her fears and a sudden panic came upon her to think what she had done, so that she turned away and began hurriedly to wipe a fleck of dust from the telephone table with her gingham apron.

It was almost dark, at that, when the big Endicott limousine floundered slowly through the half broken road and stopped before the cottage. The snow-plow had been by, and a hardy car or two, but the road was still well nigh impassable on the side streets. The Macdonald street was a side street.

Tasha's maid came breezing in with French epithets about the storm that created an entirely raw atmosphere, and Marget set her lips and went meekly on with what she was doing. The maid was one who put all but the wealthy on a plane so far beneath her that they were not even in the same world.

She hurried up to the room her mistress had oc-

cupied, and began to unpack the things she had
brought, casting a contemptuous look at the soft black
silk that Tasha was wearing, and taking command as
if she owned the place. She stripped off the offending
silk and flung Lady Macdonald's garments on the floor
in a corner as if they were cast away forever. Then she
set about arraying the young woman in a soft coral
wool frock with a dashing blouse of coral and cream
and brown with a glint of silver in the gaudy weave.

Marget brought the drabbled rose silk, and patted
it lovingly out on the bed.

"I doubt not it'll need some reconstructing," she
said sadly. "A pity! Such a pretty little dress! You
looked like a flower in it."

Tasha smiled in appreciation, a quick glad light
in her eyes. What was it in this plain old woman that
made her seem like nobility? Why was it she was glad
to have had her commendation?

Quite unlike her usual thoughtless self, she went
and picked up the borrowed clothes from the corner,
and smoothed them out carefully laying them in a neat
pile on the bed.

"I don't know what I should have done without
these," she said gently, patting them as they lay together.

Marie, the maid, gave a contemptuous glance
that slithered like a knife past Marget's consciousness.
Marie sniffed significantly.

"I wish I had had something more fitting—" said
Marget with a gentle dignity, looking toward her black
silk wrapper deprecatingly.

The maid was giving attention to the party frock
on the bed.

"It's scarcely worth bothering with, Miss Tasha,"
she said haughtily. "You'll not wear it again. We might
as well leave it—!"

"No!" said Tasha quickly. "Don't leave it around
in their way. Besides, I want it. I—mean to keep it!"

"Yes, dear! Keep it! It's too pretty. You can do
something with it sometime I'm sure. I'd like to see you
in it once more."

"Oh, very well," said Marie frigidly, and folded the poor drabbled rose petals as carefully as if they had just come from the store.

"I don't see your other slipper," said Marie, pausing in her rapid ministrations.

Marget felt her heart give a jerk and go on again. Ought she—? No, she could not say she knew where it was. She could not bring it forth from her son's bag. What should she do? Was it honest—? Honorable? But—she was not supposed to know where it was. And what would Thurly think if he found it gone? Could she make it seem natural that she had been unpacking his bag and had taken it for granted that he had found the slipper in the snow, as doubtless he had, and had restored it to its owner? Could she bridge that way of knowing where it was hidden, and make it right with Thurly without his seeing her fear in her eyes?

But while she hesitated the calm voice of Tasha answered as she turned swiftly and went toward the head of the stairs:

"I lost it off in the snow, Marie. Never mind. Come, it is getting late! We should be gone!"

Marget had not seen the sudden paling of Tasha's cheek, the quick-drawn breath before she spoke. Marget was wondering even yet if she ought not to go into her son's room and get that slipper from its hiding place. But how could she do it now, since no one knew that she knew it was there?

The cold hard voice of Marie broke in with a cutting glance at Marget that almost seemed like suspicion, as if it were all her fault.

"It's a pity, Miss Tasha. Those were your diamond slides."

"Oh—!" breathed Marget, paling. "They'll—maybe be found!"

She pronounced it "foond" and made it like a croon.

"It doesn't matter," said Tasha sharply, feeling the blood sting into her cheeks, and lowering her eyes as she hurried down the stairs.

Marie brushed past the hostess rudely with the suit case she had brought and hurried after her mistress. Marget lingered with a helpless glance toward her son's door, and a bewildered idea even yet of doing something about the slipper, then hurried down after them.

"Take it out to the car, Marie!" Tasha was saying as she held the door open and motioned to her maid. "I'll be out in a minute."

Then she closed the door abruptly and turned toward Marget, the look almost of a child on her face, a child who was sorry to leave.

"You've been so nice," she said simply, coming toward Marget with her hand out for good bye. "I don't seem to be able to thank you enough!"

"My dear!" said Marget, suddenly folding her arms about the astonished girl. "My dear!" and kissed her tenderly on her warm young lips.

Tasha had never had a caress like that. It thrilled her. It was like what she thought a mother's kiss would be, and for an instant she yielded herself to it warmly, eagerly, then drew back almost embarrassed, speaking quickly to hide her confusion.

"You'll thank your son for me, too—" she said. "He was—wonderful—!"

There had been a stamping at the front door, and now the two turned at the breath of cold air that blew upon them, and there stood Thurly! How much had he heard? Had there been too great fervor in her voice? Tasha's cheeks flamed like to the color of her coral dress, and she stood there in her confusion before him, beautiful in her bright frock and little close coral hat, as she had been in the rose petals Saturday night.

The young man, tall and brawny in old gray trousers and sweater, with a gray woolen scarf still bound around his neck, thick leather mittens on his hands, snow still caked all over his garments, his face ruddy and tired, and his hair sticking out rampantly, stood and looked at her, severity and wistfulness mingled in his gaze.

She was lovely! Oh, yes, she was lovely!

Tasha rallied first.

"I'm glad you came before I had to leave," she said with a gay little laugh that somehow sounded almost near to tears.

He took her hand gravely. He did not smile. Somehow his mother wished he would smile. It would have meant less. She was thinking of the slipper. Ought she to remind him? Would it embarrass him? It would be so easy to say right now, "She has lost her slipper" and then he would remember and say, "Why, yes, of course! I found that slipper. I forgot to mention it, I will get it," and then it would all be over and straightened out and she would never have to think of it any more. And yet, somehow, she did not say it. Was she afraid Thurly was wanting to keep that slipper? Was she afraid—of what? But of course it would not be honest to keep it. She must tell him at once. He was helping Tasha on with the rich brown fur coat. He was going to take her out to the car.

She opened her lips.

"She has lost her slipper, Thurly!" but the sound was faint and tentative as if she were trying out her voice. The wind had swished in the door as they opened it, and they did not hear her. Thurly had gone ahead with his snow shovel as if she were a princess. She went and stood in the door herself, shivering, and called again, aimlessly, foolishly, "She has lost her slipper, Thurly, her gold slipper!" But neither of them heard, and she felt like a fool standing there. The engine of the car had started. It would be impossible to make them hear now. What a fool she had been! Now it was out of her hands.

"Oh, God! I ought to have said it," she murmured. "What a fool I've been. But please fix it right somehow!"

The car plunged over a drift and wallowed away around the corner into the more broken highway, and Tasha waved a small gloved hand out the window as the lights of the car vanished.

Tasha was gone back into her own world again.

Marget felt a choking in her throat, a smarting of something like tears in her eyes. Why?

Out there in the dusk, big and strong, stood Thurly. His shoulders took a tired sag, and the loosened scarf swung grotesquely about his face. He was staring blankly toward the corner round which the car had gone. The sound of its expensive engine was even now out of hearing. So she had come, and so she had gone! Like a disquieting dream. How beautiful she was! How little her hand had been as it lay in his after he had pulled off his wet mitten. Hers seemed like a baby's hand. He hadn't wanted to let it go.

It is safe to say that Thurly had forgotten all about the little slipper.

He came in at last when it had grown suddenly dark around him. His mother hurried from the window where she had been furtively watching him, and stirred the open fire which she had kept going all day. She had Thurly's slippers on the hearth, and his big warm dressing gown lying over the deep chair he loved. The coffee was bubbling in the kitchen and sending forth a delicious aroma. Marget bustled about self-consciously to make everything seem quite natural.

"Don't bother to go up the stairs, laddie," she called, as Thurly stamped the snow off and came into the living room. "Just sit ye down by the fire and I'll bring you a cup of coffee before you do another thing. You must be wearied to death and half starved."

"I must get off these wet things first, Mother," said Thurly in a voice that sounded strangely tired and old. "I think if you don't mind, I'll just get a bath while I'm up. I'm stiff with the shoveling and I think it will help."

But what Thurly did when he went up stairs was to stand at the door of the guest room for several long minutes, and stare at the vacant room. It had a storm-tossed look for a room in his mother's house, neat as it yet was. There was a scrap of paper on the floor that Marie had dropped when she unwrapped her lady's garments. There was a bit of a white box on the bureau lined with white velvet that had held the coral beads my lady wore about her throat. There was a length of string on the floor dropped from the suit case, and a large pink shred of tulle under the bed. Thurly noted with a pang his mother's silk robe, and the bright scarf folded together on the chair, but he went deliberately and picked up the piece of rose tulle and crushed it in his hand.

Even when he went at last to his own room he did not immediately set about divesting himself of his wet garments. He stood a long time just where he had stood the night before when he caught the girl hunting in his bag for cigarettes! Then he sighed and, stooping, opened his bag, with a strange unreasoning desire to see what she had seen when she looked. He ran his hand down among his possessions, and came sharp against the jeweled buckle of the little shoe. Then he remembered! He had hidden the gold slipper under his things. Had she found it? Did she know he had it there?

When he came upon her she had been standing still, looking down at something beneath the clothes her hand was holding away. Did she know it was her slipper? What did she think of him for having it there and not giving it back to her?

He lifted the foolish little shoe and held it in his big hand. Such a tiny thing, so inadequate, it seemed, to carry anyone through the world. A bauble for a dance! Just a little light dancing girl! How pretty she had looked in that pink party gown! Yes, how pretty just now in the other flaming dress that set off her beauty so fittingly, and the rich fur coat! He sighed. She was a girl of the world. Of course she was pretty. Well, what of it? He had seen pretty girls before, plenty of them, perhaps girls prettier than she was. She was positively not a person for his thoughts to linger about. She was essentially worldly. If he had not known that before last night he certainly knew it now.

The diamonds twinkled wickedly, and shot a prism into his eyes. He set the little shoe down sharply on his bureau, and began to fumble with the button of the heavy woolen shirt he had worn all day.

His mother's footsteps padded softly here and there below and paused at the foot of the stairs.

"Thurly, almost ready?" she called anxiously. Thurly started and picked up the little shoe sharply again. Thunder! What was he going to do with that shoe?

Did his mother get the girl's address? A pang went through him as he remembered that he did not even know her name. But Mother never forgot such things. She would have the address. It was going to be awkward to ask for it—but he could m. age that. He would tell her how he had found the sho and forgotten it. Then he would send it by mail. That would be best of course. By mail. Would he have to write a letter? No. Yes. What might the girl think? That he had meant to keep the shoe? Had she seen it already? Well, perhaps she thought he was keeping it for some sentimental reason. He must not under any consideration let her think that. He would just send it back by mail if Mother had the address, and let her think what she pleased. That was it—let her think what she pleased. She was nothing to him!

"Laddie, are you ready? I don't hear the water running. There's plenty of hot water, you know."

Thurly started and jabbed the shoe back into his bag under the pajamas again. He couldn't stop now to decide. Mother would think it queer.

"I'll be ready soon!" he shouted.

He dashed into the bathroom and started the hot water, rapidly disrobing. It occurred to him that in case his mother had not been provident enough to get the girl's address he could telephone to Framstead. They would know what young woman had been missing from their dance. Or would they? There might have been more than one missing on such a night as that. Still he could probably get some clue. But the idea of bringing Framstead into the problem was distasteful to him.

He was absorbed and silent when he came down,

and Marget was self-conscious too, and so for the first time in their two lives there seemed to be a cloud between mother and son, which each was too distrait to break. But when the supper things were put away, and it came the time for evening worship Marget hovered near her boy, and putting a timid hand on his shoulder said:

"Laddie, ye'll be praying for the bonnie guest that's gone, the night. Laddie, I think she needs it sairly."

A light came into Thurly's eyes, and he answered heartily, "Yes, Mother—we'll *pray!*" and so they knelt.

But it was by that fervent eager prayer that Marget knew that the little gold shoe had someway got entangled with her lad's heart strings, and she could only pray the more, that the Lord's will might be done; but oh, that her laddie might be spared making any mistakes in the things of this world!

Chapter VIII

It was three days later that Thurly made his decision. The shoe had to go back, and the manly thing to do was to take it. He had decided also that in any case, shoe or no shoe, it was only decent to call and see if the lady had suffered any damages from her exposure in the storm.

Thurly had arrived at this decision after hours of argument with himself. Now he was all contempt for the girl who had dared to enter a man's room and search for cigarettes, again he was all tenderness for the fairy-like little person he had carried on his shoulder through the storm. The matter was getting on his nerves and obtruding itself between him and his work. He felt that it must be finished up, cleared out of his system, and forgotten. He finally faced himself in the glass and realized that some inner weakness in himself actually longed to see that girl again! All that he acknowledged was probably true about her, yet he desired more than he could understand in himself, to see her once more. He finally arrived at the decision that to go and see her in her natural setting would probably be the best antidote for his foolishness that could be had.

So he came down to breakfast the next morning and asked his mother in the most casual manner if she happened to know the address of their late guest.

Marget faced about from the stove where she was dishing up the oatmeal porridge and tried to be casual too, but there was that in her tone that made her answer seem momentous.

"Oh, yes. She's Miss Anastasia Endicott, and I found her father's name in the paper this morning. It's the same I know for it mentioned her as having been a débutante last winter, and it called her by the name she said they all used, so I was sure."

The son's eyes were veiled as he asked huskily:

"What was the name?"

The way his mother said "Tasha" gave it a pagan sound, and Thurly sat looking down at the coffee he was stirring and considered it with a queer sinking at his heart. Of course! That would be she. He might have known it would be some loud dashing name like that—yet—she was so small and delicate—so lovely—!

He was suddenly roused to realize that his mother was watching him and that her face was anxious. He looked up and tried to laugh.

"Queer name, isn't it? Sounds kind of heathen. Well, I'm glad you know who she is. You see, I found her shoe."

"Yes," said Marget without interrogation in her voice.

"It's got to be returned, I suppose," said Thurly, and suddenly realized that a personal call was utterly superfluous. He paused.

"Yes," stated Marget. "I told her it would likely be found."

Another pause.

"You—would like *me*—" she hesitated. "You want me to send it to her of course," she finished blithely as if that were a sudden solution of the difficulty she had not thought of before.

"Why—would you—Mother?" said Thurly, the sun suddenly gone blank— "You—don't—think—. It won't be necessary for me to take it in person?"

Marget's voice trembled a little as she answered.

"Why, no—no, Thurly, not unless—why, no, I shouldn't see how that would be expected at all. She's not a personal friend, of course," she finished briskly.

"Of course," said Thurly colorlessly.

"I'll write her a note," said Marget happily. "I'll say you found her shoe near the station. You did find it near the station, didn't you, laddie?"

"Yes, I found it in—near—that is it was really in the station. It was dark, you know. I ran across it."

"Well, it isn't necessary, I'll just say you found it. And oh, was the buckle on it? The maid said it was real diamonds. I hope that isn't lost."

"It's there!" said Thurly crisply. "I'll get it."

He brought the slipper down and Marget held it in her hand, the diamonds sparkling gloriously in the morning sun.

"Now isn't that a pretty little trick!" said Marget, gayly twinkling the gems back and forth in the sun. "It looks just as if it belonged to her, doesn't it?"

Marget was so happy to have this slipper out from between her lad and herself that she forgot she was admiring the girl to him. The sudden light in his eyes brought her sharp upstanding, and the diamonds smote her so that she had to close her eyes. Then a new thought stung into her consciousness.

"Laddie, I don't know as it's safe after all to send

diamonds through the mail. Someone might steal them. I'm afraid I'd always be uneasy lest she never got them. I wouldn't like to be responsible for them, sending them that way. Do you think perhaps we ought to take them in?"

The sun leaped up again in the day and Thurly smiled broadly.

"Well, perhaps—" he said cheerfully. "Yes, I suppose that would be the careful, kindly thing to do," he added and rising suddenly with a hand full of dishes he made his way to the kitchen with them, as was his custom after meals, whistling gayly, like his old happy self.

Meanwhile, Tasha Endicott, as the limousine wallowed slowly cityward, had a strange impression that she was passing back into life again after a temporary aberration. She questioned her maid eagerly as to what had happened during her absence. Was the storm terrible in the city? The maid was voluble in her description of conditions.

"Mrs. Endicott got quite angry about the storm," she said. "It hindered guests from arriving. Something went wrong, too, with the heating plant and the fire was out for several hours. Mrs. Endicott was furious with Talbot and dismissed him. It was found afterward that snow had fallen down the chimney in great quantities and stopped the draft."

Marie did not express a word of blame toward Mrs. Endicott, but Tasha knew there was veiled indignation behind the maid's formal words. Marie had been fond of Talbot. And it had not been Talbot's fault. But that was Lucia! She had to take out any annoyance or discomfort on someone else, usually the servants. Tasha stared out of the car window for several seconds thinking. She was sorry to have Talbot go. He was the last one of the old servants who had been with the family since Tasha was a child. But it had been inevitable. Lucia never had liked him and was only seeking a good cause of complaint before she got rid of him. Now what would Dad say? Would he make a stand and send for Talbot? If he did there would be a storm in the house again that might last for days.

Tasha flung the thought aside and turned back to Marie.

"Is Dad home?" she asked, her tone dismissing the other bit of information without comment.

"No, Miss Tasha. He is *not*. I believe they said he was gone to New York," said Marie, her tone answering her mistress' very thought. Marie had a great way of carrying on conversations this way without actually saying anything disrespectful or presuming. It was impossible to reprove her for anything she had said. Tasha let this go by without comment also.

"There was company," volunteered Marie with a knowing twinkle and lifting of her chin. "All day Sunday!"

Tasha turned a quick glance and swept the maid's furtive face.

"The—same—one?" she asked casually, trying not to sound annoyed.

"Yes, Mr. Clancy!" There was so much understanding of Tasha's own annoyance in the simple answer that Tasha changed the subject with dignity.

"Is there much mail?"

"Oh, yes, a quantity," assented the maid eagerly. "Many invitations. It's going to be quite the gayest season yet, judging by the way it begins. Yes, and there are boxes of flowers. I've kept them fresh. Orchids from Mr. Barry, and violets and roses—"

But Tasha was not listening. She was visioning a cozy room, that she had seen that very morning, with white muslin curtains at the windows, and a potted geranium on a little stand near the snow-covered panes, cheerfully blooming, a spot of scarlet color; she was remembering a sweet-faced old lady fussing tenderly among the leaves, removing a withered bit of bloom, hovering over the great scarlet blossoms as if they were her children, beaming at them with a smile almost as warm as the sun. Somehow orchids and hot house hybrids paled in contrast; there was something so vivid and friendly in the wholesome scarlet geranium. They would not fit into the exquisite simplicity of the home where she had been staying. She tried to picture the orchids arriving and being set within one of the stately old vases painted with shepherdesses and little white lambs. They would seem strangely out of place. But the violets would fit. They would nestle in the quaint glass bowl that had held the quince preserve. They would fill the whole little sweet house with their subtle fragrance. They would tone their purple to the home-spun, and not flaunt themselves nor seem out of place. Yes, she would send some violets to Thurly Macdonald's mother! That was a pleasant thought. She could sometimes send pleasant gifts to the woman who had tucked her into bed, called her lassie, and prayed for her as if she were a little stray lamb. Her eyes grew misty with the memory.

"There's talk of Palm Beach," insinuated Marie, watching her mistress furtively.

"There would be," said Tasha indifferently.

"Oh, but Miss Tasha, you oughtn't to take it like that!" said the maid vivaciously. "It's going to be grand this year. Dorset went down with Madame and the children from next door, and he says there are so many improvements you wouldn't know the place, and that simply everyone is going to be there. You've got so much to make it nice yourself. All the young men just crazy for you, and your father just building the new villa and all. Dorset says it is sweet. He says there's nothing can touch it anywhere in that locality."

"Yes, I suppose there'll be a thrill in that. Did my things come from New York yet? I hope you unpacked. Those transparent velvets crush so easily, and the green one is the prettiest I ever saw. I couldn't duplicate it if it got spoiled."

"Yes, Miss Tasha, they're all hanging up under their covers, and there's not a crease on one. They were well packed."

But Tasha was not listening. She was hearing a sweet little old voice saying "It's such a pretty dress!

You look like a flower in it. I'd like to see you in it again—" Why was it that she could not get her thoughts away from that plain little house, and that plain little old woman, and her strong disconcerting son?

Tasha, arrived at length, entered the stately mansion they called her home, and passed through the more formal rooms. She did not enter the more intimate library just beyond the stair, though she could hear the murmur of languorous voices, her stepmother's and a male voice she disliked beyond reason. She could see the flicker of firelight through the doorway on the wall. She stood for an instant, her foot poised on the stair, listening, then with a shrug she slid noiselessly up to her own apartment.

There was a fire on the hearth here, too, and her own deep chair drawn comfortably near the hearth. A small table was beside the chair, bearing a silver tray with a tea service, a plate of sandwiches, and some bonbons. Her cigarette case lay beside it, just where she had left it when she forgot it in her hurry Saturday night. A soft light fell from beneath silken draperies, and the little shelf beneath the table held the book she had been reading on the train up from Washington. The room was filled with the perfume of exotic flowers. They smiled at her from the period mantel, from table and desk, and carved taboret, bearing the homage of half a dozen different men she knew. Several pounds of costly sweets were lying open handily, their expensive boxes blending with the richness of the room, the firelight flickering over it all. This was hers. All this luxury! And Thurly Macdonald out in the snow dug the Widow Frailey's little cottage back into life again!

The maid came and removed the traveling boots from Tasha's feet, took her wraps and hung them away out of sight, brought the mail, turned the lamp at just the right angle. She had nothing to do but sink into the downy cushions of her chair, and amuse herself, while Thurly Macdonald struggled through storms to

preach to a lot of common people who probably
wouldn't trouble themselves to come out in the snow
to hear him! Life was queer!

But here at last were cigarettes! Why worry about
it all? She sank into her chair, reached for a cigarette
and prepared to light it.

But something arrested her. Her eyes lifted involuntarily and looked toward the corner of the mantel. There, suddenly, he seemed to stand, as if he had
come quietly in, just as he had come upon her the
evening before. The rich shadows of the lovely room
gathered about the vision of him like colored mists,
and seemed to conspire to shield him, as he stood
there, in her room, his eyes upon her—*accusing* eyes!
—just as they had been last night, looking through
and through her!

What nonsense! He was not there at all! 'Twas
just the lilies in the jade bowl on the mantel against
the dusky background of the room that looked like a
face! Her nerves were shot to pieces by her late ex-
periences! She would smoke and dispel the illusion.

She lifted her hand again, but once more the ar-
resting illusion! His eyes, looking through her. His
voice, after that pointed silence: "I do not use them,"
his face flaming white contempt!

She dropped her hand once more to the arm of
her chair and looked beyond to where a picture of
gay dancing nymphs garlanded a young god, and tried
to adjust her vision to the familiar objects of the
room, differentiating the blossoms one from another,
and from their dim background, making them again
but flowers; the semblance of a tall form below the
face, only the tall carved chair with its velvet up-
holstery in black and silver!

She laughed out an empty little ripple of triumph
as she dispelled the fancy for the second time. She lifted
the cigarette to her lips with a defiant gesture, part and
parcel of her old flippant self. But again a third time,
as if an invisible hand had drawn her hand back, as if
a voice had spoken and directed her eyes again to the
shadowy corner beyond the mantel, she looked, and

still he seemed to stand there. He was searching her
through, condemning her with a look that held both
sternness and disappointment. Condemning her, and
praying for her, and yearning over her. She did not call
these things by their names, but she felt them keenly,
each one distinctly, in her soul, and she cringed in her
chair. The moisture started on her brow and lip, her
hand that held the cigarette trembled and dropped to
her lap. The cigarette fell upon the floor.

Down in a little heap she crumpled in her chair,
with her face hidden in her arms, all unhappy, disgusted with herself; all weak with a kind of moral
fright; all angry with herself. Her little hard-boiled
self. Why had that young man such power over her?
Just because he had saved her life did he mean to
hang around her psychically, and dominate her? Did
he presume to order what she would do? He had not
bought her soul by carrying her through the storm
that night. He need not think he had! Oh, she would
break this power he had over her. She would find a way
to make him cringe as he had made her cringe. She
would offer him money in return for what he had done
for her. He might be holy and self-exalted, but he
probably needed money. In fact every room of the
little house where he lived cried out that money was
scarce. His very garments showed poverty, though
they were immaculate, and well cut. They had a hint
of threadbare edges here and there. Money would
break this power he had over her. Her father was able
to pay him a large sum. If he followed her this way she
would cast his own contempt back in his face in the
form of silver and gold!

She lifted her head and looked toward the mantel
defiantly again. The lilies nodded like a white face
through the gloom, and the illusion was gone, but the
cigarette lay where it had fallen upon the floor. As if
to stamp upon him now she had downed him, she
spoke aloud:

"I will pay you money for saving my life!" and
there was in her voice all the contempt she had seen in
his eyes.

"Did you call me?"

It was Marie appearing from the next room. Her keen eyes took in the cigarette upon the floor.

"Yes! Take those cigarettes away!" said Tasha pettishly. "They make me sick!"

Chapter IX

The maid came wonderingly, and took up the pack.

"Why, Miss Tasha," she said, examining them, "they are the same ones you always—"

"I know—take them away!"

"Shall I send out for others?"

"No! I do not wish to smoke now. What time is it? Are we dining at home?"

Tasha sat up and gathered a handful of her mail to examine it.

"Dinner is ordered. I fancy Mrs. Endicott is expecting to be at home," said Marie, stooping to pick up the offending cigarette.

"Has Mr. Clancy gone yet?"

"I'm not sure. I think he is still there."

"Find out if he is staying to dinner."

The maid disappeared and in a few minutes came back.

"Mrs. Endicott has ordered the table set for a guest."

"Then you may tell her I am not coming down to-night. I wish to have my dinner sent up. I'm tired."

Marie hesitated.

"I think Mr. Barry Thurston will be in later in the evening," she insinuated. "He seemed upset that you were not here this morning when he called."

"If he comes you may tell him I'm not seeing

anyone to-night," said Tasha petulantly, her mood hardening with opposition. It helped her to keep Barry out to-night. It somehow satisfied the angry restlessness in her heart to shut them all out, to punish others as well as the young stranger who had presumed to show her contempt. Oh, he was insufferable!

Tasha sat up and drank a cup of tea thirstily, then opened her mail. There was no thrill there at all. The same round of dances and theater parties, the same bridge clubs, and pageants, and benefits. It was just going to be last winter over again! Bah! And Lucia with her hangers on! Perhaps she would ask Dad to let her go to Europe. Of course Palm Beach and the new house would be a slight break in the monotony, and there were always new things there, new people. But life was terribly tasteless somehow. What had happened? She had not felt that way when she started out for Framstead. It must be that killjoy Sunday. She must do something to get rid of this restlessness.

She took up a book and tried to read, but the book she had been eager over had now become tame, silly, a rehash of vapid doings that seemed without a reason.

She flung herself over to the telephone and called up her friend Adrienne Lyman, and after some delay was answered by a dreary voice.

The dreary voice grew a shade more interested however when she recognized Tasha.

"Oh, is that you, Tash? You're a peach, you are! What became of you? We telephoned everywhere we knew to let you know the Framstead bus was coming for you, but we couldn't locate you, and then we heard the bridge was down! Where on earth were you, and why didn't you call up? Barry went wild, till he got so stewed up he didn't know any more, and then he spent most of the night under the table. Really, Tash, he was disgraceful! Even *I* was ashamed of him. He certainly needed you there to keep him straight. And as for Ducky Duke, he was worse than usual. He and Helena Linton—but I really can't tell it all over the telephone. We had the wildest time. It was

some thrill. You ought to have been there. Gloria
Framstead simply outdid herself in costume and set
the pace, and darling, we danced all night! We simply
didn't stop! Think of it! And when morning came and
we found we couldn't get home we danced on! We
danced all day Sunday by spells, just danced till we
dropped somewhere, and then slept a while wherever
we were, and then got up and had more cocktails and
danced again. In fact we danced most of Sunday night
too, and everybody stayed till Monday morning. Sunday night about midnight we had a masked parade,
and Barry Thurston led it with Gloria Framstead. Darling, they marched right up on the table among the
supper things and threw cake and wine—Oh, it was
wild! They say Mrs. Framstead don't like it, much,
but she didn't do a thing about it, and so everybody
had a grand time. But darling! I'm *dead!* I'm simply a
fragment! I've just waked up, been asleep all day,
and I'm not in my right mind yet. I've smoked so
many cigarettes and drank so many cocktails I simply
loathe the thought of food, and I think I shall have to
sleep for a week— But darling! Where *were* you? Did
you have a frumpy time at home, or were you caught
somewhere in the storm? Explain."

And then a strange thing happened to Tasha.

She had intended to have a good laugh with Adrienne over the "quaint" old woman and "frumpy" fanatic of a son who had corralled her for the storm
time. She had hoped by trampling on all that was good
in her soul toward those who had saved her and entertained her, to dispel the restlessness that their memory caused in her. But as she listened to her friend's
account of the Framstead affair she felt a violent reac-
tion, and a keen disgust swept over her. Something
froze within her, and she answered coldly:

"Oh, I was staying with friends near Stonington.
I was quite all right and had a wonderful time. I
couldn't telephone because the wires were down, but
I was sure you would understand. Of course you must
feel rotten after all that, so I won't keep you now. I
just wanted to let you know I'm all right, and see if

you were the same. See you soon," and with a very few more words she hung up.

She stared around her luxurious room and wondered what was the matter with her. Wondered why she had hung up so soon, without asking for more details, and then suddenly was confronted with the idea that she actually had felt as if that young giant of an accusing minister were over there by the mantel all the time listening, and she was feeling his accusing eyes upon her back while she talked.

She put her cold hands on her hot cheeks and gave a little shivering sigh, then marched back to her seat by the fire and deliberately turned on a flare of light in the room. This was ridiculous! This was acting like a baby! Perhaps she was going to be sick. She must buck up!

Marie came in with her dinner, and she ate, picking at this and that, and going back over the Sunday dinner they had eaten in the little cottage at Stonington while the storm raged without, and peace reigned within. There was a wistfulness in her eyes as she glanced up fearfully toward the great bunch of pure white lilies, that shone out distinctly now in the flare of light, with no mocking face of contempt to search her soul.

But later, when Marie had drawn her bath and laid out her night things and gone, Tasha snapped off the light and sat a long time in the dusk, with the fire playing softly over the room, and the dusky white lilies on the mantel that looked like a face, just above her. She was thinking just what she should write in a letter of thanks for her visit; thinking what she would send to Mrs. Macdonald for a present.

Afterwards when she lay in her bed she thought of how Marget Macdonald's soft hands had tucked her in and how the gentle voice had prayed for her. She had often wondered that anybody could believe in supernatural things. She had laughed at credulous fanatics who had caused the Bible to become a sacred book. Now there stole into her heart a faint wonder if perhaps after all there might be something in it. Since such a woman as Marget Macdonald believed, and had taught such a son as hers to believe, it must not be so silly after all.

Not that Tasha was an intelligent unbeliever. She was entirely too indifferent a pagan for that. She had never troubled her head about such things. In college she had passed over Bible study class as too trivial and stupid for her to bother with, so that modern destructive criticism had not even touched her in passing. She had not been where it was. She had been spending her time in the froth of life too far from such questions to even weigh them and discard them. But somehow the influence of that Sabbath shut in by God's snow and cold, with its atmosphere of prayer and praise, with its Bible words and sweet old hymns, and trustful communion with the Father, had left its touch on her gay soul, as nothing had ever done before. It seemed to fill in a way the great emptiness that had always been in her soul. She thought it was because of the lack of a mother, or anything beloved, save her gay, busy, absent father, who had made up in money what he lacked time to give in love and companionship.

Tasha lay and thought about it all until her thoughts blended into her dreams, and she thought she saw Thurly standing by the door, smiling as he had done, before he found her rummaging in his traveling bag.

Then came dimly the memory of her slipper, and it flashed its way into her dreams and became a sprite that danced over a snow-lit field. She seemed to be struggling waist deep to capture it, and fell down exhausted at last, deeper, deeper, colder and colder, till suddenly she was lifted and borne in strong arms, high above the drifts, to the tune of an old hymn. What were those words? "From every stormy wind that blows!" That was it. She must not let that get away.

Marget Macdonald had taken cold, out on the back steps, trying to melt the ice off the brick walk, with just a little shawl around her shoulders, and her hands cold and wet with snow and salt.

"I'm an old fule," she told her son, with a wistful smile. "I kept telling myself to go in and get a warm coat and a hood, and my rubbers. And now, Thurly, son, ye'll have ta gang by yerself. And I'm thinking perhaps that was the way it was meant onygait. Just take the little gold shoe, and give her my best luve, and ye'll have that off yer mind. It's best not to wait. And she might be needing her shoe. I doubt not there are other dances," and she sighed a trifle sadly.

"And other shoes, Mither mine," said Thurly with a lilt in his voice. "I doubt if she'll miss this one, but it's my business to return it anyhow. So here goes."

It is safe to say that never since he faced the vast audience in his High School auditorium to voice his commencement oration had Thurly Macdonald felt so diffident and so utterly inadequate to the situation as he did when he started out with the little gold shoe in a neat package tucked away in the deep pocket of his overcoat.

Clean shaven, well groomed, clear of eye, with his crisp brown curls brushed smooth, he was as goodly a specimen of young manhood as one would care to look upon, and more than one girl tripping by on her little high heels behind her rouge and lipstick turned and looked wistfully after him. But Thurly was feeling more excited than he had ever felt before a big football game. He was going into an unknown field, and he didn't rightly know the signals.

He stopped outside on the corner and got his bearings for a moment after he had located the number. The great stone mansion loomed ominously, its stately portico guarded by a double portcullis of delicate and intricate iron work. It seemed a daring thing to do to attempt to enter there. He had not quite visioned anything so imposing, and yet her home would be like that. He ought to have known.

There would be a butler, with maybe a footman in livery. Thurly Macdonald hated running the gauntlet between lines of liveried servants. Yet his mother's last words had been, "Remember, lad, that ye come of a royal family, and hold your head high. You're a prince and your Father's a King. Look whomsoever ye meet in the eye, and no get tae thinking of yerself!"

How canny his mother was, born and bred among the heather, yet wise to the ways of this world, and knowing the human heart like a book! He gave a little quiet laugh—the one he used to use as he went into battle in the old football days—and stepped through the iron grill into the stately portico.

Thurly Macdonald had been in just as pretentious mansions as the Endicott home many a time, going home with his college friends for week ends, an honored guest anywhere; and occasionally being entertained somewhere for over night when he went to take a great man's pulpit on a sudden call; but never before had a house so overawed him. As he followed the servant through the dimness of a spacious hallway into a formal reception room at one side, he glanced about him and caught his breath. The very chime of the cathedral clock in some dim recess seemed like fairy bells. For was he not in the home of the beautiful girl who had dropped down upon his own humble home in the midst of a storm in a rose-petaled frock, looking too exquisite to be true. This was her world that he saw about him, the nest of luxury where she was bred. The other lovely homes where he had entered had been but beautiful backgrounds for his friends, but this was different. This was where the lovely worldly young woman walked and talked and had her being; it was a fitting background for surely the loveliest creature God had ever put upon this earth, even though she was wholly apart from his world. It was good that he should be here and see how she lived. It was good that he should get all ideas of friendship with her out of his head. Here was where the little gold shoe belonged, and he was bringing it home. It never belonged on his bureau, or in his traveling bag. Its jewels were not made to shine in a cottage, but to sparkle on a gay foot upon a palace floor.

So Thurly Macdonald held his head high and remembered his royal birth as he followed the liveried man to the high quiet room and waited.

It was some minutes before the servant returned and Thurly had time to get into tune with the new surroundings. He noted the rich furnishings, rare carvings and articles of vertu scattered lavishly about; a great picture so hung that its figures seemed to be living men and women going about just beyond the next room; a mirror that seemed to reach to heaven and reflect the universe; rugs that caught the sound of a footfall and choked it into silence. And then the man stood before him again.

"Miss Endicott is not in," he said in his cold mechanical voice.

"I will wait," said Thurly with a firm set of his fine lips. "Will it be long before her return?"

The man might have answered "five minutes" in the same tone with which he spoke, but he said:

"Not until Spring, probably. Mrs. Endicott and Miss Endicott have left for Palm Beach. They usually stay until the cold weather is over."

Thurly got to his feet with a sudden sinking of dismay. Gone! Spring! At the least three months, then the cold would be over!

He walked the silent hallways lingeringly, willfully, gave one quick glance back as the great grill opened to let him out, and gravely trod the portico into the sunshine of the wintry day again.

But it was not until he was seated in a bus being carried swiftly toward the station that he remembered that he was still carrying the little gold shoe tucked safely away in his deep overcoat pocket!

Chapter X

Lucia Endicott, slim, sleek, groomed to the last degree, lolled in her seat in the drawing-room compartment and smoked one cigarette after another as she idly watched her pretty, contemptuous stepdaughter. She had hair like black satin cut sharply and close to her small round head, and her sharp features were somewhat accentuated by the points of hair that lay on her deeply tinted cheeks, and by the sharp lines of the deeply red lips that were startling against the pearly whiteness of her skin. She wore wriggly clanging earrings that seemed to have personalities like serpents, hired to go with her make-up, and her eyes were like two bright black stones that imprisoned something slimy and cruel. She was sitting in the conventional fashionable attitude, with a spine like a new moon, and just the right amount of slim knee showing beneath her brief skirt, surmounting the proper length of silken limb, like two clothesprops crossed and lolling from the clothesline.

She narrowed her eyelids that were thick and white, and just touched with a fashionable amount of blue shadow, and studied Tasha, sitting gloomily opposite, staring out of the window, a closed magazine lying unheeded in her lap.

"What's the idea, Tash?" she asked at last, "trying a new pose? You haven't smoked once to-day."

"It doesn't interest me," said Tasha without taking her gaze from the window. "I'm fed up on smoke. Besides, it's a silly thing to do. Did you ever think how senseless it is?"

"You'll never get anywhere on that," advised the stepmother languidly, "it isn't good form. And besides, people don't like you if you don't do as they do."

"There isn't anywhere to get, Lucia darling," moralized Tasha contemptuously, "and why should I want people to like me? I'm bored to death with people liking me now. I don't get the least kick out of it anymore!"

"Try something new, angel child! It really is time you got married. Which reminds me. I'd advise you to annex Barry Thurston presently or you may lose him. They tell me he was devoted to Gloria Framstead at the dance you didn't attend. You know you've been out a whole year now, and it doesn't do to let the younger set come in and pick what belongs to you. I've noticed a number of times that Gloria has her eye on Barry, and if she wants him she'll get him."

"Let her have him!" said Tasha with a shrug, as she remembered Adrienne's account of the Saturday night dance. There was contempt in her eyes and voice, and the other woman narrowed her gaze.

"You're foolish!" she said sharply, "you can't count on lasting forever with a man like Barry. He likes to be flattered and Gloria flatters him. You've wiped the earth up with him for months, and he's getting fed up on it, Tash! You can't treat a man that way forever, not when there's a stunning beauty around like Gloria. I know the signs and I tell you Barry Thurston's fed up on being a mat under your feet!"

"And I'm fed up on Barry Thurston!" declared Tasha in a cold voice. "That's one reason I consented to go to Palm Beach just now. He's not the absolutely only man!"

"Don't be silly, Tash! You know Barry Thurston is your best bet. There isn't another man in our crowd can touch him for wealth and position. You could have simply anything you wanted, and go anywhere you liked. And if you got tired of Barry you could live in Europe for a while."

"What's the matter, Lucia," said Tasha, sitting up

and eyeing her stepmother sharply, "are you getting tired of having me around? Or is it that you want to stage a display wedding with yourself as loving mother? Speak out and get it off your chest. I can always go to Europe or somewhere else if I'm in the way."

"Infant!" said the other young woman lazily, "as if I couldn't give you a word of advice without your going into a fury like that. I simply hate to see you let the best catch of the season go through your fingers, with a flock of little buds just waiting to catch him as he falls. I didn't like to tell you, but I've been hearing things about that dance. You certainly ought to have got there somehow! Strange! I never knew you to give up a thing as easily as that. You surely could have got a taxi to take you around another way if the bridge was down. There is always another road."

"Well, as it happened, there wasn't any road anywhere, nor any telephone to get taxis with even if there had been taxis and a road."

"By the way, Tash, you never told me what kind of a place you stayed in. Was it a hotel? I asked Marie about it but she didn't seen to have much opinion of it."

"No, it wasn't a hotel. It was a private house near the station."

"Near the station? Stonington? I don't seem to remember any private house nearer than Framstead estate. Do I know the people? Where did you meet them? How did you come to go there?"

"It wasn't an estate, Loo, it was just a small cottage."

"Horrors! A porter's lodge, or some servant's quarters!"

"No, they were not servants. They were very nice people, but it was a plain little private house. I met the—them—in the station. It was perfectly obvious that I was storm stayed, for the station was closed and locked and the snow was almost to my waist. They very kindly—took me home!"

"You poor infant! You must have been bored stiff!"

"No, I enjoyed it," said Tasha almost to her own surprise. "There was a dear old lady who seemed like what I used to think a mother would be."

Mrs. Endicott eyed her stepdaughter curiously to see if here was a hidden stab intended in this sentence, but Tasha sat looking idly across the hurrying landscape with dreamy eyes, and nothing vindictive in her expression.

"Was there nobody there but an old lady?" asked Lucia with narrowed eyes and cunning in her voice.

"Oh, the rest of the family were all right—" drawled Tasha, "but the old lady was especially rare. She was a kind I never saw before. I got a good rest."

"It sounds sketchy to me," said Lucia. "Did you have enough to eat?"

"Oh, plenty!" said Tasha, making her lips into a little tight line that Lucia knew meant the girl did not mean to be further communicative.

"Well, if you ask me," she said with a tone of dissatisfaction, "I should say it didn't do you much good. You've been as prickly as a thistle ever since the experience."

"At that I haven't much on you, Loo," Tasha countered. "By the way, is Will Clancy coming down to Palm Beach next week?"

"I'm sure I don't know," snapped Lucia crossly, and turned toward the window to hide the quick color that rolled up under her careful make-up.

After this sudden stab Tasha settled down with a magazine and the conversation languished. But Tasha did not read much, although she duly turned the leaves from time to time. She found herself strangely stirred at the conversation. She found herself resenting her stepmother's attitude toward her rescuers, and her contempt of the little house that had given her haven during the storm, even more than the attempt to pry into her private affairs.

And back of it all there was something else. She was wondering within herself why she did not wish to reveal the fact that there had been a young man in that home, a man both interesting and well known among college people? To have told this would have explained at once to Lucia why she had not been bored. But that would have entailed endless questions. And why, then, on the other hand, was she not willing to hold him up to ridicule as a fanatic? Was it possible that she had respect for the things for which he stood?

Though he had shown contempt for her and her ways, did she yet feel that there had been that in him that she must protect from the scorn of her family?

After a time she closed her magazine and lay back in her chair, pretending to be asleep, but in reality going over her whole experience in the snow storm, detail by detail, and getting a new view of herself as well as a new view of her rescuer. But ever, her meditations came around to the same place, with the young man standing in the door of his room, looking at her with those clear, cold blue eyes, that searched her soul and applied scorn to the wounds.

As she remembered that the hot blood burned in her cheeks and her proud young soul writhed. She felt she would like to go back to his precious home and flaunt all her sins. She would like to smoke a cigarette in his face! Yes, even in the sweet face of his old lady mother! She would rejoice to defy him, and show him that his scorn meant nothing to her! She would like to ride roughshod over his soul as he had by his look ridden over hers, and make him writhe too!

Yet Tasha had not touched a cigarette since the night she saw his face looking at her from the spray of lilies in the dusk.

Then like a ray of light in the dark, there came the memory. "Well, he has my shoe yet, anyway! I can hold that over him any time I like. I wonder what he means to do with it?"

And suddenly she sat up and looked at her wrist watch.

"It's dinner time, Lucia, let's wake up."

So the cloud between the two young women was for the time dispelled.

And about that time Thurly was tramping up the steps of his own home, with a slump of weariness in his shoulders and the little gold shoe still in his pocket.

Marget had hovered near the window all day watching for her boy, and when he did not come on his usual train she brought her sewing and sat close to the window, where she could watch the street and see him as he first turned the corner.

Over and over she imagined the interview between her boy and the girl who had so intruded into their peaceful life and disquieted her heart. There really was not much to be imagined about. The mother had thought of all possibilities. Miss Endicott might be out, or be busy, and send down word that she could not see him; and at that thought Thurly's mother would lift her Scotch chin proudly, and view the girl with a scorn so fine that she might not half have understood it.

Perhaps she would invite Thurly in—and it would likely be that of course, for how could a girl in her senses not wish to be welcoming such a young man as hers? That would be it, of course. She would ask Thurly in, and they would maybe talk over the latest books, and Thurly would recommend one a bit, one that would perhaps help the young woman, for Thurly knew how. They would mayhap talk of music, for the lass had spoken of a great violinist who was soon to visit the city. Marget had read enough of the society notes to know that rich folk invited their friends to sit with them in their boxes at the Academy on great occasions like that, and Marget dreaded the thought that the girl might think to repay her son for his rescue and hospitality by inviting him to a concert with her; dreaded, yet half hoped she would. Marget liked to think of her precious son as being welcome in the grandest boxes in the land, and able to move among the world's people without shame; yet she knew in her heart that herein would lie the danger for him. He loved music, and was not able to afford to hear much.

Yet even as she longed for such pleasure for him,

she prayed in her heart, "Oh, Lord, save him! Help him! Guide him! Don't tempt my laddie too strongly! Don't let the world pull him away! She's not for him, I'm sure you think, oh Lord! She's just a worldling sent to try my laddie! Make him strong! Don't let him be led into temptation!"

All day she had dreamed and prayed, and watched, and when the dusk was coming down he came tramping slowly up the street, with no spring in his walk, and his gaze on the pavement before him; just his stubborn plod that he wore at times when things were all against him and he meant to keep right on anyway. Ah, she knew her laddie!

She hurried to open the door, and reached her warm soft arms, with their warm roseleaf touch, around his neck. She took his greeting kiss with her soft lips trembling with her love for him, against the hard ruddy coldness of his cheek, keen from the cold night air.

She waited while he hung up his hat and coat on the little hall rack, for he never would let her wait upon him. Then she saw with a start that he was bringing a package in his hand—the package he had carried away in the morning—and her heart sank for him, for she saw that his face was clouded over, and her mother love sprang at once to the defense. Had the girl been unkind to him? But no, for he would not have brought the package back again. Perhaps her eyes had deceived her. It might be something else he had brought from the city, put up in the same wrappings, or a gift the girl had sent to her. But there was no sparkle in her laddie's eye as there would have been if he bore a pleasant thing like a gift. So she waited for his word.

"It's very cold out," was all he said and laid the little package down on the table, going over to the fire and holding a chilled foot toward the blaze. "It seems to be growing colder all the time!" he added as if he did not know that she was waiting, just waiting, for his account of what had happened in the day, and especially about his visit to the Endicott house.

"But you brought the bit package back again,"

said Marget when her patience would not hold out any longer, "why did you do that, laddie!"

Thurly mustered a grave smile.

"Yes," he said languidly, "I did. I didn't intend to, but I did it without thinking."

Marget paused on this thought a moment and caught a gleam of hope from it.

Ah, then! If her laddie could forget the little shoe, surely then there was no need for worry about him.

"How about?" she asked perplexed.

"Well, you see, she wasn't there," said Thurly, as if somehow the day had been a disappointment and his thoughts were still heavy with it.

"Not?" said his mother sympathetically. "Weel, could ye na have left the bit shoe? It seems a long way to plod back again."

"Why, you see, Mother, I forgot I had it with me when I came away." Thurly laughed foolishly as if he knew he was showing his keen old mother how he had been upset by the whole matter.

"And was the house so grand then?" she eyed him tenderly, proudly.

"Grand. Yes. It is grand. It is—" he hesitated and said almost tenderly, "it is such a place as she would belong in, Mother."

"Yes, it would be, laddie!" sympathized his mother, and neither of them seemed to realize that they were making a queer meaningless conversation, for each knew what the other meant.

"They had a serving man, Mother, who rather magnified his office," explained Thurly half sheepishly.

"I see, laddie! And so ye forgot. Well, mayhap it's juist as weel!"

Marget relapsed into the vernacular of her childhood on occasion, when she would be deeply stirred. She brushed the tip of her finger across her misty eyes, and smiled thoughtfully.

"There must be a way to send it safely," she mused, caressing the package. "I'll find a bit box and some cotton and put the pretty trick up safely, and it'll

maybe be more dignified to send it, after all! Isn't there
a way to insure it or something, lad?"

"Yes, we can insure it, or register it. Oh, it'll be
safe enough I suppose!" And there was that in Thurly's
tone that made his mother not so sure after all that
Thurly was safely past this rock.

"Well, we'll think about it, lad. Were ye thinking
of going again? Perhaps after all——" She eyed him anxiously. If Thurly felt he ought to go, she must not seem
to hinder him. "Could ye make it to-morrow morn
again? Ye can ill spare anither day from the study I suppose."

"Why, she'll not be home to-morrow, Mother.
She's away until Spring the man said, gone to Florida
till the cold is over; and I was so surprised that I stupidly
carried off the shoe again and didn't realize it till the bus
was half way to the station. Of course I didn't just see
going back then. The next block after I discovered it
one of the professors from the University got in the bus
and wanted me to take lunch with him, and go with
him afterward to meet a man who is interested in a
church, and I've been with him ever since till I ran
for my train."

"Well, come now, laddie, the dinner is all but
dished. We'd best sit down, and we can talk while we
eat."

So the little shoe lay on the parlor table while
mother and son went out to dinner.

"And so it was a grand hoose!" mused Marget
when they were both served and had begun to eat.

Thurly described as best he could the glories of
the Endicott mansion, and Marget sat and watched her
son, analyzing his every intonation, the turn of his
smile, the lift of a lash, as if her senses were a ther-
mometer that could register the state of his heart.

They spoke no more of the girl that night, though
the little shoe remained between them on the table all
the evening. But when it came time to go upstairs to
bed, Marget lingered.

"You'd best take it up with you, Thurly," she
said pointing to the little package as if it were a great

responsibility, "we're not used to having diamonds in the house. I feel we should get it to her as soon as possible. She'll be needing the shoe. A bit trick like that must cost something."

"She's plenty of shoes, Mother, don't worry about that! She'd never miss this one if it never reached her at all."

But he said it a bit bitterly, as he picked up the package to carry it up stairs.

Far back on his closet shelf he hid it, and piled Jamieson, Fausset, and Brown's *Critical and Explanatory Commentary on the Bible,* Young's *Concordance,* and *The Works of Josephus* in front of it, not because he was afraid of his mother's burglars, but because he wished to dispel the bright radiance of the glittering gems that seemed to emanate from even the brown paper parcel of it.

But though the gems were guarded safely by the most orthodox brand of theology, yet there was little sleep that night for either the young minister or his mother. They were trying to decide what to do with that little gold shoe. It seemed such a simple matter, just to send it back, or take it back—which? And then they would go back to the beginning of the argument and have it all over again, both from their point of view and the girl's point of view, and perhaps several other points of view.

The mother, used to yielding her will to the Higher Will, made out to set the whole matter in wiser Hands than her own, and fell asleep at last, but it was not till toward morning that the young man got out of bed and down upon his knees.

"Oh, God. That shoe has to go back! But oh, Father! Save that girl!"

After which prayer, the young man too slept.

It was the next morning that Marget found Tasha's picture in the paper with an account of her migration to Florida, in company with her stepmother. Marget, after a thoughtful look at the pictured face, folded it open upon the breakfast table where Thurly could see it the first thing when he came down.

After he had read it she said in a quiet voice:
"I guess, laddie, after all, we'd better let the bit
bootie bide until the lassie gets home."

Thurly assented gravely, and by common consent
they laid the subject aside.

It was while Thurly still lingered at his late breakfast that there came a ring at the door. A messenger
boy from one of the great city florists had brought a
big box of sweet violets for Mrs. Macdonald from Miss
Endicott.

Marget put them in a lovely old pewter bowl that
she kept hoarded away on her pantry shelf, and set
them on the little parlor table, from whence they
promptly filled the house with wondrous fragrance.

Marget stood and looked at them long and buried
her sweet old face in their purple depths. After she
was gone back to the kitchen to finish her dishes Thurly
came and gazed down upon them, drew in a deep
breath of their sweetness, flicked one purple blossom
from the rest, brought it up to his face for an instant,
with closed eyes, and then slipped it away in his vest
pocket for further reference, and went his way into the
world to his belated work. But Marget spent much
time that day, smelling of those flowers, and looking
at them, half in awe and fear, and half in a great delight of the beauty which her soul loved.

Chapter XI

Tasha plunged into the gayeties of Palm Beach with a
restless energy that made her as usual the center of
the gay set. Her followers and her frocks were the talk
of the town. Nevertheless her heart was not at rest. It

was as if she were ever seeking some great thrill which would satisfy, and drive the fever from her soul.

Perhaps part of her restlessness was due to her having broken her habit of smoking which truly had been heavy upon her. Several times she was on the verge of going back to it, but always there seemed to come that vision of the lilies in the dusk, and as if to prove she could she seemed to dare her soul to keep free from it. Just what her own idea in doing so was she was not sure. Sometimes in the small hours of the night as she crept to her couch she wondered over it, half thinking it was a silly superstition from which she should rid herself. But always the thought of the cool, steady contemptuous glance brought her back to her first decision, and she came to acknowledge to herself that her real reason was that she might exorcise that glance by one as cool and steady and as clean. "I do not use them." Well, she could say so too, now!

It was after she had come to that point of understanding that the vision came again.

She was standing in a brilliantly lighted room among a lot of other dinner guests, awaiting a late arrival, and the cocktails were being passed. She accepted her glass with her usual grace, and lifted it with a gay word to Barry Thurston who had come down that day and was giving her news of Gloria Framstead.

But as she did so her glance went to the wide doorway opening into the spacious hall, and there, quite distinctly, she seemed to see Thurly Macdonald, standing under the archway, not in evening dress like the other men, but dressed in his fine dark blue serge as he had stood that Sunday night at Stonington. One hand was resting lightly against the door frame, and his eyes were upon her as she lifted the wine glass to her lips. In those eyes was that terrible glance of mingled yearning and disapproval that searched her vapid young soul and turned existence into ashes.

The laughter died on her lips and her eyes took on a frightened look. She forgot her friends all about her, and the gayety that rang through the house. She stood, and stared across the room with paling cheek and lips that wanted to tremble, and slowly, almost mechanically her hand with its glass went down from her lips.

"What's the matter, Tasha!" cried Barry, "you look as though you saw a ghost."

Tasha became suddenly aware of her position and rallied, trying to laugh, and lifting the glass once more. She must get herself in hand. She must swallow the liquor quickly. Perhaps she was going to faint. But involuntarily her gaze went again to the door, and there those eyes seemed now to hold her own, and control her gaze. She could not take her eyes away, though she tried. She knew it was but an illusion, yet it had power over her. Her hand went slowly down again, and her eyes took on their stunned look once more.

"Why, Tasha, are you sick?" It was Barry's voice that recalled her again, with real anxiety in it now, and Tasha turned and held out the glass to him.

"No, not sick, Barry, just trying to find a place to set this glass down. Won't you take it for me?"

"But you look white," said Barry. "Why don't you drink it? It's the new cocktail. Haven't you tasted them? We had them up at Framstead after you left. They're great! Just taste it!"

"Not to-night, Barry. Take it for me, please. I want to speak to Lucia a minute before we go out to dinner. That's a dear!" and she pressed the glass upon him and slipped away toward the doorway. He saw her presently standing there with her face turned partly away from him, her hand resting lightly against the door frame, a strange smile upon her lips, but she was not talking to Mrs. Endicott who in slight draperies of cloth of gold, and green emerald serpents in her ears and about her neck and wrists, was discoursing eagerly to their host a few feet away. Tasha seemed to be suddenly detached from the company with which she was surrounded, and to be alone in a little world of her own. He could not quite understand it; but meanwhile, why let a perfectly good cocktail go to waste? He slipped his own empty glass behind a picture on the mantel, and working his way around into the sun porch he found a secluded spot in which to imbibe Tasha's cocktail.

But to Tasha, standing in that doorway where the vision had stood, with her hand where Thurly Macdonald's hand had seemed to be, there came a thrill that surpassed all the artificial thrills she had ever manufactured for herself. What it all meant she did not stop to question. She might be going mad, or turning sentimental, or about to die; but it was sweet, and she had the consciousness that she had conquered that cold stern look in the young man's eyes, and done something with which he would have been pleased if he had really been there. Her eyes might look back to his now, clean and free. Why, yes of course, he probably didn't use cocktails any more than he used cigarettes. He probably did not approve of women who drank any more than of those who smoked. It was incredible that there was a man like that, but it seemed to be true, and somehow she liked it in him.

Well then, she would not drink cocktails either. She did not stop to ask herself whether it was going to be a hard task to give them up, whether it would bring ridicule upon her, and put her in embarrassing situations. She just registered a resolve that she was done with that, and the firm set of the pretty lips would have told anyone who knew Tasha well that it was of no use to argue with her. She was doing this thing as a challenge to a young man who had affronted her with his eyes, who had charged her with being unfine, unwomanly. That was what his look had meant that night. It was what it had meant tonight as he looked at her from the doorway as she was about to drink.

That it was all a sort of mirage, a figment of her imagination, made no difference. That the young man in all probability would never know of her resolve, would never likely see her again in this life, and if he did would not know what she had done because of him, did not enter into her calculations. She had conquered and set right something in herself to which he had objected, and she felt not only her self-respect rising, but a kind of new joy—or was it just elation? At least it was something precious to keep and turn over in her soul.

Standing thus alone, within that doorway, all in misty white with something sparkling about her throat and in her hair, and that misty look in her eyes, more than one in the gay assemblage looked and called attention to her. "Isn't Tasha lovely to-night?" And Barry emerging from his ambush in search of more cocktails caught a glimpse of her and swore softly to himself, with a vague fear, and murmured:

"I'll gamble there's another man! I'll make her answer me to-morrow. Gloria isn't in it with Tasha, and that's a fact!"

But although he took her out to dinner, and she was gayer than usual, yet Barry got nowhere with her. Tasha was jubilantly, brilliantly floating along in a world all of her own in which Barry had no part.

It took some days for her friends to realize that Tasha was neither drinking nor smoking any more. They thought it was just a whim at first, for she was given to whims and odd doings, but had ever been the daringest of the set. Then one and another began to whisper it about, to watch her and question.

It was their laughter and utter contempt for her new fancy that finally riveted her half formed purpose, and made her declare that she was fed up on smoking and drinking, and had decided to cut them out. She was one of those whom opposition makes but the stronger, and so several of them set about arguing the matter with her, and trying to show her that she could not keep that up and hold her position: that it was an impossible situation. One could not go against fashion and custom. It was rude. It was impolite. As if any of them had ever bothered themselves much about good manners in this day and generation! But then perhaps they thought they did, and they certainly were outraged by Tasha's stand, insomuch that she grew quite firm in her laughing statements, and finally declared that if they did not like her as she was she would seek other company.

So she went her way as always, gay, beautiful, gorgeously dressed, entering into all the sports, present at all the functions, notable for her high spirits, yet in her heart strangely restless and weary of it all.

For now that she was entirely sane and sober when the rest were drinking she began to wonder if she too had talked such vapid nonsense at the close of a dinner? Or was it that they were all just a stupid lot and she had not had sense enough to know it before? She began to grow silent as they grew hilarious, and then her stepmother took a hand and remonstrated once more.

"Tasha, you really are acting like a spoiled child. What is it you are trying to put across, anyway? Can't you see that Gloria is just putting it all over you, the way she is leading Barry around by the nose?"

Tasha's answer was to whirl around from the balcony where she was overlooking the sea, watching the white sails dip in the wind, and face her stepmother down with a straight steady look.

"Lucia," she said, "get this. Gloria isn't putting a thing over on me. I'm putting it on her, if there is any putting at all. I sent Gloria off to walk with Barry last night on the beach because I simply couldn't stand their idiocy any longer. They were both of them silly drunk and it made me sick."

"Nonsense!" said Lucia sharply, a bright red spot on either cheek beneath the rouge, "I've seen you in just the same condition!"

Tasha eyed her quizzically.

"I wonder!" she said, "well, I'm glad you told me. You won't see me that way any longer. And now, Loo, you've given me a good deal of advice, perhaps you'll take a little from me. If I were you I wouldn't be seen with Will Clancy any more. People are beginning to talk and Dad is coming down next week."

"Nonsense!" said Lucia, angrily, "you don't know what you are talking about! Everybody goes around together. I'm not with one any more than another! There's absolutely nothing your father could object to in our friendship."

"Cut it, Loo, you can't put anything over on me. I cut my eye teeth long ago. But I mean what I say. You better watch your step. Dad divorced Marietta for less than you are doing, and you know Will Clancy hasn't enough to keep himself, let alone buying cigarettes and imported gowns for you. You can't get away with it and you'd better take my advice and cut it!"

With which sage advice Tasha walked jauntily across the porch and went up to her room, where she locked her door and flung herself across the bed.

"There, I've done it, but what good'll it do?" she asked herself. "Poor Dad! He's never had half a chance!"

Then quite unexpectedly she burst into tears and hid her face in the pillow. Decidedly Tasha was not herself.

She did not go down to dinner that evening, but had something sent up to her room, and then, arrayed in a simple little blue frock that was as much like a home house dress as anything she owned, she slipped out while the rest were at dinner, and walked fast and far.

The smell of the sea was good, the soft perfume of the yellow jessamine, the whisper of the pines, above her among the great southern stars, the silken swish of stiff palmetto leaves outlined against the night sky, the soft black darkness, as she walked away from the brilliant lights and came toward the plainer less populated portion of town all rested her feverish soul. The sea could be heard out here, away from the numberless orchestras, and sounds of luxury.

There were plain little houses, with lights in cozy rooms, and children running in and out the door calling to one another. Their voices sounded distant in the clear atmosphere as if they stood beside her. The fragrance of a simple vegetable stew floated out appetizingly, reminding in some subtle way of the Sunday dinner at Macdonald's, and strangely softening her heart toward these unknown dwellers in the humble homes.

She stumbled on, sometimes walking in the sand now, for she had strayed beyond the sidewalks and come to where there were mere paths along the edge of the road.

And now a little light sprang up in a tiny chapel, twinkling feebly, and spreading from window to window, till the whole little frame structure stood out like a toy church on a sandy plain, almost isolated save for a group of palmettos and a lofty pine waving gray arms of moss among the stars. Stark and lonely it stood, yet beckoned her as if there were something warm and human and true inside, and a little steeple pointed whitely, with a star twinkling just above the apex.

Tasha to her own surprise began to take her way across a sandy space shredded with coarse grass and wild pea blossoms, and bristling with sand spurs. She got sand spurs on her stockings, all the way up to her knees, and sand inside her small white slippers, but she kept on like a hungry person to a meal.

There was a little street presently that led past the tiny church, and she filed down with a few other stragglers and entered the building, sliding into a back seat and looking about her.

There were about twenty people in the church, and a few more entered as she sat down. A girl somewhat older than herself was at the organ, a plain girl without style, who was turning over the pages of a hymn book. An old man with white hair and a saintly look sat by the table in front of the pulpit, and he presently announced a hymn.

There seemed something familiar in the strains

that quavered out from the organ. It was a poor organ, and rather badly played, but the girl kept good time and seemed to enter into her task with spirit. Someone with squeaky shoes came down the aisle and handed Tasha a hymn book open at the place, and then they began to sing:

> "From every stormy wind that blows,
>   From every swelling tide of woes,
> There is a calm, a sure retreat,
>   'Tis found beneath the mercy seat."

Why, that was the very hymn they had sung at Stonington that Sunday night, Thurly Macdonald and his mother! Tasha sat remembering every little happening, every turn of a note, the wailing of Thurly's violin, the placid look of his mother's face, the sweet voices blending with the violin, and the way Thurly's hair fell over his forehead when he stooped to pick up her handkerchief that had fallen to the floor. It set her heart a-throbbing.

The little scattered flock in the church were all singing, and Tasha found herself trying to sing too. They were not all singing on the key. They were not all keeping time. Some dragged fearfully. Some voices quavered and broke. Others were shrill and unmusical, but all were singing with their hearts. One tall thin old lady with a queer combination of ancient fashions in garments, and a hat of the vintage of the *most* Victorian ages perched high on a notably false front was shrilling out a high tenor above all the others, her eyes shut, and her book held upside down, but the words she sang were clear and distinct, though they were off the key.

> "And heaven comes down our souls to greet,
>   And glory crowns the mercy seat."

Tasha did not mind the harsh singing, nor the voices off the key. She was back in Stonington singing with the Macdonalds, singing the words this time

with a groping yearning to know their meaning. All
these people, even the woman with the funny hat and
the tenor voice seemed to be singing with a meaning,
singing with their souls. She wished she knew just
what this mercy seat was they were talking about.
Why hadn't she asked Mrs. Macdonald? She had wondered then what it was. But she sensed that in some
way it was connected with worshiping God.

Quite unconsciously she bowed her head, because her spirit was listening, when the old minister
began to pray. He had a voice that was feeble and
monotonous, and now and again she would lose
several words or a sentence, but she could see that he
took the same general tone of intimate converse with
an invisible One that Thurly Macdonald had done.
It was all strange and mysterious, but it hushed her
impatient, wild, young soul, and gave her a thrill to
hear them.

They sang another hymn after the prayer, "I
need Thee every hour."

That was one of the hymns they had sung at
Stonington too. Did all religious people use the same
hymns, she wondered? Tasha's experience with
church had been very slight, mainly confined to being
a bridesmaid at weddings, and having to be very
conscious of her step and how she managed her train
and her flowers.

The minister opened an old soft Bible that looked
as if it was ready to fall to pieces, and seemed to
know itself where to fall open at the right time.

It was not the same scripture that Thurly had
read and it meant very little to the devotee of the
world. She got but one sentence out of it, and that
did not convey a very clear meaning. The droning
voice read about a corruptible body and an incor-
ruptible body, and Tasha did not get a thing out of
it. But the sentence that stuck and remained for
weeks afterward was "Now this I say, brethren, that
flesh and blood cannot inherit the kingdom of God."

In a vague way she struggled for a meaning to
it, but was glad when they sang another hymn. And

then a strange thing took place. The minister asked
all who would to pray, and those men and women,
sitting right in their hard little benches, bowed their
heads in a long silence. Tasha bowed hers too, wondering what was coming to pass next. Then almost
in front of her an old woman began in a low quavering voice:

"Oh, our Father, we thank Thee that Thou art a
prayer-hearing, and a prayer-answering God. We
thank Thee that we can come to Thee in all our need,
and that Thou wilt supply us. I thank Thee for the
way that Thou did'st answer my prayer this day, and
send me that money in my sore distress. I can never
thank Thee enough, dear Lord. I will praise Thee
while my breath lasts. I thank Thee for the mercy
seat where I can come with all my troubles, and
where Thou hast promised to answer my needs—"

Ah! So that was a mercy seat! A sort of a
throne where a King sat to grant petitions!

Tasha opened her eyes and looked curiously at
the old black bonnet in the seat before her, trembling
with the emotion of the little old woman, whose
prayer had been so low that Tasha was sure nobody
else in the room but herself could have heard the
words, unless it might be true that there was a God
who heard such pleadings. A mercy seat! And Thurly
Macdonald and his mother believed in it, that was
sure.

The low thankful voice in front of her had ended
in a tiny sob of gratitude, and an old man with a
quavering voice took up the sound. Before he was
finished a third had begun, and voice after voice
took up the low weird cry. Even the young organist
prayed a sharp little prayer full of neat pious wishes
for her neighbors, and a sparse plea for her own
spiritual growth.

Tasha was glad when the closing hymn was
announced. She had been almost afraid they would
expect her to join in the service. She had glanced
furtively toward the door for a way of escape.

After a quiet benediction, something about,

"Keep us from falling and present us faultless—" Tasha turned to hurry out, but found the old woman of the rusty black bonnet intercepting her with a black cotton gloved hand held out.

"We're pleased to see you here," she said shyly.

Tasha ignored the hand in the cotton glove. She did not rightly understand such salutation, but she smiled and said thank you.

"Are you staying in the village?" went on the woman affably, and Tasha perceived that there was still a tear glistening on her cheek from the prayer time, a tear from that sob that had meant joy.

Tasha assented.

"Oh, then you'll come again perhaps."

"Why, I don't know," said Tasha pondering, "I'm rather busy. I don't get down this end of town very often."

"But you're one of His," the old lady said with a smile. "I know you are or you wouldn't be at prayer meeting. They don't when they ain't."

"Was this a prayer meeting?"

"Why yes," said the old woman eyeing her curiously. "Didn't you know?"

They had passed out the door together, and the old woman stumbled. Tasha caught her arm and guided her down the steps.

"Thank you, dearie!" she said, "I ain't so keen of eye as I used to be. Sometimes I can't get down those steps alone. My daughter usually comes with me, but to-night she had a sick child and couldn't."

"Which way do you live?" asked Tasha, moved by a sudden kindly impulse, "couldn't I walk home with you?"

"Would you, dearie? I'd be wonderfully obliged. I'm most afraid to go alone, and Martha she begged me not to, but I says, 'Martha, the Lord has been so good to us to-day, sending us the money for that operation for the baby, that I wouldn't have the face not to go to meeting and thank Him.' "

"Do you mean," asked Tasha curiously, "that you really had some money sent in answer to prayer?"

"I really did," said the old woman eagerly. "You see we hadn't a cent. We'd spent everything for medicine and doctors, and a big bill at the grocery too, and when the doctor said an operation was the only thing would save Timmy I says to Martha, 'Martha, there's only one thing to do. I'll go ask Father.' So I did. And this morning there come a letter from Kansas City from my Cousin Harriet. Five years ago she borrowed two hundred dollars off us when she was about to lose her place that was mortgaged, and we ain't thought to ever see it again, 'cause Harriet, she ain't forehanded, and the man she married didn't turn out to be much of a business hand neither, but here, didn't she send me a check for the whole thing with interest! And now Timmy can have his operation, and they say he'll walk again! Ain't that grand?"

They had come to the door of one of the very humblest of the humble homes, where a light in an upstairs window showed the room of the little invalid, and the grandmother turned in eager haste to say good night and be back in the sick room again.

Tasha impulsively held out a little purse.

"Here!" she said putting the beaded trifle in the astonished woman's hand, "won't you let me help too? I'd like you to get a little something for Timmy with that. It isn't much but perhaps it will get something to amuse him at least."

And then with the woman's thanks ringing in her ears she fled away toward the lights of the town.

A great moon like a burnished plaque had come up in the heavens during the meeting, and flooded the world with almost daylight brilliance, and Tasha flitted along in its radiance like a little white moth, thinking of what she had seen that evening, and wondering what Thurly Macdonald would think if he knew she had been to prayer meeting.

Chapter XII

The little gold shoe remained on the closet shelf, perhaps not forgotten, but hidden. Jamieson, Fausset and Brown, and Young's *Concordance* were forced to come down and assist in preparing a sermon, but Josephus stayed on the job, and so thoroughly protected the small package done up in brown paper, that no one would ever have suspected it contained a valuable diamond buckle.

Then one day there came a letter for Marget from Florida, just a note, in a high scrawly hand on queer big expensive paper:

"Dear Mrs. Macdonald:
  I'm sending you a little trinket, just to remember me by. Please don't think I ever can pay for all you and your son did for me when I was storm-stayed, but I want you to have this just to know how grateful I am.
                Sincerely,
                    Anastasia Endicott."

The little trinket proved to be a tiny platinum wrist watch set about with twinkling little diamonds. More diamonds! *Diamonds!* Diamonds for Marget Macdonald! Hitherto diamonds had only meant a gem reserved for the heavenly city. Now she looked at hers in amaze, doubting if it were quite right to enjoy such rare and costly things.

But Thurly's eyes shone, and Thurly told her yes, she must keep it. He put it on her wrist under the cuff of her little gray mohair she was wearing that morning, and showed her how to fasten it, and

how to wind it. Without any key. Such a dear little
trick! And for her! What would Thurly's father say
if he could look down from heaven and see his Marget with a little pretty thing like that on her wrist?
Diamonds. Bonnie little trick! Her eyes filled with
tears. Her John had always meant to get her a watch,
a round gold one with a long chain, and a pocket
sewed in her basque to carry it in; that was the kind
they wore then. But this was so handy! And so neat
and hidden like, right under the sleeve till you needed
it, and ready there without undue display to tell the
time of day.

She cast a sweet grateful thought to the lovely
girl who had sent it, and then she lifted anxious
eyes to Thurly's face. How was Thurly taking this?
This would be one more thing to make her lad think
of the lassie who was so far out of his world. Ah!
He must not! What should she do about the watch?
Send it back and put the thought out of his mind? But
no, she could not do that and hurt the wee young
thing. She would have to pray about it. Just ask the
Father.

Two hours later there came a telegram from
Chicago. One of the Christian workers in a noted or-
ganization had been called away by severe illness
in his family, and might be gone from his classes for
weeks. Could Mr. Macdonald come on at once and
fill his place indefinitely until his return?

They talked it over hastily, anxiously.

"If it's the Lord's call you must go, laddie,"
sighed Marget, sore perplexed, "and no, lad, I'll bide.
We couldna tear up the hoose for an uncertainty, and
we couldna leave things as they are without somebody
here. It's cold weather. The pipe would freeze up and
spoil our wee hoose. You go, lad, and I'll bide."

"But I'll not leave you alone, Mother."

"Nonsense, laddie, I'm best by myself. You mind
I don't like a stranger butting about telling me
what I shall do in my ain."

"I know, Mother, but this time you'll have to
stand that for a little while if I'm to go. I simply

won't leave you alone," and Thurly put on his stubborn Scotch tone that his mother knew meant business.

Marget got up and dusted the parlor table nervously, as was her wont when she was disturbed about anything. Then she looked up.

"Weel, then laddie, we'll fix it. We mustna go against the call of the Lord. I'll just send for Martha. You mind she wrote me she was coming to pay me a visit. Let her come noo."

Marget sighed as she gave her word. Her son knew that she was not greatly fond of this friend and neighbor of her childhood who had married and come to this country to live.

"If you mean that, Mother, I'll get her on the phone and arrange it at once. I've no time to lose if I'm going. I'm afraid it'll be a trial for you, Mother, but I can't leave you alone."

Thurly went to the telephone and arranged everything.

"She says she'll start day after to-morrow morning," he announced with satisfaction. "I'll get Jimmy Fargo to sleep here those two nights. No, Mother, don't say a word. I couldn't rest easy a minute if you were alone. Not in weather like this. There's liable to be another storm you know—"

So Thurly had his way, and with a heavy heart Marget went up to pack his bag, and see that every button was in place, and every sock well mended.

Thurly left on the evening train, and after Marget had made up the cot in the little room off the dining room for the high school boy Jimmy, she felt very forlorn and alone. For the first time in several years Thurly was away, really away, for more than a night or two, and the worst of it was she did not know how long it would be before she might look for him back again. A kind of feeling as if she were bleeding in her heart came over her, but she put it resolutely away.

"It's of the devil," she told herself. "He's just foond the weak places in me, and he's romping all over my puir soul. I'll away to my Father!" and she hurried upstairs to her trysting place.

At last with peace upon her brow, the peace of an utterly yielded will, she went down stairs and looked about her for something to occupy her hands. This first night was going to be the hardest, and she must keep busy until she was weary enough to sleep.

Then she bethought her of the treasure that was in the house. The little slipper with its diamond buckle. What had Thurly done with it? She had forgotten to ask him. Of course he went away in such a hurry that he never thought. But she ought to know where it was, even if he had hidden it safe from burglars, for in case of fire she would want to rescue it first of anything because if was not her own and she was now responsible for it.

So she trotted over to Thurly's room, and was glad for the chance to be among his things, and work around putting things to rights as usual, just as if he were coming back next morning; meanwhile hunting for the slipper.

It would be in his bureau of course.

She opened all the drawers, but only neat piles of summer clothing were left, and some outworn collars that he considered not good enough to take with him. She got away with one fifteen minutes happily enough going over the summer things and finding a torn buttonhole, a missing button and a small place in the shoulder of a shirt that needed darning. Tomorrow morning she would sit down with her needle and set those right, then they would be off her mind.

But the slipper.

It would be in a drawer of his desk, of course, and she went confidently to the little desk where Thurly wrote his sermons. The drawers were locked. Yes, of course they would be with the diamonds inside. But the key was in the little top door by the cubbyholes. That was careless of him. But he must have intended to give it to her and had forgotten.

She fitted the key in the top drawer and looked in. Nothing there at all but some bundles of old letters and receipted bills, neatly strapped with rubber bands and labeled. There was correspondence with "Marathon Church," "Hutton's Mills," "Chester," all places where he had preached from time to time. "College." Those would be from his professors and classmates. "University," "The Mission," "Bible School," she knew for what each one stood. She shut the drawer and locked it again.

The next drawer contained sermons. A glance showed that there was no place here for hiding diamonds or a little high-heeled shoe.

The bottom drawer had nothing but a pile of writing stationery, a box of envelopes, another of pencils and some old pens. She even opened the box of envelopes and poked them to see if the slipper was hidden in there, but of course it was not. In dismay she turned back to the room.

Then she searched the bed, thoroughly, underneath the pillow and mattress. He might have kept them there for safety, though it was not like Thurly to make much thought of a burglar. But still he might have put it there to be out of the way, and safe. But there was no slipper.

Last, she went to his closet, for all else in the room was open to the casual glance, and no slipper could be hidden there without her being able to see it. She cleared all Thurly's old shoes out and took the little flash light he made her keep by her bed, to look in and be sure a diamond buckle was not hid in some corner; the little slipper was so small. Yet of course that was foolish for it would still be wrapped in its papers. Then she took all Thurly's old coats, and his old flannel bath robe down and looked through their pockets, but no slipper!

She glanced at the shelf above her head. Thurly kept books up there but they were mostly gone. The shelf seemed empty save for an old felt hat that had so much the slump of the way he wore it that it brought the sudden tears to her eyes. But she climbed on a chair and continued her investigations. The left hand side was deepest, because the closet went back beyond a niche in the chimney, but she turned the search light deep into it. She moved away Thomas a' Kempis, Keith on the Prophecy, and Life of the Early Christian Martyrs, but there was no sign of a little gold slipper belonging to the elite. No little package tied up with string. Only the sturdy red bricks of the chimney and a crumbling chunk of mortar fallen from its crevice. Well, if it were some people she might think Thurly had gone to the trouble of removing a brick and hiding the diamonds in the very edge of the chimney. But Thurly would never do a dramatic thing like that. She knew her boy, and though she searched the chimney keenly with the bright eyes that needed as yet no glasses to see anything less diminutive than print, she turned from that end of the shelf, leaving the early Christian martyrs and Thomas a Kempis where she had found them.

The other end of the shell seemed to have only one big fat book, "Josephus," for "Cruden" and "Jamieson, Fausset and Brown" had gone to Chicago with Thurly. But Josephus was standing in such a manner, with his gold letters glittering in the flash light, that he seemed to be plumb up against the end of the closet wall.

At that psychological instant the doorbell rang through the house, and with another quick scan of Josephus, Marget climbed nimbly down from her chair, closed the closet door, shut off her flash and went down stairs. There really wasn't any other place to look unless Thurly had pried up one of the boards of the floor and put the slipper under it, and she was sure her fearless son would never have been as anxious about it as all that.

But the thing which caused her to catch her breath and almost fall as she got down from the chair and hurried down the stairs, was a new idea entirely. Could Thurly have taken that shoe with him? Surely he would not do that. Not even to protect the shoe. Not even to protect her from a burglar getting in and frightening her—though how a burglar would know whether Thurly had the shoe or it was still in the house, she did not stop to reason out. But she was immediately alarmed for Thurly.

True, he had carried that shoe in his bag once before, but there was excuse for that. He had just picked it up, and might have forgotten that he had it after he came into his home. But the fact that it had lain in there once before a day or two; that it had been hidden under his garments as if he wished no one to know he had it, made her more than uneasy, and immediately all her alarms for her precious son returned in full force. If Thurly had taken that shoe with him it must show that he was more than just casually interested in the "bit lassie." He maybe intended to send it to her from Chicago, but how would that look? He surely should have told her what he was doing. Poor bit mannie, he would never think how queer it would look to the lassie that he should carry her shoe off away to Chicago to send it to her, when he should have sent it from home.

So thinking her distracted thoughts she came to the door and let in her young protector, who had arrived early according to arrangement and demanded a place to study his lessons for next day.

Marget established him at the dining-room table under a good light and went her way about the house, doing whatever little things she could find to do, and they were very few for Marget's house was always in the pink of order. But that was more than Marget's thoughts were the night. If it was true as she thought that worriments were but teasings of her enemy the devil, then surely the prince of this world was romping all over the old battle ground with her that night.

As she pottered about in her kitchen, changing the arrangement of some of the dishes to make work for her nervous hands while her thoughts castigated her, she went back over the night of the storm when Thurly had brought the wee drabbled lassie into her house. She forced herself to remember his expression, one of high disapproval and extreme annoyance, as he set her down and told his mother in the same breath that he must hurry back or he would lose his train. Certainly up to that moment he was not interested in the little painted woman of the world.

She went carefully over her first impressions, the messy little face with the paint all spotted with the weather till she had washed it off. The dripping rosy gauze in tatters round her little frozen feet, the naked look of her as she stood forth from her fur trimmed wrap and seemed not a whit embarrassed at the slim expanse of bare flesh; the lack of adequate clothing, showing that modesty was not one of her particular charms. The way she talked of her parents, especially her stepmother, calling her by her first name. The flip little way she had with words, and the lack of respect she showed for anybody or anything.

And yet as she pondered there grew in her heart the warm pleasant charm of the lovely child, as she had nestled her in blankets and folded her in the great old-fashioned gown, several sizes too large for her. The love that had come to her in spite of everything as she tucked the little lost lassie in the blankets and kissed her and prayed for her there beside the bed. Something warm and tender that wanted to stay in her heart pled for the child, and asked not to be banished.

Yet Marget knew that she must not keep this stranger in her thoughts even, if it meant danger to her own child. Such a subtle thing is love. Marget felt that it was the only temptation of the world that she really feared for her strong young consecrated son. Just why she could not trust the Lord to protect him from this danger as well as all the others that a wicked world could hold, she never reasoned out with herself, but surely it was that Marget allowed herself many hours of misery over the one possibility that her precious son would marry the wrong woman who would lead him into trouble and temptation. It had never occurred to her that this attitude argued that perhaps she was trusting Thurly himself to keep himself from evil, rather than his Lord. After all it takes a canny soul to read her own heart. Though Marget Macdonald was cannier than most people, at that.

In due time she got her high-school boy to bed on his cot, and herself to bed in her own room, but not to sleep. There she lay hour after hour, staring blankly at the opposite wall where the electric light in the little street cast shadows of bleak bare branches, waving weirdly; and when she at last fell asleep toward morning it was to dream that there were burglars in the house tearing up all the floor boards to find the little shoe.

But she had the courage to laugh out at her fears and say to herself:

"Well, and what a little old fule I am to be sure! As if the Lord couldn't look after that shoe, as well as my Thurly."

So she got up and went about getting some breakfast for her young lodger so that he might get off to school in due time.

She had decided in the watches of the night that she must not mention the matter of the shoe to Thurly in a letter, for if he had carried that shoe off to Chicago with him, he did not want her to know it, and she did not want him to think she had thought he did, in case he had not. In fact she did not want to bring up the matter of the shoe at all.

So once again the little gold shoe became a golden wall between this wonderful woman and her son; and a heavy heart she carried about her work, as she began to prepare for her unwelcome guest.

The guest room had not been in use since Tasha had occupied it. There were things that Marget felt she ought to do to it. She remembered Martha as an indefatigable housekeeper, critical to a fault and she marched to the door of the room and surveyed it with the cold hard look of a stranger just entering. Yes, the paint was a bit dusty, the windows could bear a little shining, and there was that place on the door where the paint had been cleaned so many times it had worn thin and showed the lumber through.

She went to the telephone and ordered a can of white paint that would dry quickly, and a brush.

She would soon remedy the paint. There would be enough to go all around the base board and windows and touch up the two doors.

She took the rugs out on the back porch and flung snow upon them, giving them a good sweeping in it. She made up the bed in her finest linen sheets, and got out the rose blankets with the pink bindings, the same ones that had tucked so tenderly about Tasha when she slept. She put fresh covers on the bureau and wash stand, rubbed the windows, and did up the two curtains crisply, looping them back with clean cords from her sewing basket.

And all the while she was doing it, she was searching furtively for that little gold shoe. Twice she went into Thurly's room and gazed about her as if somehow the four walls would give forth the secret if she looked hard enough, but Josephus remained at his post and never said a word. Josephus was a good warder.

The day passed and the night came. The high school guardian returned and silently studied his lesson beside the plate of gingerbread that Marget had prepared for him, and another night was lived through, but still the little gold shoe had not been found, although Marget had not lost sight of her search for it for a single instant all day long. She had even gone to the extent of tapping every board in Thurly's floor, and closet, to make sure he had not hidden it somewhere. She had taken out and searched behind every drawer on the upper floor. It certainly was perplexing. She wondered if perhaps she had missed it in her excitement. Perhaps she should begin again and go over the places she had looked the first night. But the anxiety and the housecleaning, and her wakefulness of the night before, one or all, put her to sleep the minute her head touched the pillow, and when she woke in the morning she felt saner and stronger to bear the new day.

She got up and prepared a lunch for her night's guardian, thanked him smilingly for his care, and gave him the money Thurly had left in an envelope for him, bidding him good bye. Then she set about preparing such a dinner for Martha, as would forestall any criticisms of her ability as a housekeeper once and for all.

Meanwhile, as a certain Western train hurried on its way toward Stonington, a surprise was nearing Marget which was destined to fill her thoughts pretty well to the exclusion of everything else, for a time at least.

Chapter XIII

The night before Martha Robertson was to take the train to visit her old friend Marget Macdonald, she fell down stairs and broke her leg!

Out of the bewilderment and pain of her first oblivion, Martha roused with stern Scotch promptness to attend to her duty, and early next morning sent for her niece Hesba Hamilton.

"How'd you like to take my place, Hesby?" she gasped from among the pillows, her thin lined face anxious with her responsibility. She had promised Marget's son to stay with her till he returned.

"It'ud be a nice vacation for you, Hesby," she added anxiously as Hesba hesitated.

"Yes, but you know, Aunt," said Hesba turning her round serious eyes toward the sufferer, "I'm right in the midst of my course of study in the training school, and it might put me back a whole year, if I go."

"Oh, no, Hesby," argued the old woman crossly, "you're real bright. You can take your books along. Besides, there's likely just as good a training school put in that city as here, and it's a good thing to see the world a little, especially if you're going off to teach in some college in China or Turkey. You're young yet, you know, and you better see what you get a chance to see."

Hesba considered.

"I might—" she said. "Of course I'd have to ask our dean. I could telephone him," she glanced at her wrist watch. "He's in the office usually at this hour. I'd like to help you out of course if I could. How soon would I have to start?"

"The train leaves at five o'clock," sighed the sufferer, a twinge of pain making her close her eyes and wince. "You'll find the ticket and reservation in my purse in the upper drawer. You can take the hand bag right along. It's all packed ready with everything, money, time table and all, clean handkerchief, and my travelling comb. Just take it. That will save you some time. I'll be so glad to have you go. I couldn't go back on my word you know. You see Marget and I used to go to school together back in the old country, and I've always meant to visit her. But this is just my luck. I'll tell you, Hesby, if I get better before that son of hers gets home, I'll come on and relieve you."

"Son?" said Hesba, turning her round shell-rimmed eyes on her aunt. "Has she got a son? What's he like?"

"I never saw him," said the aunt wearily, "but they say he's a fine fellow. He's studying to be a preacher. You two ought to know each other, seeing you are both thinking of being some kind of a missionary some day. He might get back while you're there, too, and take you round a little. It might turn out to be real pleasant, Hesby."

"Oh, well," said the girl strong mindedly, "I'm not in this life for pleasure, you know, Aunty. But I'll do my best to help you out at least till somebody else can be found to stay with your friend. Of course if I can get transferred to another training school that would be great. I'll see what I can do."

Hesba went calmly out and in half an hour telephoned she would go. Methodically she set about her preparations, and by five o'clock she was seated in the sleeper, rolling eastward, complaisance in her round gray eyes. This was one of the advantages that had come for her further education, and she meant to make the most of it. Incidentally of course she would do her duty as it came, no matter how unpleasant it might be, and do it thoroughly and well.

In due season, in fact earlier than due season for Marget, she arrived in Stonington, an hour before Marget had calculated she could possibly get there.

Being young, and being early, she missed Jimmy Fargo entirely, who had promised to meet Martha Robertson's train and convey her safely in his uncle's Ford to the house.

But Hesba Hamilton was always sufficient to an occasion. She stared around the station mildly for a moment, surrounded by her two sensible pieces of baggage, and then she corralled a passing truck and compelled its driver to convey herself and her two suit cases to the Macdonald home. The driver agreed that he knew the house, said he was in the habit of delivering coal and wood there. Nothing daunted the young woman swung her suit cases up to the swarthy youth who was driving, and then climbed up beside him. So she arrived at Marget's door, paid her chauffeur twenty-five cents, and strode up the steps, a suit case in either hand, staring around her interestedly through her shell rimmed gray eyes. She was wearing a thick gray tailored suit, and a tan felt hat that was unbecoming, but it was a matter of the least moment in the world to her. She felt herself to be on a higher plane than most poor mortals. It was virtue and intellect that counted in this world, not the outward show.

Marget went to the door with a dab of flour on her cheek, and a flush from the oven in her face. She thought it was the paper boy with the evening paper, and she wanted to tell him that the paper had not come that morning, and he must be more careful and lay it under the door mat where it would not blow away. She opened the door and there stood Hesba with the two suit cases in her hands.

"Is this Mrs. Macdonald?" asked Hesba. And when Marget assented with a kindly smile, Hesba walked in.

"Well, I've come to stay with you," she announced, setting down her suit cases and looking frankly around. "What room shall I take? I suppose I might as well go right up and get washed before we talk."

"You've—come to—*stay* with me?" said Marget wheeling round from the door which in her astonishment she still held half ajar. "Why, who are you?" There was dignity, and a bit of severity in Marget Macdonald's tone, which was wholly lost on the guest.

"Oh, didn't I explain? Well, you see it's a long story and I thought I might as well get cleaned up and tell it calmly. Why, you see my aunt Martha was to come, and she fell down stairs last night and broke her leg, so she asked me to come in her place. It wasn't very convenient of course, but I managed to arrange it so I could. She didn't like to disappoint you. We didn't telegraph because there really wasn't time, and it seemed a waste of money, as I was coming anyway."

"Fell down stairs!" exclaimed Marget sympathetically, closing the door now and coming over to the girl. "The puir buddy! Now isn't that fearsome! And to think she broke her leg! That's just what Thurly's always expecting of me to do. It's a sair thing for a buddy at our ages to have to lie abed when we'd rather be round doing our daily stint. But you needn't have bothered to come all this long way to stay with me, my dear. I'm grieved I did not know, and I would have wired ye. Didn't yer Aunt Martha need ye to nurse her?"

"Oh no, she has a trained nurse, and Uncle Geoffrey is there. I shouldn't have been with her in any case. You see I have my training school to attend when I'm home, and that was one reason why I thought I couldn't come when Aunt asked me. I couldn't miss my school. But she suggested I might find another school here, and I talked with my dean. There is one, and he's arranging for me to be transferred, that is if you can spare me during the day, and occasionally in the evenings perhaps—but we can talk all that over afterwards. I'd better get my things off now—"

"Oh, my dear, it's not necessary for anyone to stay with me—not in the least—it was just a whimsy of my son that it would be nice for my old friend to visit me now while he's away for a wee while. But it's all right, Jimmy Fargo will sleep here, and I can bide. You stay over night and get rested a bit, and then you run back to your school, my dear. I'm obliged, but it's not in the least necessary!"

"Oh, that's all right," said Hesba easily, swinging her suit cases a trifle impatiently, "if you'll just show me, is it upstairs I go? I can find my way—" and Hesba moved toward the staircase.

"No, wait!" said Marget desperately, as a strong spicy sweetness suddenly penetrated to the hall from the region of the kitchen. "Excuse me a minute, I've a pie in the oven—!" and she turned to fly to the kitchen.

But Hesba set down her suit cases and kept easy pace in long strides, with her quick little steps.

"Let *me* go," she said, and her voice though loud and distinct enough to be heard as they went, was still calm, as if she had grasped the situation fully, "I always tell my mother she should never leave her oven while she's baking without turning the gas down, even if the house is on fire. They always draw up when you least expect it. Here, let me do this, you'll burn yourself. Shall I take this cloth?"

She had swung into the kitchen at a good pace, and now she seized on Marget's fine white apron with hemstitching across the bottom which she had discarded on a chair as she went to answer the bell. Before Marget could open her mouth to stop her, the girl had flapped open the oven door and seized the rich blackberry pie with the folds of the fine linen apron, bringing it forth from the oven triumphantly.

"There!" she said calmly. "Where shall I set it? Here?" and without more ado she plumped it down on Marget's nice newly covered white oilcloth table, where it promptly stuck to the white surface, and sent up a smell of burnt paint to mingle with the blackberry juice that was dripping down to the bottom of the oven.

"Oh, my dear!" said Marget aghast, "the pie is only just put in. It's juice that has run down a wee bit and is burning, not the pie at all. Here, let me take the apron. It's all sticky." She surveyed her best white apron in dismay.

"But, my dear, you've juice on your dress, and on your shoes. Oh, I shouldn't have let you——" she added politely—as if she could have helped it!

"It's of no consequence," said Hesba, still calm, "I presume it will clean. Boiling water will take out blackberry stain, and the shoes are old ones. You shouldn't fill your pies so full, and then this wouldn't happen. Shall I wash my hands at the sink?"

Hesba was running true to form. It was her habit to ask permission for what she was already doing.

Marget herded her out of the kitchen at last and up to her room, her heart boiling with indignation, as she strove to hide her annoyance, and then she hurried back to her little white kitchen and essayed to undo some of the damage.

She lifted the pie back into the oven with the little patent lifter that hung by her range, grieving at the havoc wrought on her new white oilcloth which was badly scorched and stained, deprecating the sticky pan which would be to clean on the bottom as well as the top from the oilcloth adhering to it. And the "bit pannie" would never be quite so bright again. She moaned to herself as she wiped up the path of juice from the stove to the table, and then dropped her pretty white apron into a pan of boiling water to soak till she had time to try and get the stains out. Such a mess! And all because the poor mistaken stranger had a mind to help! Well, she mustn't be too hard on her. Her soul was just being tried a bit more, that was all. She had lived so long alone, and had things her own way, and the bit girl had wanted to be kind.

So Marget soothed herself into calm once more, and went on with her dinner preparations.

Meanwhile, upstairs, the "bit girl" was taking a survey of the new land in which she had come to dwell for a while. She removed her hat and coat and tidied herself briskly. Then before she even hung up her coat in the closet Marget had showed her, she went out into the hall with catlike tread, and made a careful investigation of the rest of the second story, not excluding the store room and linen closet, though she opened their doors cautiously, and noiselessly. Then she went back to the guest room and brought her suit cases and her coat and hat into Thurly's room, hanging the coat and hat in the closet, and standing her baggage beside the bed. She gave the room a careful survey, examined minutely the several pictures of college life on the walls, and especially the picture of Thurly in his football regalia, and then went down stairs, stealing upon Marget in the kitchen so silently that she jumped and almost slopped over the pitcher of cream she was carrying to the dining table.

"Let me take that!" demanded Hesba as if it were her right: "You're tired, I can see, or you wouldn't have jumped. You sit down now and I'll finish getting dinner. By the way, ought I to have dressed for dinner? Aunt thought you did, but I didn't see any use if we're all alone, unless you think I should."

"Dress for dinner?" said Marget perplexed, "why, you are dressed, I'm sure."

"All right if you're satisfied," said Hesba, "I wanted to do the right thing, the first night, anyway. Now, where's your bread box? I'll cut the bread."

But Marget at last roused to the occasion.

"You will not cut the bread, my dear," she said, and looked her guest in the eye with battle, gently shown, "I prefer to cut my own bread, and to get my own dinner. It will please me far better if you will sit in the parlor and rest yourself until I call you."

"Oh, very well," said Hesba coolly, "then if you don't need me just now I'll go up and unpack. I hurried down because I thought I could help, but if you've everything nearly ready why I suppose you would rather finish. However, I'll take over a good part of the work tomorrow."

"No," said Marget smilingly, "no, my girl, you won't take over my work. I never let anyone take over my work. And you'll go in the parlor now, or up the stair, and make yourself contented in any way you like, till I call you."

Greek had met Greek, and Hesba looking into Marget's eyes said, "Oh, very well." Hesba was not a fighter. She was a doer. She usually worked so quickly that one had no time to prevent or to battle. She turned and went upstairs.

Half an hour later when Marget rang the little tea bell that usually summoned Thurly from his study, Hesba came down stairs quite complaisant.

Marget, her face a little red from worry and flurry, presided at her table with dignity. She put all the serving at her own place, and kept a firm hand on things. She kept the lead in the conversation too, asking quick discerning questions that kept the guest busy answering, while they ate.

Hesba talked frankly about herself.

"You know I'm in training for some kind of social service. I've been attending a school, and I'm going to keep up my studies."

"Yes?" said Marget quite interested for a moment. "Yes? It'll maybe be like the school where Thurly was teaching last winter. It's a wonderful school—" and she launched into a description of the curriculum and the teachers, and the good they were doing, that showed she was well acquainted with the facts.

"Oh," said Hesba coolly, "I never heard of it," and then she went on with her own plans. Her teacher was to write her, and get her in touch with the dean of this school in the city near Stonington, a training school just like the one she had been attending.

Marget chided herself that she felt somehow an antipathy toward this girl who was so serious and well informed, and so evidently right minded. A girl who was planning to devote her life to Christian work, even to social service, must be a girl of true worth. And yet she found from the first an aversion to her. Why was it? She was not ill to look upon. Her features were good, her complexion was fair with healthy color in her cheeks, she wore no rouge, and did not deck herself out as if the life of the flesh were all that was worth while; and yet, she could not to save her, like this girl. Why was it? Was it just that she was perverse?

Look how she had loved the bit lassie from the world that had dropped down upon them through the storm! And she was avowedly the world's own, with no attempt to even pretend to be making her life worth while.

Well, it must just be that Marget Macdonald was perverse in her thoughts, loving the world herself and the things of the world. For if this new lassie was the Lord's own treasure, as she was like to be if she was devoting her life to others, why then it just simply must be all wrong that Marget Macdonald didn't love her, and she must get to work, and find out her lovableness.

She suffered her to help with the clearing off of the table, saying nothing when her assistant suggested putting things in another place than was her custom. It would be easy enough to put them back where they belonged when the guest had gone upstairs, and she must not antagonize her this first night. She must remember that the girl was trying to be kind and help.

They had family worship together. It had worried Marget to think about it, but if this was another child of the kingdom of course she would be in hearty accord.

Hesba seemed indifferently willing, and they read

in turn verse about, a portion of the fourth chapter of John, the story of Jesus at the well talking to the woman of Samaria. When they came to the twenty-ninth verse, where the woman of Samaria came to the men and said: "Come see a man, which told me all things that ever I did: is not this the Christ?" Hesba read it and then paused and added:

"You know our professor in Bible says that that is a mistake of course, for Jesus had no means whatever of knowing all that that woman had done, unless of course He might have heard some gossip about her as He passed through the village."

"A mistake!"

Marget Macdonald looked up and something blazed in her soft blue eyes that resembled fire mixed with steel.

"A mistake, did ye say? A mistake in the blessed Buik? Why, now that is strange! A mistake! Why, it cuid na be! Why, have ye na heeard how not even one dotting of an 'i' or one crossing of a 't' shall be changed in the Word of the Buik till all be fulfilled? Girlie, ye may be ignorant and therefore not culpable, but ye canna say such like things again the Buik in this hoose. This hoose is a hoose of prayer and faith, and neither I nor my laddie will list to sayings of unbelievers. Yon is atheism, pure and simple, and if ye dinna know better, ye'll mind and keep it to yersel' while yer here!"

"Now, Grandma, don't get excited!" said Hesba soothingly. "I was only telling you the modern view of things. Of course you're old fashioned and like to think of things as you used to know them, and I don't suppose it will hurt you any, but you ought to be broad minded enough to listen to the other side. However, if you don't wish me to—"

"Broad minded!" said Marget Macdonald rising, closing her Bible with a snap, and laying it on the table. "Dinna ye know, poor buddy, where the broad road leads to? 'Wide is the gate and broad is the road that leads to *death*, and many there be that go in thereat—' Lassie, we'll kneel and pray now." And Marget Macdonald knelt and prayed such a prayer for the erring young soul as would have melted a heart of stone.

But Hesba Hamilton was quite unmoved as she rose from her knees. She turned to her hostess, all weak, and tearful with her emotion, and said quite calmly:

"Grandma, you're very amusing, but don't you think it's bad for you to get so excited? I think religion is largely self-control, don't you?"

"There's a deal of that needed sometimes," said Marget, and went and dusted off her little table with her best pocket handkerchief.

Having gained the needed control she sought to get rid of her guest.

"Ye'll be weary with the journey," she said kindly, "and I've a bit sponge to set for my bread the morn. So ye'll juist feel free to go to yer bed without waiting for me."

"All right," said Hesba, "I guess I will retire. I like to read a while before I sleep. You needn't bother about waking me in the morning. I always set myself to waken at a certain time. Good night!"

Marget gave a sigh of relief and slipped out to her kitchen pondering how she was to get rid of this unwelcome visitor and send her on her way without hurting either her feelings or those of the woman whose place she was supposed to be taking.

She tiptoed upstairs cautiously, not to waken her guest, but found her precaution unnecessary. Hesba, in a mannish kimono tied about her waist with a cord and tassel was awaiting her in the hall.

"I thought I better tell you," she said, "in case you should want me in the night. I looked about a little and found that this front room which has evidently been your son's room, is much nearer to you, right across the hall from your door, where I could hear you if you moved, so I took the liberty of moving into it. I moved the bedclothes too, so there's nothing for you to do, and I've been cleaning out the closet and hanging up my clothes so I'd be ready for living in the morning. I've stacked those pictures and college things in the other room on the bureau, and tomorrow I'll move all the things in the desk drawers for I'll want to study at that desk. Here's a shoe I found on the shelf in the closet behind a book. You might take care of it, or maybe you'll want to throw it away. I opened it to see what on earth was hidden so far back. It's likely some souvenir from a dance your son went to. They collect all sorts of queer souvenirs now. I guess likely he didn't want you to know he had it."

She handed out Tasha's little gold slipper with the gleaming diamond buckle, half hidden by the wrappings.

Marget had been trembling so with anger during this speech that she was ready to fall down the stair, but when the little gold shoe appeared she grasped it with a relief that was almost like a shout of joy, and with it in her hand, as if it had been a sword she stood forth.

"This is the slipper belonging to a friend who was visiting us, and who left in haste leaving one of her shoes behind her. She is getting it when she returns from Florida. Meantime it was hidden away in what we supposed was a safe place from prying eyes, for the diamonds in the buckle are valuable. But girlie, this is my son's room, and no one else occupies it, *ever!* He likes not to have his things disturbed, and you may take your bag and baggage and go back to the room I gave you, or you may go out of this hoose." With which ultimatum Marget walked majestically into Thurley's room, gathered the maiden's garments from the hooks in the closet, in one wide swoop, her brushes from the bureau, and carried them into the guest room dumping them unceremoniously upon the chairs. Then she took her arms full of the pictures and things of Thurly's that had been taken out of his room and brought them back, while her guest stood and watched her, finally saying:

"Oh, very well, if you feel that way about it. I'm sure I thought I was doing the right thing," and picking up her empty suit cases she marched back to the guest room.

Marget had by this time rolled up the bedding for her son's bed, brought it back, and sweeping the few things from the closet went into her son's room and locked the door, leaving her guest to do what she pleased.

Marget, as she worked, swiftly, eagerly, putting back her son's Lares and Penates into their accustomed places, was singing a little paean in her heart. The slipper was found. She had it stuffed safely away in her apron pocket, the dainty little trick! And Thurly hadn't taken it with him at all! Thurly hadn't kept anything from his mother! Thurly was all right! The slipper was found! The slipper was found! It was not stolen, it was not strayed, it was here, here, *here!* Safe! Safe! *Safe!* There was nothing to worry about that little shoe any more. Diamonds and all it was found! And even if it did take a little huzzy of a thing to discover it, the Lord had lifted her worry and set her up above even a girl like this one that had come down upon her determined to manage her. Well, she might try, if she could, and Marget would hold her peace, and stand as much as she could, but there were two things the girl could not touch. She might not speak against God's Word, and she might not enter Thurly Macdonald's room any more.

So Marget locked her son's room door, after all was in order again, and then went across to her own room, and locked *her* door, a thing she had not done since she could ever remember.

But she lay down and slept the sleep of the just, and the little shoe was with her, wrapped soft in a silk handkerchief, and then in cotton wool, and tied with a "bit ribbon," blue like the eyes of its owner, and hid under Marget Macdonald's pillow.

Chapter XIV

Marget awoke with a start next morning, with the knowledge that she must have overslept. Dismay came over her as she gradually realized the situation, for she had intended to forestall the visitor and have breakfast all ready when she should wake. Now she would probably find that forward young woman sitting primly in the parlor reading the newspaper, with reproach in her eyes for a housekeeper who rose so late. Her only hope was that the girl might be human enough to be weary herself from her journey.

She jumped out of bed cautiously, and listened. The house seemed to be perfectly quiet. Still, that would be the case if the guest were reading the newspaper. Nevertheless she clung to the hope that she was still asleep, and got dressed in haste and with the utmost quiet, tiptoeing out into the hall. cautiously when she was ready.

Hesba's door was wide open, and in dismay Marget noted that the bed was made up most precisely, and the room in absolute order. With mingling emotions she descended the stairs, and looked into the little parlor. But there was no one sitting there. What had the girl found to do? With rising apprehension for her own order of things she hurried into the kitchen, but again order reigned, seemingly as she had left it, save that the dishcloth hung limp and damp on its little rack, instead of stiff and dry as it usually was in the morning. A quick glance around showed a cup and plate out of order on the shelf. Ah! The guest had eaten her breakfast, for there was the coffee pot on the back of the stove, and she had probably made the coffee with cold water instead of boiling water as Marget had always done. They mostly did when they preferred to put in cream afterward, instead of pouring it in the bottom of the cup before pouring the coffee, so that it would better blend.

Then suddenly the old saint began to marvel at her own smallness. What were such things compared to peaceful living. She must not let the enemy blind her with trifles so that she would sin. Better have all the coffee spoiled and take it pleasantly, even if it was her own house and her own coffee, and her own right to have it as she liked, than to soil her soul with fretting and rancor over a trifle.

"Surely He shall deliver thee from the snare of the fowler." If this wasn't just like the little snare that a bird catcher would set in the grass to trip the unwary bird to his capture, then she did not know scripture, and it was quite plain to her suddenly that she was being tried. After all these years of peaceful quiet living, having her own way, and being respected and tenderly guarded by an adoring son, she was having to be teased and tried by the little trifles of life. She had had many a big trial in her life, like the noisome pestilence in its overwhelming suddenness, and devastating sorrow; but her life had been singularly free from the little annoyances that make up the whole existence, seemingly, of many of God's children.

She must beware. "Your enemy the devil, goeth about like a roaring lion, seeking whom he may devour," but she remembered that he often came in sheep's clothing, or as an angel of light. She decided that as soon as she could occupy her guest contentedly in something for a little while, where she would be out of danger, she would seek the mercy seat, and find strength for the day, for she suddenly felt most inadequate to meet it.

But where was the guest? She couldn't have gone out to survey the back yard for the back door was duly bolted as she had left it the night before.

Going back into the dining room she discovered a note propped up against the sugar bowl, and for an instant her heart leaped up with joy. Perhaps the "bit girl" had taken offense at the way she had ordered her back to the guest room last night, and had taken herself home! Although she would always feel ashamed that the exit had been a matter of offense, still it would be a great relief to have her out of the house. It certainly would, and Thurly none the wiser. She could get along perfectly well alone, with Jimmy Fargo nights. And Jimmy would like to stay. She was sure of that. She would put him in the guest room and let him study there evenings, and he wouldn't be a bit of trouble, just a bit pan of gingerbread now and then, or a plate of cookies, to please him.

All this she thought while she was getting out her spectacles and framing them on her nose with excited hands that trembled in their eagerness.

Then she read the note:

"Dear Grandma:",

Marget felt a twinge of dislike at once. She wasn't anybody's grandmother yet, certainly not this prim maiden's. But that was an unworthy feeling. The old enemy again! She must put away such ungodliness! She read on:

"I've gone in town to arrange about my school. The coffee pot is on the back of the stove, and there are some fried tomatoes in the warming oven. I'll be back in time to help get dinner.
                                                    Hesba"

"The dickens, you will!" said Marget aloud, "I'll make me a pot of soup and have it hot on the back of the stove whenever she comes. I'll make me an apple pie, and some cottage cheese from the jar of soul milk, and that's enough dinner for anybody, for the bread'll be fresh. I've no call to let her ramp all over me in my own hoose, even if this is a trial set for my training. I must keep my identity, and my self-respect. I'm sure the Lord would tell me that!"

So Marget went eagerly and hurriedly about her work. There was a pot of soup stock already in the house, for she always kept all the bits of meat and used every drop of nutriment. She went to the telephone and ordered a piece of meat to make the soup more tasty, and then she set about preparing her vegetables, and making her apple pie and cheese, and while she worked, she planned how she might send that girl away to her home again, without having to be disagreeable about it. Perhaps the Lord had sent her for a double reason. It was quite evident that her teaching had been all wrong. It smacked of what Thurly called "modern." She might be right intentioned, and if she only knew the Lord Jesus, it might make all the difference in the world. There was no limit to how the Lord might change a buddy, once He had them.

Then she recalled how easily she had felt about that other lassie that the Lord had sent her there for a purpose. How eager she had been to teach the pretty child, and to pray for her and love her in spite of her paint, and silly clothing, and her being a little pretty worldling. Was she to do less for this other girl because she was less weak, less appealing, less lovely in her ways?

This really was probably a stronger minded girl, more capable of developing into a fine character, with teaching; more the kind of girl who would make a good mate for Thurly! She winced over that thought. Suppose Thurly was home and she had to worry over that too! Suppose she had to look forward to having her for a daughter-in-law! Ah! then! That would be a trial! And yet she had half toyed with the thought of having a daughter like the other little lassie, so bonnie, and dainty, and graceful.

This girl was not bad looking either. She had nice eyes if she wouldn't stare so much, with that look as if she knew it all and everybody else was all wrong, but she must set them right. As if she had been sent into the world just to set everybody else right!

Ah! But she mustn't think of her that way! It was

not Christian. Perhaps she was prejudiced just because of that little incident of the pie right at the start of their acquaintance. They began wrong. That was it. She must be more longsuffering and kindly. Perhaps she would grow to love the girl. For after all a girl who could give up the world, and look forward to a life of sacrifice for other people was not to be despised. She certainly had chosen more wisely than a child of frivolity, whose only thought was to amuse herself. Yet she was cherishing the thought of the girl who had worn that little gold shoe, in spite of all her fears for Thurly. What a mystery was the human heart! Yes, even one's own heart. There were things hid away in the corners of it that one never suspected. But God must see them clearly all the time. One ought to pray without ceasing as the Bible said.

Nevertheless it was not to be thought of that the present incumbent should remain with her during Thurly's absence. It might even open the way to further acquaintance, and force Thurly somehow into her company; and while Marget was ready to submit to the Lord's will if He had picked out this girl for a future mate for her beloved son, still she did not want it to be *her* fault, just because she had to be taken care of. And she must find a way, to gently, kindly, pleasantly remove her. "Oh, Lord, please show me how to get rid of the little huzzy!" she prayed with a deep sigh of trouble, and then caught herself in the act and anxiously added, "unless it be Thy will, Oh, Lord, and then give me strength to submit, for ya ken I'm dinna able to bear wi' the nagging, high handed ways of her alone, dear Lord."

Marget reflected that this summary taking of things for granted by Hesba, and going ahead with her school, was going to make it harder. If she only knew the name of the school to which she had gone she would telephone and try to reach her, and tell her not to make any arrangements until they had talked together. Then there wouldn't be anything to undo. But there was nothing she could do about it until the girl came home, so she worked hard and the morning passed rapidly. She scarcely stopped to take a bite herself at noon; till the kettle of soup began to send forth savory odors; two apple pies stood cooling on the pantry shelf, their tops all frosty with powdered sugar, their spicy juices making little appetizing gummy streaks around the crimps; three loaves of perfectly baked white bread browned to a nicety, cooling across their pans on the kitchen table, and a bowl of cottage cheese in the refrigerator.

After she had taken a cup of tea to hearten her up she added a sponge cake to the list of her deeds, and when that was baked and cooling in the pantry, she went up stairs.

Hesba arrived at five o'clock promptly.

Marget had taken the precaution to put the night latch on that she might not be taken unawares. She did not like the feeling that a stranger had stepped into her home, and might walk in on her at almost any moment. If the girl had the ordinary polite ways of a well bred person, it wouldn't be so hard, but she seemed to think that coming here to be a companion constituted her housekeeper, and general reformer, and there must be some way to show her her place while she remained. Marget meant that she should not remain long. Of course she could not just ship her back over night. She must be hospitable, yet she would make it very plain that she was not needed.

Marget went to the door, in another nice white apron, the mate to the one that Hesba had done her best to ruin the night before.

Marget had rested fifteen minutes, even falling into a restful doze, and now she had just finished setting the table, even going so far as to pick a couple of her best geranium blooms and arrange them on the table with a bit of asparagus fern in a tiny crystal vase, for good cheer. She had done this to prove to herself that she was going to be cordial and pleasant to this girl thus thrust upon her.

Hesba walked in with her arm full of books. She had the sharp, worn, alert look of an old blackbird who had been out scratching too long for worms.

It was sharper than the quick sharpness of youth, that passes, and leaves the soft smooth contours again. It was almost careworn, in one so young.

"I'm late!" stated Hesba, as she laid down her books on the table and began to take off her strong sensible fabric gloves. "Your trains don't run on schedule. I waited fully three quarters of an hour for the train gate to open. They made some excuse about trouble on the road, but it really is inexcusable I think on a big road like this one. However, I've planned what I can get in a hurry. I'm used to thinking up quick make shifts, and I'll have dinner ready on time. Have you got any parsley?"

"Parsley?" smiled Marget, gazing placidly at her young tormentor, the peace of her recent quiet hour in her eyes. "I'm afraid not, I've just used it all getting dinner."

"Getting dinner!" said Hesba in a vexed tone. "But I told you I would get it! When I make a promise I always keep it, and if I can't do it one way I can another. I would have got it in time. You needn't have got worried."

"Oh, I wasn't worried about that at all, my dear," said Marget pleasantly, "I got dinner quite early this morning, that is I prepared for it. I usually do. You see, my dear, however kindly your intentions may have been in offering to get dinner, I would prefer that you don't worry yourself about the hoose. This is my home and I have always run it in my own way, and prefer to do so. When I need help I will ask it, but while you remain here you are my guest. The hoose and its arrangements are mine."

"But I should not feel right not to help with the work. That's what I promised Aunt I would do."

"But *I* should not feel right if you did, lassie, so we'll talk no more aboot it. And noo, whilse we're speaking of it, I may as weel tell you that I've been thinking it over, and I feel it's best for you to go back to your home after you've had a good rest from your journey, for this is no place for a young thing like you, and I can't see my way clear to keeping you. I'm a home buddy, and not used tae having young things around."

"Oh, you'll find I'm not much of a young thing," said Hesba looking firmly at Marget through her round rims. "I've got serious work to do. Look at all my books! I'm to go in town three days in the week, so I'll have plenty of time to help you around the house in what ever you want done. You ought to begin to learn to let someone else do some of the work. You're getting old you know, and you'll have to give up pretty soon."

The color flamed softly in Marget Macdonald's cheeks, but she kept her tone steady and even smiled a bit as she said:

"Well, when it coomes it coomes; but it's na coom yet, and I'll bide as I am whiles I can. There's nothing I want doone for me."

"You'll find I can do things exactly as well as you can—" argued Hesba crossly, "I'm quite capable."

"I've ne'er thought ye were not capable," answered Marget, "ye might be able to do things better than I, but it's my work, and I likit to do it myself. So that's settled."

"Well, I could take more classes by going in *every* morning," said Hesba practically, "if you really don't need me."

"I dinna need ye," said Marget firmly, "but I think, my girl, ye better return to yer ain schule. Our winters are bitter up here, and it'll be hard gaeing to the train some morns. Besides, as I said, I prefer you should go. I have other arrangements. After of coorse ye've had a proper resting space before you take the big trip again."

"It's quite impossible now," said Hesba just as firmly, "I've paid my tuition in advance. You should have thought of this before you telephoned my aunt. I came on in good faith, and I spent the money for the trip, and for my school, and I've made all arrangements to be transferred. I couldn't go back of course. And I should miss the whole term and be behind."

"That'll be too bad," said Marget with a troubled look, wavering. "It's been a mistake, a great mistake, but I'd no idea of coorse your aunt would send a young person. It doesn't suit me at all."

"Well, the tuition is paid and I'm under promise to stay. I guess you'll have to make the best of it," said the girl. "I really wouldn't know what to do if you didn't. I couldn't afford to pay my board. The tuition is almost twice as much at this school as it was at home."

"Tuition?" said Marget puzzled, "why it doesn't cost anything for tuition at those Bible schools. You should have asked me aboot it before ye started oot. You see my son taught at the Institute all last winter."

"The Institute!" laughed Hesba half scornfully, "Oh, I wouldn't go to a school like that! I've heard about that! They were laughing about it in the office this morning when I registered. They say those schools don't teach you anything but the chapter and verse of a scripture reference. It's not to a school like that I'm going. It's a *Training* School. You get a lot more than the Bible. You get Training, and other Cultural branches, pedagogy, and social science and things like that. We have Bible interpretation of course, and Critical Study, and all that, and it's very interesting, but we get a lot more than juist Bible."

"Most Bible students find that they have their hands pretty full with juist the auld Buik," said Marget dryly, and then remembered suddenly her resolve and sheathed her sharp tongue.

"We'll speak na more aboot it," she said. "Ye may bide a few days at least, till we see. It may be that my son will return within the week."

"I should have been told that then, and not made all these arrangements," said Hesba crossly, as if she had been greatly wronged.

"There are several things that should have been told," said Marget with a sigh, "but it's too late for that now, my friend. We'll juist have to bear with things as they air till the Father changes it!"

Hesba laughed harshly.

"You're awfully funny, Grandma, thinking God attends to things like that. I think it's our own look out when we get into scrapes. It's somebody's fault and ought to be set straight."

"You'd be in a sairer strait yet, I'm thinking, if the Father didn't attend to a' things. That's where you make your mistake. And I'm thinking it doesn't matter sa mooch what you or I or onyboody *thinks* aboot it, the Father attends to it, juist the same. For He says so in the Buik. Noo, if ye'll wash oop and be ready, I'll pit the dinner on."

And with dignity Marget walked out to her kitchen and began to dish up the dinner.

Chapter XV

Letters from Thurly, two of them, came promptly, one to announce his safe arrival, the second to describe his first impressions. He spoke enthusiastically of the work, his colleagues, and his classes, described his pleasant location, and the first dinner he had eaten in his new quarters. His mother sighed and wiped away a tear. Here was she, far away, having to cook for this little huzzy of an alien, who debated everything she touched from the way to draw tea, to the meaning of a text of scripture; while Thurly, her own son, ate dishes prepared by strangers, and got the indigestion from sour bread and heavy pancakes. Ah, Thurly! Why had she not accepted his invitation, just closed the house and gone with him for a while? What joy it would have been to see Chicago under his guidance!

But of course that was all foolish. They couldn't have afforded to close the house and pay her board, not until Thurly had a church of his own and a regular sal-

ary. She must just bide and do the Lord's will, and
Thurly would come back by and by. Pain did not last
forever. Who was it said "This too shall pass"? But ah,
there was a better saying than that: "He knoweth the
way that I take: when He hath tried me, I shall come
forth as gold!"

Having taken her stand on the three things that
lay closest to her heart, the matter of Biblical interpretation, Thurly's room, and the conducting of her
own household, Marget determined to bear with all
the rest, wherever the unwelcome guest's ideas did
not verge on vital matters. But there was no end to
the ways in which Hesba Hamilton tormented the soul
of Marget Macdonald.

Marget was glad that the sessions of the school
began early and lasted late in the afternoon, glad that
Hesba was a perfect shark for study, and spent many
hours in her room, growing wiser, more round eyed,
and critical, as the days dragged by. But at least Marget had the better part of the day to herself, and she
managed by much Bible reading and prayer to keep
sweet the rest of the time.

It was late one afternoon that the postman
brought a parcel. Hesba happened to be home that
afternoon on account of a half holiday at school. Of
course she took it upon herself to go to the door, and
to demand that the postman account for being so
late.

"He *says* the train was late," she said, returning
primly with the mail, "but he's probably lying. They
all do. He just got lazy and didn't pep up! Just look
at this big thin package, Grandma! What is it, do you
suppose? It looks like a photograph, and it's from
Florida. 'Palm Beach,' it says. Mercy, do you have
friends rich enough to go there? I thought they were
all multimillionaires!"

"Palm Beach!"

Marget's heart took a sudden leap, and a light
flashed up in her eyes. She even forgot to notice that
Hesba had called her "Grandma" again. She wiped

her hands on the immaculate roller towel and came forward quickly, but Hesba was too quick for her.

"I'll open it for you," she said like a mother to a little child. "It's one of those patent envelopes for photographs and you won't know how." Zip! the envelope was ripped open and a photograph brought forth and opened up, its protecting tissue paper front floating lazily off to the dining-room carpet where it lay unheeded while Hesba gazed in amazed contempt at the lovely face of a girl about her own age with a string of pearls about her slim neck, "Anastasia" was written in a careless but characterful scrawl across one corner, and beneath in very tiny script "Just to help you remember me."

"Who on earth is that?" said Hesba contemptuously. "She looks like a movie star!"

Marget was vexed beyond words. She had a childish impulse to cry with indignation, but she managed to control herself and say nothing. She stooped to pick up the tissue cover, and when she lifted up her head was able to answer Hesba's exclamation quite pleasantly.

"Oh, that is just a little friend of mine, Miss Endicott."

"Mercy!" said Hesba again, eyeing the other girl enviously, "she puts on a great deal of style, doesn't she? Does she live down in Palm Beach all the time? I suppose there are some regular all-year-round residents."

"No," said Marget composedly putting a few of the dishes on the sideboard straight, "no, she lives in the city. She's down there for the winter—that is—" remembering what she had gleaned from the society notes she had been reading lately—"The Endicotts have a winter home in Palm Beach!"

"Mercy! You don't mean it!" said Hesba still studying the picture though Marget had not as yet been able to give more than a casual glance, "then I suppose those must be real pearls she has around her neck. Are they very rich people?"

"Well, I suppose they are comfortably off," said Marget. "They have a very handsome home in the city."

"Do you visit there?" she asked, giving Marget one of her round searching glances.

"Well, no—" said Marget uneasily, feeling that she was getting into deep water. "You know I don't go out much. I'm a real hoome buddy."

"Well, how do you know it's handsome then?"

There she was, put in a corner again. That direct huzzy was always delighting to get someone in a tight place!

"Oh, my son has been there, of course," she admitted. "He has told me about it."

"Oh! Is she a friend of Thurly's?"

Hesba had taken quite easily to calling the absent son by his first name as if she had the right. Marget had never been able to quite understand why this should annoy her, but it did.

"Why—yes—" she answered slowly with somewhat heightened color, "I suppose she is," and wondered if she were quite telling the truth, and whether she ought to admit it even if it was the truth, to this prying creature.

"Are they engaged?" came the next thrust.

Marget's hands trembled so that she dropped the fluttering tissue paper again, and was glad to have the opportunity to bend down and hide her startled face.

When she had picked up the paper she turned quite away from her questioner and opening the sideboard drawer began to rearrange the napkins as if it were a work of immediate necessity, trying to make her tone quite casual as she answered:

"Why, no—not that I know of." And then was filled with compunction at the impression she must have conveyed. Yet she knew not how to change it without making it ten times worse, so she changed the subject.

"If you'd like me to turn up that hem on your new dress for you I can do it now, Hesba," she said.

Hesba laid down the photograph quickly and hurried upstairs for the dress. But after it was on and they had decided on the length and Marget on her knees was carefully measuring with the yard stick and setting pins five inches apart, Hesba resumed just where she had left off, tone and all:

"Do you like her?"

"Like her? Like whom?" queried Marget to make time. The question seemed to stir some hidden depths of her heart that she did not understand, between joy and fear.

"Like this Anastasia?"

"Why, yes, I like her," said Marget resuming her casualness.

"Does Thurly like her?" was the next question, put bluntly.

Marget was almost at the end of her patience, but she managed a smile.

"Well, Hesba, I doubt me if my son would care to have me discuss his likes and dislikes with onybuddy," she said gently. "Turn a little to the left, won't you? It seems longer right by the seam does it not?"

Hesba turned sharply but continued:

"You're funny, Grandma," she said, "you're as close mouthed as a clam. I don't see why you shouldn't discuss things with me if you choose. Anybody might ask that question. Why should he mind you telling me that?"

"Well, perhaps he wouldna," said Marget easily, "but I always think the least said aboot those absent, the better. Would you like me to sew it? I've a bit spool the color."

"Thanks, Grandma, I wish you would. I'm not keen on sewing. I always buy my things ready made and have alterations made at the store when they are needed. But they didn't seem to have that kind of service in this store, so I had to take it as it was, it was such a bargain."

When Hesba had gone upstairs to take off the dress Marget went and stood by the table and looked into the sweet picture-face with a long anxious glance. Sometimes a photograph will bring out in a face something that is hidden in the flesh, and Marget was involuntarily searching for some flaw in the girl that her heart had gone out to; for her reason told her that Anastasia was not a girl she should take too deeply into her heart of hearts, unless she wished to face keen disappointment in the future. But Marget found nothing like that in the photograph, and with a kind of triumphant satisfaction she took up the picture and went and stood it on the mantelpiece in the little parlor, where it seemed to glorify the room just as the violets the girl had sent had done.

She would much have preferred putting the picture away where no alien eyes should look upon it, but she thought that might arouse the suspicion of her mentor, so she placed it out in the open and went on about her work as if nothing out of the ordinary had entered her home with the gift of that charming pictured face. Just as if her heart had not throbbed with a curious triumph to know that little lassie had not forgotten her. Just as if it had not also throbbed with a curious kind of fear with the instant question that came: had the girl sent it that *Thurly* might remember her also, half hoping that she had, half fearful lest she had. Oh, a curious thing was Marget's heart, and that was a fact she had begun to recognize quite clearly for herself.

Quite clearly Marget was beginning to see that she herself was beginning to be in danger of falling in love with the little worldling, and if she could not withstand her charm, how could she hope that her son would? Oh, the little gold shoe, the little bonnie shoe, with its flashing stones! What havoc had it wrought in their quiet household!

But Thurly was away for a time, safe! Why might she not enjoy the sweet face for a season, watching her from the mantel as she went about her house? If only that other girl did not have to be here too, with her eagle eyes watching Marget's every glance!

There had been one or two short letters passing between Palm Beach and Stonington, during the weeks since the storm. Marget had written a characteristic letter of thanks for the violets and again more at length for the watch, after Thurly had decided she must keep it. Tasha had written back telling of the summer weather she was enjoying, of the sea bathing, and tennis, and all the gay doings. But now this picture began to look as if the little brilliant butterfly had some real attachment for the friends of a day, and wanted to keep up the friendship.

So the picture remained on the mantel, and the two girls eyed each other furtively, the one on the mantel and the one behind the shell-rimmed glasses.

For Hesba had not budged for an instant from her determination to stay and keep on with her new school. Faithfully every morning she arose and made the coffee—*her* way—leaving the coffee pot on the back of the stove, never knowing that Marget had taken to tea for her breakfast, and got immense satisfaction from emptying the coffee pot, and washing it clean. It might be a bit wasteful, but it certainly did her soul good to throw out that coffee that was made the wrong way and had a wrong flavor.

For Marget after a few mornings' protest, had succumbed to letting Hesba get her own breakfast and depart, and for the first time in her life Marget slept till after seven, partly because she wanted to cut down the points of contact with her ruthless young governor whom she could not seem to dislodge without an actual battle, and partly because she did not want to fight about how that coffee should be made. If it pleased Hesba to think she was helping a little by making the coffee, and if she liked her coffee better made that way, why surely she, Marget, did not need to be so narrow about it. Let her go on and do it.

So life in the little Stonington cottage had settled down to a routine, not without a kind of outward peace. Now and again there would be a theological brush at the evening worship, for Hesba was persistent in trying to introduce modern ideas into the reading of the scripture, and Marget waxed hot when the inspiration of the scriptures was attacked; but for the most part, there was peace because Marget was daily and almost hourly praying for a higher strength than her own wherewith to walk her difficult way.

Then, one day, there arrived a delivery car from one of the big florist's establishments in the city. It happened to be the one that Hesba passed every morning on her way to school, and she had therefore acquired a knowledge of its importance. It was a large handsome box that was delivered to Marget, and Hesba as usual did the opening, though Marget stood back with her sweet soul boiling at the rudeness, and her fingers fairly itching to untie those ribbon knots and open her own flowers. Only a few flowers like that in her lifetime and she not allowed to open them! Hesba broke the ribbon, too, with a strong right thumb and finger, instead of untying it carefully and saving it for a treasure box.

But even Hesba was overpowered for a moment with the vision that was revealed as she lifted the lid of that box. Yellow and white and green, a perfect mass of glory and beauty! Roses and lilies and daffodils, starry narcissus, and freesias, masses of white lilacs and more roses, great yellow buds!

"Mercy!" said Hesba, "what a waste!"

"A *waste?*" said Marget starting back sharply from her first sweet breath of them with a hurt look in her eyes.

"Yes, sending all these *here,* with just us two. Not even a party or a wedding or a funeral! Mercy! Do you know what those yellow roses cost, those with the yard long stems? I priced them the other day, just for curiosity, and they are seventeen dollars a dozen! Just think of that! I say that's *wicked!* Think of the heathen!"

"The heathen?" said Marget puzzled. "What about the heathen?"

"Why, think what that might do for them!"

"What would it do for them?" asked Marget burying her face in the mass of lilacs, and wishing she might keep it there awhile and not listen to the grilling of Hesba's questions.

"What would it *do?* Why feed them, and send

them to school, and put decent clothes on their back, and teach them to be respectable citizens in the world."

"Is that all?" asked Marget with her eyes half closed, looking at the flowers dreamily.

"*All?* What more do you want?" asked Hesba indignantly. "Isn't that about all one needs in life?"

"I was thinking you might be saying it would send the knowledge of the Lord Jesus to them," said Marget, lifting a stately lily and gazing into its golden heart.

"Oh, that! Of course, that goes too. But they have to *live* you know. They *have* to have food and clothes."

"You think that comes first?" said Marget, laying her lips to the soft yellow coolness of a rose bud.

"I *think* so! I *know* so! How queer you are, Grandma! You are always saying such unusual things. Of course you don't mean them. You're trying to kid me I see. But really, what was the reason for sending a great lot of flowers now? It isn't even Easter. It couldn't be your birthday because you said that was in the Fall! Mercy! I call it extravagant. I hate to see waste! That's what it is. Do you know who sent them? I'd like to tell them so. It wasn't Thurly of course."

"No, it wasn't Thurly," said Marget smiling, "though the dear lad would like to send twice as many to his mother every day in the week if he could afford it."

"Well, I should hope he'd be more sensible. Who *did* send them? Was it that *girl?*" nodding toward the picture on the mantel. "Because she looks as if she'd have just about that much sense!"

But Marget with her face buried again in the lilacs and her eyes closed, was breathing in deep breaths of fragrance, and trying to keep from saying what she thought.

Just one more thrust the girl gave her.

"Say, was that gold shoe hers, the one I found on Thurly's closet shelf?"

And when she got no reply from Marget she added with a calm sneer,

"You needn't tell me she isn't interested in Thurly,—and *he in her!*" With which fling she walked upstairs and left Marget with her flowers and her thoughts.

Chapter XVI

The winter was broken at last. Drops began to drip from the icicles on the eaves, and little rivulets appeared in the gutters of the streets. Someone said they had heard a bird's note, and Hesba brought home some stalks of pussy willow she had bought on the street.

Marget took them pleasantly, with as much fuss as if they were roses, and put them in a vase, feeling of their silky little blossoms and cuddling them as she would have done any flowers. But she could not help thinking that these little harbingers of spring were like Hesba, hard and tight and tailor-made.

Marget was beginning to try to excuse some of Hesba's trying ways. It was almost time now, surely, for her to go back to her home, and she wanted her to leave as pleasantly as possible. She hoped against hope that she would go back for the Spring term at her home school; but Hesba had begun to talk about staying on until Commencement. She said she thought it would probably be better not to change again.

It was quite evident that she was planning to stay until Thurly returned if possible. She openly said she wanted him to take her around the city and show her some of the sights that she had not had time to see, and did not care to visit alone. In dismay Marget offered to get some neighbor to go with her at once, or even to go herself, much as she dreaded going out in bad weather; but Hesba said she hadn't time yet, that she had to study hard. She was taking two courses in one and hoped to get enough credits to finish her course in one year more.

Thurly had written that the professor for whom he was substituting was to return in ten days now, and he would probably be able to come home. He would likely know very soon whether the man could take up his work at once, but it was generally supposed that he would. His mother could read between the lines that while he was eager to get home to her, he yet was disappointed not to be able to carry his students through to the logical finish of the year's work, to show what he really could do with them in a year. It would be far more to his credit, and add to his reputation more than if he but substituted for a part of a year.

Marget would not have believed that the time would ever come when she would actually be willing to have her son remain away a little longer than was necessary, but she was in a real panic now as she thought of the possibility of Thurly's returning while Hesba was there. Not that she could see anything in Hesba to attract a young man beyond the fact that she was young and strong, and supposed herself to be consecreated to a Cause with a capital C. But the longer she lived with Hesba the more she felt what a dire calamity it would be to have Thurly fall in love—No —she couldn't quite fancy anybody falling in love with Hesba, but she could imagine Hesba forcing a man into the frame of mind where he thought he was doing the right and proper thing to marry her. In fact she was so persistent that it was hard to see how a gallant gentleman could well escape her clutches if she should once set out to capture him. Hesba would make herself seem so eminently fitting a match for a man who was contemplating Christian work. She was so practical and matter of fact, that she could well nigh make a man forget there were such things as love and romance, and think that the only qualities in the world that were worth while were practicality, and devotion to a Cause.

Marget had come to feel that Hesba was no nearer being a mate to her son in spiritual things than was the little beautiful worldling who had dropped down upon them that night in the storm. For Hesba had no Bible for a foundation, no real Christ in her heart to build upon. Hesba was building upon theories of men and science so-called, and moulding the old Bible over to suit them; consequently the ground under her feet was shifting sands, and she was acquiring more and more the habit of cutting loose from former things and finding new paths, which sadly enough did not lead to old truths. Hesba was a devotee of organizations, and uplifts, and effort of every sort to save one's self, and to save the world. Thurly was a devotee of the Lord Jesus and a believer in the old Book from cover to cover. No, they were not fit mates; and Marget, though she knew and believed that her Lord could guide her son, and was able to keep him from falling, yet she hoped he wouldn't come home while Hesba was there. She did not like the idea of Thurly and Hesba under the same roof together.

Daily she prayed for Hesba, daily besought the Most High to deliver herself from rancor and hard feeling; from being unjust to one of God's children; to give her love, like His, for the girl who had seemingly been sent to her. Daily she sought in little ways to show forth the Lord Jesus, and witness as to what he had done in her life, but Hesba only smiled wisely, and called her "grandma" and went on her high, soulish way. It would seem that her eyes were blinded that she could not see the light. Marget groaned to herself in spirit daily that the girl could not have chosen a school from among real believers, rather than the one to which her home professor had sent her. But Hesba was never one who could be advised, and she would spend hours of time trying to convince Marget Macdonald of some trifling interpretation in scripture—an interpretation that took all the spirit from the passage, and spelled destruction and distress for Marget.

It was in vain that Marget tried to show her from

the Bible that no man had a right to explain away the plain truths that were written for our instruction. In vain did she quote "No scripture is of private interpretation." Hesba would smile in her superior maddening way and say, "Oh, Grandma, you're so literal! But you know of course that the Bible would be very different if it were written to-day!"

And then Marget Macdonald would quote: "Jesus Christ, the same yesterday, to-day and forever!" and Hesba would say, "Oh, but Grandma, that's a very different matter. You don't really understand what that means. If you would take up a correspondence course in our school you would learn that a lot of things you used to think were so are all changed!"

Then would Marget Macdonald look out of her window sadly toward the faraway hills and acknowledge in her heart that all her talk, and all her argument were of little avail. This girl was entrenched behind a lot of sophistries that she had been taught as if they were based on truth, and she did not want to see the right. Poor child! And she was going out to teach others, blinder than herself! The blind leading the blind. No wonder that the world was getting topsy turvy and going after new gods, when the old ones had been dust covered in an attic of antiques, and everyone had to hunt a new god for himself.

In these days Marget Macdonald spent much time upon her knees in prayer, finding out her own follies and failures, yes, and her own weaknesses, and praying to be given the victory through Him who has vanquished our enemy, the prince of this world, once and for all, and through Whose victory we have a right to triumph too.

She would have been surprised if she could have known, however, how deep an impression her life was making on this self-centered girl. In her practical, blunt way Hesba was becoming fond of Marget Macdonald, and almost regretting the time when she must leave her. Several times she went out of her way to bring some token home with her. It was always a tailor-made tribute, like the pussy willow, but it was nevertheless a tribute, and as she went forth into her self-made future she would always remember "Grandma" as one who was wholly sincere, and lived up to her narrow beliefs with a steadfast self-forgetfulness that would always cause a little question in her mind, whether after all there had not been *some* truth in the things she believed. Hesba was one who took in all "religions" into her kingdom of love, and believed that even a false belief was better than none at all, and to be respected with equal reverence with a belief in the saving death of the Lord Jesus Christ. She had hitherto shut out what she chose to call fanatics from this broad inclusiveness, but now she began to see that even a "fanatic" might be allowed to come inside the pale if he was sincere, as "Grandma" Macdonald seemed to be. But to her credit be it said that she had no idea whatever what a trial she had been to that same sweet saint.

And through it all Marget was led to a place where she ceased to argue, ceased to protest, just held her peace. Sometimes she even prayed for Hesba at their evening worship together, bringing her so tenderly to the mercy seat that Hesba would rise with tears in her eyes. Once she stood a moment afterwards brushing away a tear, and then said in her blunt way: "I'm sure I thank you, Grandma."

Marget felt a thrill of something like pleasure at that, a kind of love for the girl's soul, even though she had not yet got to the point where she could enjoy being in her company.

The day came when Tasha Endicott finished her play in Florida and came home for the tail end of the season in the city.

It was Hesba who first discovered and announced the fact. In fact all winter, if there was any particular thing that Marget would have liked to be silent and a bit private about, Hesba always managed to hale it forth and make much of it.

Hesba had gone out Sunday morning and purchased a Sunday paper the first Lord's day she was in Stonington; and because she found that a Sunday paper had not been approved at the cottage where she was saying, she considered it her God-given duty to purchase one quite ostentatiously every Sunday thereafter. It had been one of the many trials that Marget had submitted to, because she felt she had no right to impose her conscience on another.

So this Sabbath Hesba had taken her usual Sabbath morning walk to the news stand and come home with the fat flaring sheet tucked under her arm. She sat down in the parlor to read as it was not yet time for church going, and she seldom favored Marget's church when she went, but took a train to the city to attend some noted speaker, or some gathering of a queer cult which she said she attended for "experience" whatever that was.

So Hesba read her paper.

Suddenly she turned a page and gave an exclamation:

"Mercy! That must be your friend, Grandma! Yes, it is, the very same one. Look at the picture. It's got the same string of pearls around her neck, and the very same dress, although it's not the same pose. The face is more profile. But it isn't the same name. Look, Grandma, isn't that queer!"

With a sense of portending disaster Marget looked up at the paper that was being held for her inspection, and there, sure enough was the little lassie's picture, right in the midst of the society column.

"It doesn't say the same name that's on the picture," exclaimed Hesba gain, excitedly, as if she would draw some information from her silent hostess. "It calls her Tasha! Mercy! What a queer name. That's worse than the other. Perhaps it's her younger sister, but I'm dead certain that's her picture. See! The nose is the same too, and that flower on the shoulder of her dress. Listen! 'Mrs. Endicott and Miss Endicott have returned from Palm Beach where they have been spending the last three months in their new villa, and have opened their home on Waverly Drive where they

will be until after Easter, when they are planning to
sail for Europe for the summer!' Mercy! Think of
that! What's the use of having a home if you don't stay
in it? I think that's wasteful. Even if you are a multi-
millionaire, that's wasteful! Don't you think so, Grandma?"

But Marget did not answer. She was trying to
keep her thoughts steady, and her heart from excitement. So, the little lassie was back once more, and
there would be the matter of the little gold shoe all
over again! Thurly was away— She was both glad and
sorry that Thurly was away. The matter of the shoe
would devolve upon her and what should she do about
it? Would she have to go to the grand home by herself
and take the little shoe? She shrank inexpressibly from
such an experience. And there would be the great lady
Mrs. Endicott that the paper spoke about. That creature that the girl had called Lucia, who had been
divorced so many times and married again, or was that
the husband? She could not remember, but she did not
want to meet her. Oh, she did not want the peace of
her heart broken up again by the nearness of that girl.
That lovely worldly girl. She could not help loving
her, but of course they had no part with her. She was
of another universe, the pretty lassie!

So Marget was paying little heed to Hesba's questions until she asked a second time:

"Don't you feel that is awfully silly, Grandma,
having all those homes? I call them snobs, don't you?"

Then Marget looked up and smiled mysteriously.

"Not just snobs," she said. "She's been in this
simple little hoose, and partaken of oor plain food, and
sung songs thegither with Thurly and me, and she's
been a parfect little lady. She's oor friend, Hesba, and
I'd rather ye didn't ca' her names. You don't know her,
that's a'! And now my dear, it's full time I was getting
my bonnet on for church. Will you go with me the
day?"

So Hesba was silenced for the time. But Hesba was
never silenced for long.

It was only at dinner that same day that she

looked up from the excellent dinner she was eating and asked:

"How did she come to leave that gold slipper here with all those jewels in the buckle? You never told me."

"No?" said Marget with rising inflection. "Weel, there was nothing to tell. She juist left it. That was a'."

"But didn't she miss it? Didn't she write for it? Didn't she even know she had lost it?"

"Oh, yes, she knew she had lost it. She said however it didn't matter. She has plenty of shoes. She didn't seem to worry about it, and of course, noo she's hame she'll get it again!"

Hesba eyed Marget dissatisfied. She never was willing to leave a subject till she had poured it to the dregs, even though it might make a bitter drop for someone.

"Well, I think it was awfully queer, Thurly having it up on his shelf there. Did you know he had it? What did he say about it? What does he think?"

"Certainly I knew my son had it," answered Marget serenely, "I gave it him to put safe awa'. But what does he think? Why, what shud he think? I doobt if he ever remembers the wee bit shoe at a'. Will you have anither bit of the lamb, Hesba?"

But the very next afternoon Tasha came to call, regally garbed in velvet and ermine, driving her own little extravagant car, with a light of real gladness in her eyes as if she enjoyed coming.

Marget took her in her arms, and kissed the soft cheek, that was free from make-up for the occasion, or was it so subtly put on as not to show to her untaught eyes? At least she looked fresh and wholesome to Marget who was glad to get the lovely lassie in her house again, looking even lovelier than she remembered her.

Tasha was childishly happy to be in the cottage again, and moved around touching things, saying, "There is the hymn book we sang from! And oh, I have heard several of those hymns since! I've been going to church. Did you know I went to church in a queer little chapel down in Florida? And they said some of the same things you did."

She stood before her own portrait seeming pleased that Marget had cared to set it up, for she could not have failed to see how it crowned and dominated everything else in the room.

She fluttered over and sat down beside Marget on the couch with the old book of college photographs in her hand and turned the pages as she talked, lingering, Marget noticed, over some of the groups of football laddies where Thurly stood in the midst as their captain.

They did not speak of Thurly, not directly, yet. They talked of the winter, how cold it had been in the North, how lovely and summer like in the South. Tasha told of her winter sketchily, not much more than she had written, till she came to the tale of the old woman in prayer meeting, and her subsequent interest in the little sick grandson who had to have an operation. Tasha told of her visits to the child; how she had enjoyed taking him toys, picture books, flowers; how he was getting well now and beginning to walk like any little boy. Marget caught her soft little hand and held it, watched the color come and go in the pretty cheeks and the light in the stormy young eyes, and wondered.

Then, suddenly when they had only begun to speak of Thurly, and Tasha had put her hand out to rest on his violin case which stood behind the couch in the corner, in walked Hesba!

The light went out blankly in Tasha's face, and her chin went up haughtily. She gave one look at Marget, and then back at the girl again, questioningly.

Hesba looked at Tasha too, but not as one taken unaware. One never took Hesba unaware. She was always prepared for everything under the sun, and quite equal to any occasion.

"Oh!" said Hesba, coolly walking up to the visitor, "you're Anastasia, aren't you? I've wanted to meet you to see if you looked like your pictures. You do, only you're better looking of course. You really are. I wouldn't have believed it, for they generally are not. How's Florida?"

Tasha rose, with that little tilt of chin that gave insensibly the touch of hauteur and breeding. She looked at Hesba, and then at Marget questioningly, then back to Hesba.

Marget rose quickly but Hesba burst in before she could speak.

"Oh, I'm Hesba Hamilton. You must have heard of me if you're such a friend of Grandma and Thurly. I came on to take care of Grandma while Thurly's in Chicago teaching this winter. I'm attending training school in the city, getting ready to be a social service worker or missionary or something. My school will be over pretty soon, but I intend to stay a while after Thurly gets back and have a little fun when he can run around with me. I've been doing some pretty stiff studying all winter and need relaxation to keep fit. I'm glad you've come back. I hope we see a good deal of each other."

Tasha surveyed the other girl and froze visibly. So this was the kind of girl Thurly liked to run around with! She looked her keenly through, managed a haughty little smile and turned back to Marget who read the occurrence like an open book, and flew into a panic, though preserving an outward calm. She essayed to explain.

"Miss Hamilton came verra kindly in her aunt's place. Her aunt was an old neibor of years back in Scootland, and my son would na leave me alane, so he telephoned Martha who promised to coome, but the verra night before—"

Just here Hesba broke in eagerly,

"The night before she was to start she fell downstairs and broke her leg. So of course I had to come. It was all in the family you know!" and by this last sentence Hesba wiped out all possibility of Marget's delicate explanation getting across and put herself in the foreground again as an intimate of the Macdonald family. Marget looked at her guest with distressed but mute appeal and apology in her eyes, but Tasha was again looking coldly at Hesba and did not see it.

Hesba was by no means mute however. She always rushed in where the proverbial angels feared.

"You came after your gold slipper, didn't you?" she offered affably. "Well, it's here all right. I haven't let any burglars get in since I've been here."

Tasha's gaze grew colder.

"My slipper?" She glanced at Marget in a half surprise, saw the rising crimson in her cheeks, and turned sweetly back to Hesba with scarce a second's hesitation.

"Oh, yes, my slipper. I had forgotten about its being here. Of course. No, I did not come for the slipper. I came to see my friend. But now I think I must be going at once. It is getting late and I have one or two other stops to make."

"Oh, but aren't you going to stay to supper!" cried Hesba with a determined note in her voice. "Of course you are. You sit here and talk to Grandma while I put supper on!"

"Thank you, no, it is impossible!" said Tasha, the words like icicles.

Tasha took Marget's warm little trembling hand for farewell, and Marget murmured a little plea in a low tone, "I'd love to have you stay."

"I know, dear, some other time," said Tasha. "Some time when you're all alone and need me," she added in almost a whisper.

Hesba standing jealously on the outside, studying the cut of the Endicott garments, hurriedly, avidly, perceived that the visitor was really going, and going too, without the golden shoe.

"Oh, you mustn't forget your slipper!" she exclaimed, as Tasha moved swiftly toward the door, "I'll run right up and get it. Where is it, Grandma? Did you put it back on Thurly's closet shelf? Because if you did you'll have to tell me where to find the key. You locked the door you know."

"Sit down, Hesba, I will get the shoe," said Marget, her voice rising severely above her excitement with the old Scotch dominant note.

But Tasha put up a protesting hand.

"Please don't, dear," she said, "I'll get it another time. I must hurry now. I promised to meet a train and I'm late. It really is of no consequence at all. Good bye, dear little Mrs. Macdonald," and Tasha caught Marget in a sudden quick hug and kissed her soft wrinkled cheek. Then she was gone, the door shut behind her, and Marget and Hesba were left alone, two vexed, disappointed women.

"It would be better," said Marget when she had got control of herself, and could keep the angry tremble out of her voice, "if you would let people manage their own affairs!"

"Why, Grandma, what did I do? I'm sure I was only trying to be polite to your guest," and her voice was aggrieved.

"If your own inner sense of the fitness of things does na teach you, I'm afraid I canna explain," said Marget with dignity, and went out to her kitchen and her neglected dinner, her heart sore with the sudden termination of the pleasant call, yet warm with the thought of Tasha's kiss.

"The wee lassie!" she said, winking the mist from her eyes at the remembrance. "The wee bonnie birdie!"

Hesba stalked up to her room, but came down at the tinkle of the supper bell with a self-righteous silence upon her that made the meal anything but a pleasant one, but Marget's thoughts were in a tumult and it did not matter. She was trying to think if there was anything she could do to eradicate the impressions made on the caller that afternoon, and her cheeks burned with mortification as she realized what a position her Thurly had been placed in by the thoughtless words of Hesba. Or were those words so thoughtless after all? Sometimes she wondered if Hesba did not often have intention in some of the ill-timed things she said.

Marget went early to her room that night and after much deliberation wrote a short note in her stiff little cramped hand on queer thin foreign stationery she had brought with her from Scotland years ago.

> "My Dear Miss Endicott:
> I so enjoyed your visit to-day, and was sad to have you leave so suddenly. I hope you will pardon what occurred. Miss Hamilton does not understand. I will explain more when I see you again, and I hope you will come to me soon. I am always alone in the mornings.
> > Very sincerely,
> > Marget Macdonald."

The only answer to this was another large box of flowers containing Tasha's card and the word "Sometime" written across the back. It arrived in the middle morning, and for once Marget had the pleasure of opening the box herself, and arranging her own flowers, although she was certain that Hesba would try to rearrange them when she came home. Hesba could take the poetry out of a bunch of flowers with less effort than anyone Marget had ever met.

Chapter XVII

Thurly was coming home for Easter. A telegram had arrived telling her so, and Marget stood at the window and read it and wiped a tear of joy from her eyes. Even the presence of Hesba on the scene could not quite blot out her joy in his coming.

Thurly said that the returning professor was taking his own classes, so he would remain at home, and Marget's heart sang a paean as she went excitedly about her house putting it in fine array for her son's return.

During the morning she thought up a way to get

rid of Hesba, at least she hoped she had. She would offer to pay Hesba's way home to visit her family for Easter vacation. Of course if Hesba insisted on returning to finish the spring term of her school she would pay her way back again, but there was a slight chance when she once got home that she might stay there. Anyhow, Marget would have a full week of time all alone with her boy, and get to understand everything before they were interrupted by Hesba's return, and who knew what might develop in a week?

But Hesba returned from school early that day, by reason of the illness of a professor, and clipped Marget's hopes in the bud.

"No, I don't care to go home at this time. Nobody expects me, and I hate to surprise people. Besides, I couldn't anyway. I've made two dates. I'm going to a symphony concert, and a lecture with one of the young men from my class, that will be Tuesday and Thursday evenings, and I may go in to a social the class is planning, I'm not sure; that will be Friday. Thank you just the same, but I think I'll stay right along till school closes."

Marget's lips drooped with disappointment; but at least Hesba would be out of the way two evenings, and perhaps three. She was glad for that. Marget had not told Hesba that Thurly was coming. She had an innate feeling that if she did Hesba would remain in spite of her. Hesba's interest in Thurly had been most marked.

"I hope you won't mind being alone those evenings," went on Hesba, "and I may not come home even to dinner those days; he wants me to take dinner with him. I could try to get somebody to stay with you. Who was that boy you had stay nights before I got here?"

"That isn't at all necessary, Hesba. Besides, I may as well tell you, I'm—rather—expecting my son soon. He—might be here the day, or the morrow—!"

"Oh!" said Hesba with a sound of almost dismay, "if I had known that I wouldn't have made those dates. You see he's here away from his folks, and he's lonely—"

"Oh, that's all right, Hesba! It's bonnie fer you to

be kind to him. And I wouldna have ye stay home for Thurly. He's naething to you, nor you tae him, and he wouldna expect it. In fact, we likit tae be alane thegither after the lang separation. Juist gae tae yer pleasure, and have a good time!"

But Hesba stood a long time looking out the window, thinking that for once she had messed her plans.

Marget, with glad heart went about preparations in the kitchen, making pies, cake, biscuit, getting ready the things that her son best loved to eat, killing the fatted calf as it were, and did not notice the dismayed look on the face of the solemn-eyed girl behind the shell-rimmed glasses. Presently Hesba turned with a sigh and marched off upstairs to her room. Afterward that sigh came back and smote Marget's consciousness, and she tried to be kinder to Hesba at dinner that night, but apparently Hesba was the same matter of fact creature again that she always had been, and Marget put away the momentary anxiety on her account and let herself rejoice in anticipation.

The next morning after Hesba had gone to school Marget opened up Thurly's room and cleaned it from top to toe. But the little gold shoe remained in her own room locked safe in her treasure box, with the key on a ribbon around Marget's neck. It would be inevitable that Thurly must know the history of that shoe since he left, so there was no point in returning it to the care of Josephus. If Thurly had taken the shoe with him, Marget would not have felt that she could open the subject between them, but since he had not, since he had cared so little about it as to actually forget to speak to her about it, her heart felt free to do with it as she thought wise, and she felt that the long absence must have caused Thurly to forget the owner of the shoe as well as the little shoe itself, therefore she had naught to be worried about from that quarter. In truth, she had come to feel very differently about the girl, Anastasia, of late.

As she went about her work she was constantly

thinking of her and of her visit cut so abruptly short by Hesba's ill-timed appearance. Once as she stood by the window, pausing in the polishing of a pane of glass, she looked off to the hills across the valley which were her constant delight, thinking what the lassie had told her of her winter's experience, and she said to herself aloud, rejoicing that no one was nigh to hear her:

"Anastasia. Convalescent. I doobt na she's cooming back tae health, the bonnie little lamb! Anastasia. It's a bonnie name! I like it weel!"

So, when night came, Marget had the room all sweet and fine, ready for her laddie, and she locked the door and went down to prepare the evening meal with a great joy upon her. Sometime on the morrow Thurly had said he might arrive, or it might be the next morning. He had not been sure. But the air seemed full of song, and the sunshine sparkled precious gems to her glad eyes.

Thurly Macdonald had bought a car. It was not a perfectly new one, nor very grand in its way, but it was one of the better makes with a reputation for comfort, mileage, endurance and speed. He got it at a bargain from one of the professors who was going abroad and could not take it with him. And he was driving home to surprise his mother. For he meant that car to be a great comfort to his mother as well as to himself.

Thurly would not have been human if he had not dreamed dreams sometimes, and often as he drove along through the country that was practically new to his eyes, there would come to him the thought that sometime he might find another one who would go with him on these rides, along with his mother. Someone who loved to have his mother along, and who was altogether all the wonderful things that a man dreams his mate will be, before he has ever set eyes upon the girl he finally asks to be his wife.

But the thing that troubled Thurly's dreams, and made him feel almost guilty whenever he indulged in them, was the fact that the dream face and form of the girl who was to love him, and be all these wonderful things he hoped for, seemed always like just one girl—the little worldling whom he had brought in out of the terrible blizzard; who had left her little gold shoe in his heart, the feel of her little cold silken foot in his hand, and the weight of her slender figure on his shoulder as he bore her through the storm.

Now he had told himself more times than he could count that the girl he had taken home that night was no more all the things he wanted in a wife, than he was what she wanted in a husband. She was rich and haughty and proud—although she had had courtesy enough not to show it in his home. But she was a worldling! That one word told it all. She belonged to the world, the flesh and the devil as represented by her life of frivolity and pleasure. Her very errand in that storm had been to a Framstead dance, and Framstead dances were well known in the home neighborhood as being the very height of extravagance and license. Framstead! That told it all!

He belonged body and soul to the Lord of all the earth, but she did not even know that Lord. She had shown that plainly by her walk and conversation that day.

Yet how lovely she had been! What charm the world put upon the human form! Yes, and into the human spirit!

Oh, he had put her away, out of his thoughts! Many times he had put her away, yet she always came back to tantalize him. And though he recognized her as a temptation to take his thoughts away from his work, yet he thought he had conquered her. He thought that her pretty spirit had been exorcised. Put out of his heart forever. It had always been the utmost folly anyway! As if she would have ever looked at him, a poor young minister, whose calling she likely despised.

But there was one fear that had begun to possess him, and that was that though he had succeeded in putting the thought of her so far from him that he had not even remembered about the little gold shoe—not very often—he might perhaps never be able to get the vision of her out of his eyes enough to see any beauty in the right maiden when God should send her. And daily he prayed that her face and her smile and the vision of her as he had seen her at different times, might be taken away from his thoughts so that he might recognize good in other girls, if they should come his way. For that a man should love one woman, some time in his life, cling to her, protect her, and make her the companion of his years, he firmly believed. It was a principle that his mother had taught him from his youth, and he had put it off until now, feeling that there was plenty of time, and that the right one would come some day.

These thoughts were with him more or less as he drove along at a flying pace toward home.

It was almost midnight when he reached a city less than a hundred miles from home. Common sense bade him stop and rest for the night and take the last lap of his journey in the early morning. Yet the sound of familiar names, and the sight of familiar roads had set him longing inexpressibly for home, and after a bite to eat he decided to push on. He knew his mother would not mind being waked to greet him. He knew his bed would be waiting, all turned down, and his things ready. He would go and surprise her!

It was between two and three in the morning that he came to a place within thirty miles of Stonington where two main highways crossed, there were lights, and voices and confusion; two cars overturned and a third badly smashed. There had been a drizzly rain all the evening and the roads were slippery as glass with the spring frost coming out of the ground, and the spring mud beginning to ooze.

Thurly came to a halt and looked out, his own lights bringing out the scene more clearly.

One man was lying across his path in a limp heap, another had been thrown in the ditch with his head badly cut. Two others were stumbling around as if half dazed, and the sound of a woman's scream mingled with oaths from one of the overturned cars. The road was covered with splintered glass, and the voices that cried out showed that most of the party were under the influence of liquor.

Thurly got out and threw his flash light on the different faces. He went first to the car that was overturned in the dark, and managed finally to get the door open and lift out the struggling, frightened inmates. They came forth cursing and weeping, young men in evening clothes, and girls in party dresses and rich furs. They fell upon him and besought him to do something about it, and some of them even blamed him for the accident. He was forced to shake them off for there was one more person in the car and he must go to the rescue.

She had crept up to the opening when he turned back, and he pulled her out and set her on her feet.

"Are you hurt?" he asked gruffly, for he was filled with disgust. This was some more of the young generation engaged in having a good time, breaking the law to do it! He had little sympathy for them in the calamity that had overtaken them. They were all headed for destruction and did not seem to care.

But the girl that stood beside him shuddering did not answer, only put out her hand gropingly and touched his arm.

"Are you drunk too, like all the rest?" he said gruffly, and turned his flash upon her face that was white to the lips with a trickle of blood from the forehead down the cheek.

Then for an instant all the strength in his body seemed to be leaving him as he gazed on that face.

"*You?*"

He uttered the word like a cry of anguish.

For an instant he longed to turn and flee from the sight of her. Then he said it again, like a wail of something dying, "*You!*"

She choked in a sob, and tried to speak.

"Take me away, please, quick! Oh, take me

away!" and she shrank suddenly toward him as he saw a dark young fellow lurching toward her.

"Tashshsesh! Where you? Live'n kicking? Here I am. Here's your Barry! Close call, Tashesh! Where—are—you?"

Thurly caught the girl in his arms and dashed by the drunken youth, pushing him toward the ditch to be rid of the outstretched hands which would have prevented him, and Barry toppled backward and sat down against the muddy bank of the roadside; but Thurly had Tasha safely shut inside his car.

He went back to the others, and did what he could to help. Several of the party were badly hurt and one was probably dead. But there was need of an ambulance and doctors at once so he left the party in charge of the soberest man and went back to his car, promising to send relief from the nearest town at once.

Tasha was crouched in the corner of the seat, white and still. He almost thought she had fainted, till he touched her and she opened her eyes.

"Are you hurt?" he asked sternly.

She shook her head.

He stepped on the gas and they shot out over the dark road. He did not speak, but gave his entire attention to driving. Only once he turned toward her again and said: "You are sure you are not hurt?"

"Just bruised a little on my arm," she said with a catch in her throat like a sob.

She could see his face stern and white in the dim shadows of the car, but he said no more till the lights of a town came in sight. Then he turned again to her, though he did not slow down his pace.

"Now, suppose you tell me just what happened. We'll keep you out of this thing if we can."

"Oh, don't mind me!" said the old Tasha tone of a good sport, as she caught her breath in another smothered sob.

Thurly longed to take her in his arms, and comfort her, but he held himself firmly in check. To have found her in such company! He had needed this. He was appallingly conscious that he had been thinking of her all the time underneath the surface of his mind. Even when he thought he had conquered the thought of her, she was there! And now this!

"What happened?" Thurly asked again sharply.

"We were coming down the highway pretty fast. We had skidded several times. I saw another car coming down the crossroads at top speed. It came too fast to know just what did happen, but they struck us and we overturned. I heard the brakes screaming and felt us skid and turn, and then the jar of the car behind hitting us. After that I don't remember anything but darkness and being smothered, till someone burst open the door and let the air in, and they took the people off from me."

"Were you all drunk?" asked Thurly sternly.

"I was not drunk," said Tasha speaking with a sweet sort of dignity. "I don't drink—any more!" she added.

"You go with people who do," said Thurly still sternly.

"What else can I do?" defended Tasha in a little gasp of indignation that was pitiful. "They are the people I know, the ones I was born and brought up with."

"You need to be born again," said Thurly his voice still sharp like a surgeon cutting an open wound.

"I ww-w-wish I could!" sobbed Tasha, her face down in her hands.

"You can!" said Thurly. "It has been done. It is up to you," and suddenly he reached out one arm and drew her up sharply, bringing his car to a standstill, tilting her chin and turning his flash light full in her face.

"You are hurt!" he said, "there is blood on your face!"

"It is only a scratch!" she gasped, trying to stop her falling tears, and shuddering into the haven of his arm to stop the trembling of her body. Little hard boiled Tasha Endicott, crying like a baby, and glad of an arm to steady her!

"Poor child!" he said, and there was infinite tenderness suddenly in his voice, as he looked down at her.

Never in his life had Thurly Macdonald wanted to do anything so much as to gather that child close to his heart and kiss her lovely trembling lips, her sweet misty eyes, and comfort her.

But Thurly Macdonald was built of sterner stuff than most men, and he had the fear of God ever before him. He still knew that Tasha Endicott was not one that he should kiss, and he still could feel the strength of a Power higher than his own weak flesh.

For an instant he kept his strong arm supporting her, searching her face in the light of his flash to make sure she was right about not being hurt, then gently, he sat her back in her corner, and put his hand on the wheel.

"We must push on to the rescue!" he said tersely, and started the car once more.

Two or three minutes later they came into a town, and found a policeman.

Thurly did not speak to Tasha again until they had seen the chief of police, with two doctors in his car, and an ambulance following hard behind, start back to the scene of the accident, with another ambulance to follow in five minutes.

"Now," said Thurly, turning to Tasha, who sat white-faced in the shadow of the car, "do you want to go back to your friends?"

"Oh, no!" said Tasha. "Must we? Ought we?" He could feel she was trembling at the thought.

"Not unless there is someone there for whom you —are responsible—someone you want to be with—"

"Oh, no! I have been frightened and disgusted all the evening! I was afraid to come home with them, but I was afraid to remain where we were. I did not know before I started that we were to go to that roadhouse. They said we were going to a house party. Oh, could I go home, or would it be—would it be running away?"

"I think not," said Thurly. "We have sent help enough for them all, and in any case you could not do anything except identify each one."

"Ned Norton can do that," said Tasha. "He was the one walking round in the road when we left. He never quite loses his head."

"Then I shall take you home. This thing is liable to get in all the papers, and you might as well keep out of it if possible. I fancy there are some pretty well known people in that bunch."

"Yes," said Tasha, "but I was a part of them all the evening, perhaps I ought to go back and stand by them. They are my set, and I don't like turning yellow. Turn back, please. I guess I must!" she said, and dropped her head back against the cushion of the car.

"You're not going back!" said Thurly sternly. "You're not fit. I shall not let you. See," and he stepped on the gas, "you are being carried away by someone who came along and picked you up. It is not your fault. You are not able to go back, and you could do nothing if you went. I am taking you home. Will anyone be up to receive you and look after you?"

"Yes, I can call my maid," said Tasha, with thankfulness in her tired voice.

Thurly spoke no more till he drew up in front of the Endicott mansion.

Tasha wondered how he knew where she lived, and hid that thought away in her heart for further meditation.

"Have you a key?" he asked gravely.

Tasha produced one.

Thurly helped her out and up the steps, unlocking the door for her.

"Now, are you sure you will be all right?" he asked anxiously.

He took her hand and held it for just an instant, her little trembling hand, and looked down at her gravely.

"If you should ever need me for anything will you promise to let me know?" he said, and his eyes searched her face hungrily.

Tasha promised, and with a quick handclasp he turned away.

"Good night, now, I'm going back to see if there is anything more I can do for any of those folks."

And he was gone.

Chapter XVIII

It was still dark when Thurly arrived at the scene of the accident once more, though the East was beginning to show a faint light at the horizon. He found the chief of police still on the job, for it had been a heavy task to identify all the people of three cars, and get them to their several homes or hospitals.

The police eyed Thurly suspiciously.

"You back?" he said with a frown.

"Yes, I had to take the lady home who was with me, but I thought perhaps there might be something I could do."

"Well there is. Take that fella in the car there home. He ain't hurt, that is not bad, but he's bound he won't leave till he finds one of the ladies. He says she ran away from him. I ain't had men enough to send him off yet, but ef you can see him home I'll be obliged." .

It was Barry Thurston who was reclining in his car, now righted upon its wheels, but badly smashed as to running gear; Barry heavy with sleep and liquor and stubborn as a mule.

Thurly and the Chief had to fairly carry him to the other machine. Thurly drove to the address he gave, when they could rouse him enough to speak at all. But once roused Thurly had all he could do to keep the drunken man from trying to seize the wheel and run the car, for he seemed to fancy that he was still

in the midst of an accident which he must do something to avert. And whenever Thurly coaxed him back
in the seat, and told him to sleep he would babble
about Tasha. It filled Thurly with indignation to think
of the frail young girl in such company, for he learned
from the drunken babblings that this was the man who
had been Tasha's escort for the evening. So this was the
life she had been born to! This was the kind of company she had been in the habit of keeping! His heart
sank. All that he had feared about her was true and
yet more. Had the Lord brought him through this evening's experience to show him once and for all how
far she was out of the way, and how utterly she was
unfit for a companion to one who had chosen the way
of the Kingdom?

Before he had Barry Thurston back to his apartment, and in the hands of his valet, he was heart sick
and dog weary. It seemed to him that the world was
too wicked a place to stand any longer. How did the
Lord bear with me all the wickedness that must come
up before Him?

The day was dawning when he at last came out
to his car, free to go to his home. But how could he
go to his mother at this hour without explaining all
that he had been through in the night? It would only
distress her. Also half the pleasure in taking the new
car home had been to see the light in her eyes when
she looked from the window and saw it standing there
in front of the door, her car come home to take her
riding. This was no hour to appear, anyway. He
would just drive to some hotel and get a snatch of
sleep before he went on out to Stonington.

And so, too weary to care what he did, Thurly
stopped at the first hotel he came to and went to bed.

It was broad day when he awoke, and his senses
were so benumbed with sleep that it took some minutes
to know where he was and what had happened, but
when he came fully to himself he found that it was
nearly eleven o'clock.

He dressed hastily and hurried down to his car,

not even waiting for a cup of coffee. He wanted to get home, into the atmosphere that was safe and sweet and sane, with his mother's eyes, and his mother's smile, and her tender love about him. His spirit felt all bruised and bleeding.

He would have liked to call on Tasha and see if she was all right, but he felt she might still be sleeping, so he drove straight home.

Hesba had been away to her school for two or three hours when he drove up to the door of the cottage, and Marget, hovering all the morning between her work and one window or another, sighted the car at once and shaded her eyes with her hand to look.

Ah! Yes, that was her Thurly getting out of the car! What a blessing that he came while Hesba was away and she might have him all to herself for the greetings without having Hesba intrude upon every word they spoke. Marget had carefully refrained from saying much in her letters about her young companion beyond the mere fact of her presence, and that she went to a training school that Thurly wouldn't approve. But Thurly gathered much between the lines, and Thurly knew his little mother well. Ah! Thurly understood what a sore trial that young presence had been to his mother all winter, and he too was glad that they might be alone for their greeting.

So Thurly took his mother in his arms as if she had been a child, and she laid her cheek against his. The comfort and the healing of each other's love went through them both, just as it had done when Thurly was a little child, and the mother had been the strong one to lift and comfort and protect.

And then, before he told her anything, he had to wrap her in a shawl and take her out to see the car.

She exclaimed in wonder.

"And is it really your ain, laddie? Now what do you think of that! Thurly Macdonald with a real chariot! Isn't it beautiful! Every line of it! I couldn't have dreamed a better if I had been choosing from the world of cars!"

Marget could not say enough. And then he had to put her in the soft cushioned seat and drive her around the block.

"But are ye shure ye know how to drive her, Thurly lad? There's ower mony accidents these days. I read them in the paper. There was one bad one last evening, with a man killed and a lot of silly young folk hurt. I mind ye was always a bit venturesome, laddie; ye must have a care."

"I'll have a care, Mother dear," laughed Thurly, "never fear. I've driven all the way home from Chicago, and I can surely drive you round the block."

But when they came back from the brief ride and Marget discovered that her lad had had no breakfast, she would have no more words until she had put his lunch upon the table, and then they sat together, and drank in the joy of each other's presence, talking of bits of this and that, too eager and excited to tell all at once about any one thing.

It was after the lunch things had been cleared away, and Thurly had put the food in the refrigerator for her, wiped the two cups, two plates, and the silver as she washed them, and they had walked together into the little parlor and sat down upon the old couch side by side. It was not until then that Thurly saw Tasha's picture on the mantel.

Marget had thought to put it away, perhaps, before he came, yet for fear of Hesba's sharp eyes and Hesba's sharp tongue she had foreborne. And there smiled Tasha, true to life, with the little string of pearls about her throat, and the little crushed rose on her shoulder.

But when Marget saw the look in her boy's eyes, those eyes she had watched from his babyhood, her heart stood still in a kind of happy consternation, and she wondered whether she had done well or ill to leave the picture out.

"How did that come here, Mother?" he asked, a sound almost of awe in his voice. Rising he went and stood where he could look at it the better.

"She sent it herself from Florida," answered the

mother proudly, "and see what's she writ beneath. She's a bonnie wee thing! Thurly, I'm thinking you'll have to be taking the little gold boot into town again, now, for she's back at her home."

"And how did you know she was back in the North again, Mother?" asked the son with a twinkly smile, "have you been up to your old capers, reading the society notes in the papers again?"

"Na, laddie, I had a far better w'y of knowing this time, not but what 'twas in the papers too; but she came her own bonnie self to call."

"Here!" said Thurly startled, looking around as if somehow he expected to see some lingering radiance from her presence.

"Yes," said Marget, watching her boy yearningly, scarce understanding her own feelings.

Thurly looked about the room and back again to the picture struggling to get his thoughts arranged. Suddenly he faced his mother with a quick question:

"Then why didn't you give her the shoe, Mother? Why do you say I must take it to her?"

"Ah!" said Marget, "see I must tell it ye. But it's a lang tale, and I'm sair worried ye'll be vexed. 'Twas a the fau't of that huzzy Hesba. Ye'll mind I've not said mooch aboot her in the letters—"

"You don't have to say much, Mother," laughed Thurly suddenly as if somehow he was glad about something. "I've formed my opinion of the lady already so don't be troubled. Speak out your mind and let's get the tale over with. Come sit down, Mother, and tell it out from beginning to end. What did the huzzy do?"

"Mercy!" said a voice in the dining-room doorway, "has he come already? Now isn't that just like a man to turn up when you didn't expect him? Introduce me, can't you, Grandma? We can't stand long on ceremony in a family you know, and Thurly and I know each other pretty well already, I imagine."

Marget sat frozen with dismay, her sweet face actually white with disappointment. Now what was Hesba doing home at this hour, and how did she man-

age to get in without being heard? Also, how much
had she heard? Now Hesba carried the key to the side
door, that entered the dining room, and came in the
same way she did when Tasha had called.

Thurly, annoyed to be interrupted, but courteous
as ever, and conscious that some of his last words
might have been overheard, rose to the occasion.

"Miss Hamilton, I presume," he said bowing dis-
tantly. "I'm sure we're indebted to you for your will-
ingness to cheer my mother's loneliness. It's been most
kind of you to remain away from your home so will-
ingly, so long. But I'm sure you'll be glad to know that
I'm home to stay now for a while, and you can have
your freedom as soon as you like."

"Oh, it hasn't been a bit of trouble," smiled
Hesba, "I feel that it was quite an opportunity to get a
new point of view from another training school, but
please call me Hesba, won't you? I have been calling
you Thurly all winter."

"Have you, indeed!" said Thurly, and gave the
young woman a good square look with a twinkle of
amusement in his eyes. His mother saw the twinkle
and took heart of hope.

"Yes, and you're not rid of me yet, either,"
laughed Hesba gaily. "My school doesn't close for
sometime, and after that I've arranged to stay for at
least another week and play around with you. I haven't
really had time to see the sights of your city yet. And
you know it's no fun to see them alone."

"Indeed!" said Thurly with lifted brows, looking
the young woman over with rising amusement. "Well,
I shall be rather busy myself I'm afraid, and later
even more than I am now, but if you and Mother want
to go anywhere in particular that would not be safe
for you to go alone, why I shall be glad to arrange
to accompany you sometime when I can spare an hour.
I'm not just fond of romping much myself, but perhaps you and Mother might play around a little."

Hesba stared at him with her round, shell-
rimmed eyes that would have been pretty if they had

not been so presumptuous, and then laughed at what she perceived must have been meant for a joke.

"Oh, you're clever!" she said. "You didn't tell me he was clever, Grandma!"

"Grandma?" said Thurly, and gave his mother a quick questioning look. "I should think aunt would be more appropriate if you must have some title. Well, Lady Mother," he said turning toward Marget, "shall we go now? Get your coat and bonnet and I'll be waiting outside for you, Mother o' Mine. Better put something warm on, the sun is beginning to go down and there's a chill in the air. You'll excuse us, Miss Hamilton, my mother and I have an errand out—"

Marget turned amazed eyes to her son's face, but got to her feet and went for her wraps. Nobody noticed that the countenance of Hesba Hamilton lost several degrees of confidence as she watched them climb into the car and drive away.

"Now, Thurly, my son, was that quite the square thing?"

"Why not?" grinned Thurly.

"We haven't really an errand, my son," reproved Marget anxiously.

"Oh, yes, we have, Mother Mine. We're going to buy—what shall we buy? I know, a yeast cake for you to make old-fashioned buckwheats for breakfast in the morning. I haven't had a buckwheat since I left. Now out with your story, Mother, for we'll not go back till it's finished."

"But I'm sair troubled, laddie, that I oughtn't to tell it at all," said Marget. "It's sure to vex you one way or the ither."

"Well, I'm vexed now, Mother, so go ahead. She's a huzzy all right, I can see that at first glance, and needs a good taking down. Leave her to me, Mother, and don't worry any more."

"But, laddie, you mustn't be hurting her feelings. I'm sure she has them somewhere, and I'm not doubting that she meant to be kind."

"All right, Mother, but now for the tale. I'm

growing impatient, and I'll just stop the car till you begin."

So, laughing she told her tale in her own quaint way, till Thurly saw the picture of the girl as she came to call, in her velvet and ermines, saw the tint of her cheek, and the glow of her eye, through his mother's quaintly chosen words.

But his face grew grave as he heard how Hesba entered, and fetched the little gold shoe right into the conversation.

"But how did she know about the shoe, Mother?" queried Thurly amazed. "You surely never told her!"

"No, son, I did na tell her onything. You do not need to tell her, she was uncanny w'ys wie her. So lad, I'll have to tell ye the *whole* story. And here's where ye were to blame, Thurly, by not taking heed to the wee bit slipper before ye left and teeling me wher it was hid."

So she told of Hesba's change of rooms, and how she found the slipper and brought it to the front. Thurly listened, his brow in a frown.

"You're right, Mother, she *is* a huzzy," he said at last when the story was finished. "And you needn't excuse her by saying she's stupid for she's not. She thinks, Mother, that it is smart to bring things out in the open like that and put people to shame. Well, now that's bad, isn't it, Mother? The little lady thinks you've told everything to the other girl. She probably thinks this Hesba's an intimate of the family. And what does she think of me, hiding her shoe in my room? That's bad!"

Thurly was still for several seconds, his brow drawn in thought, and his mother watching him anxiously. At last he turned with a laugh.

"Well, it can't be helped this time, little Mother, we'll just have to make the best of it. The right will come out somehow in the end I guess. And now, I suppose we'll have to get our yeast cake and go home to dinner, won't we? We're a good thirty miles away and it's getting dark."

"Thirty miles!" marvelled Marget. "Just think of it!" but there was a great relief in her voice that Thurly was taking the annoyance this way. Somehow the burden was only half as heavy now that Thurly shared it with her. Surely he was right and there would be a straightening out of the thing. Hesba would not be allowed to put them to shame this way.

Hesba came down to dinner vivaciously. The grace was scarcely said before she burst forth eagerly:

"I forgot to tell you the news about your friend this afternoon," she said, "it's terribly exciting, but then I thought all along she'd be that kind of a girl. Your Tasha Endicott has been caught in an awful round up. There was a double smash-up, they say, last evening; a lot of society folks out joy-riding, and all of them gloriously drunk. They killed a man who was driving along slowly, and trying to keep out of their way, and then they all got broken arms and legs and heads and everything. I say it was a good lesson for them! They ought to all get killed off and then perhaps the world would be safe for the rest of us." She finished with a little excited laugh.

Marget looked up with her eyes full of horror, and her face white. She kept on pouring cream till it ran over into the saucer and she never knew it. She turned her frightened glance toward Thurly.

But Thurly did not seem to be so upset as she expected. He was looking sternly, it is true, at the narrator, and with a kind of amused contempt in his expression.

"Where did you hear that, Miss Hamilton? It was not in the papers." His voice was quite calm. "And how did you happen to connect a tale like that with our Miss Endicott?"

"Why, I heard it at school this morning. There's a young man studying there who has a job at the apartment house where this Tasha Endicott's fiancé lives. Thurston, his name is, Barry Thurston, and he didn't get in till almost daylight, and was all lit up. He said it was awful the way he was going on about Tasha Endicott. She must have been pretty well stewed herself, from all accounts. Say, I wish you'd remember to call me Hesba, Thurly. It sounds more friendly."

"It is a pity that any young person who is study-ing to make something of himself, should lend his in-fluence to create gossip like that!" said Thurly severely. "Because you see as far as Miss Endicott is concerned the story is not true at all. She was not drunk last eve-ning. I happen to be in a position to prove that, for I spent several hours in her company, and she was quite sane and sober. In fact I happen to know that she does not drink."

"Oh!" breathed Marget in a soft little breath, and a flood of relief came into her face as she turned amazed eyes to her son's face. It was just then that she discovered the cream running over her thumb, and had all she could do to keep it from going on the cloth.

"Oh!" exclaimed Hesba, the wind suddenly gone out of her sails. "Mercy! How on earth could you have been with her last night? I thought you didn't get home till late this morning."

"I had business in the city last night that detained me," Thurly answered coldly. "You'll oblige me by con-tradicting any such talk about Miss Endicott that you may happen to hear in future. She is not that kind of girl. And the young man had better be informed that it is rather dangerous to spread such stories unless he has accurate information, which he evidently did not have. What news do you hear from your aunt, Mrs. Robert-son? Is she able to walk at all yet? Has the bone knit satisfactorily?"

Hesba was most thoroughly squelched for once and retired into an amazing silence, leaving the conversa-tion unbelievably in the hands of Marget and her son.

After Hesba had withdrawn to her room to study, Marget's eyes sought her son's face with a question written large, which she would not utter.

Thurly smiled.

"It's all right Mother Mine, you needn't worry. What I said was true. But we better not discuss it to-night. Even the walls have ears at times. I think I'll take that shoe back to-morrow and break the spell that seems to have come over this house."

"I would, laddie," smiled Marget, and was content.

But up in her room Hesba was doing some hard thinking, and before she slept she came to a great resolve, and sat down and wrote a letter which she mailed in the city the next morning on her way to school. The letter reached its destination about noon.

Chapter XIX

Thurly took his mother to market next morning and while she was selecting meat he made occasion to telephone from the drug store to Tasha. He hoped to make an appointment to see her if possible that afternoon.

But Tasha, it appeared, was occupied at that moment and could not come to the telephone.

"Is she—well?" asked Thurly anxiously.

"So far as I know, she is," replied the voice of the servant.

"Will you say to her that Mr. Macdonald will call this afternoon if convenient?"

"I will, sir. Good bye, sir," and the man hung up before Thurly realized that he had not made the servant understand that he wanted to know whether Tasha would see him or not.

"Dumb!" said Thurly to himself as he hung up the receiver, "dumb, that's what I am. Now why do I have to get things all balled up just because I know that the man at the other end of the telephone wears a livery and would probably despise me if he knew I wore a threadbare overcoat?"

At first Thurly was inclined to call the number again and make his wishes clear. Then he decided that he would let it go. It would be a good way to find out whether Tasha wanted to see him or not.

Marget, when she came out to the car, wondered why Thurly seemed a bit absent-minded, but she said nothing about it, and he was presently smiling and joking like his old self.

As he helped her out of the car at home he said gravely:

"Mother, if you'll get that slipper ready for me to take I think I'll drive in this afternoon and get it off my mind. I'm going over to arrange about a garage now, and I'll be back in half an hour. Will that be all right for lunch?"

She assured him it would and went happily upstairs to pack the little shoe for another trip to its owner. Somehow she felt strangely elated by what Thurly had said about the little lady last night at supper. She had been looking all the morning for him to explain it but he hadn't said a word, and she felt it better to wait for him to speak. He would likely tell her all about it when he got back from his call, and she remembered that this was the evening of Hesba's symphony concert. She would not be coming home. They could have the evening to themselves!

So Thurly had his lunch and went his way with the little slipper in a white, new, shiny box that Marget had hunted up. In due time Thurly's car drew up in front of the Endicott mansion and Thurly went up to the door with a feeling that somehow this was to be a momentous call. He was gravely happy over it, and not in the least overawed this time by the grand house and the men in livery, for he had something better to think about.

But when the door opened Thurly was met by the announcement that Miss Endicott had left town.

Left town!

Thurly looked blankly at the man as if he could not have spoken the truth.

"When did she go?" he asked crisply, feeling somehow that there must be a mistake.

"Only about an hour ago, sir," answered the man

eyeing the caller disparagingly, his glance lingering for just the fraction of a second on the worn place in the young man's overcoat cuff. None but a trained eye would have noticed it, and Thurly himself was not even aware of it, but he felt the glance and it made him impatient. He was not to be put off. This was not the same servant who had opened the door at his last call.

"Did she leave a message for me?" asked Thurly, hope springing anew. "My name is Macdonald."

"Not that I know of, sir," said the servant looking into Thurly's keen brown eyes and feeling an added respect. "I'll go and see, sir. Just step in, sir."

Thurly sitting impatient in the same chair he had taken on his last visit looked about him on the garish luxury but it did not impress him as it had done before. There was more cheer in his mother's little cottage than in those lofty rooms filled with the treasures of Europe and the richness of the orient.

The servant came back to report that no message had been left.

"Did you give her my message when I telephoned this morning?" asked Thurly looking at the man sharply.

"I wasn't on duty this morning in the house, sir," answered the man. "I was out on an errand for Mrs. Endicott. I'll ask, sir."

But he was back in a moment to say that the servant who had answered the telephone was out at present and no one else knew anything about a telephone message. Neither could the man tell him when the young lady was expecting to return.

Thurly went disappointedly back to his car, the little shoe still in his hand. Not that he forgot it this time; but he had decided that having waited so long to return it, he would keep it as his excuse for coming again and making certain explanations which he felt he owed to his self-respect, on account of Hesba's rudeness.

So he drove back home again, with the little gold shoe snugged close beside him on the seat. When it came right down to it he would not care to surrender that little shoe to anyone else but its owner.

The letter that Hesba wrote reached Tasha about half past eleven that morning, a few minutes before Thurly telephoned, and read as follows:

"Dear Anastasia:

You did not tell me I might call you that, but I like to be informal, and I hope you won't mind.

I'm going to be married, and I'm telling you first for a very special reason, because I'm going to ask you to be my maid of honor. I hope you'll be willing, for I've set my heart upon it. You're the prettiest girl I know, besides a favorite of the family. None of my friends from home will be here at the time, so I wanted somebody that sort of belonged. Of course since you're such a good friend of Thurly's it seems about as if you were a relative already, so I thought even if you were very busy you'd be willing to put something off to help me out; for of course it means a lot to me to have someone like you at my wedding, right in it, a part of it. I'm not very good looking myself, I know, and I've always thought it didn't matter much, but here just lately, I've begun to find out that beauty matters a lot to some people, so I thought I'd like to have someone who was really beautiful to take the attention off me. Of course, there won't be many there, only the family, and I'm not wearing orange blossoms and all the fol de rols, it wouldn't suit me. So if you just wear the dress you had on when you came out to see Grandma it'll be all right and not make you any trouble, unless it's too warm for that and you've got something else you'd rather wear.

You see, I'm writing you first, because I haven't even told the groom yet, what day I've set. I wanted to make it sure you could come before I said a thing to him, men get so set, you know. If you'll please let me know by return mail whether you are willing to serve, I'd like to tell them as soon as possible now. And I know Thurly and Grandma are going to be awfully pleased if you say yes, for I've discovered they think a lot of you and then some.

So, if it's agreeable to you, I'll set the date for Wednesday two weeks from to-day at noon. Then we'll have a wedding breakfast and everybody can get back to whatever they have to do without losing time. Of course if that isn't convenient for you I can make it either the day before, or the day after, but if it's all the same to you Wednesday would suit me better.

Hoping you'll answer right away when you get this,

Affectionately,
Hesba Hamilton."

Tasha read this letter which a strange mingling of feelings, a mild amusement at the audacity of the request, and the frankness of the flattery, passed quickly into bewilderment and consternation. Could it be then, that it was really true that that splendid young man was going to marry a girl like this?

And suddenly she realized that she had grown to consider Thurly a splendid young man. She thought back quickly over her brief acquaintance and tried to reconcile everything she knew about him, with the fact of his engagement to this girl, rude and crude, and ill-bred. There was nothing of that in Thurly Macdonald. Yet of course she had known him so little, and there had been the glamour of his having saved her twice from terrible situations. She drew a deep sigh of disgust, and the world somehow looked blanker than ever to her.

When she had read the letter over the second time and perceived that it was something she must answer at once unless she wished to practically affront two people who had been most kind and lovely to her, she roused to think up an excuse.

It was just at that moment that Thurly called her on the telephone. When she heard the name of Macdonald she was positively snappish in the way she refused to answer the call. Here then, was the bridegroom, probably having discovered what his fiancée had done, and come to urge his plea that she would function at his wedding! She turned hard at the thought. It seemed to her she wanted never to hear the name of Macdonald again. The romance and joy had been torn from the memory of them by their connection with that girl. Even the holy memory of that Sabbath day was blotted out in the thought that henceforth Hesba Hamilton was to share in all that pertained to these two people. She could not quite understand why she disliked that girl so. Was it the fact of her being so forward, so intimate, even before she had been introduced? Or was it that she had dared to bring out the fact that her lost slipper had been found and was hid in Thurly Macdonald's closet? It argued a coarseness about the soul of a woman who would fling intimate things into public view. Even if she were jealous at finding the shoe, even if she wanted to show the other woman that she knew all about her, there was no excuse for what she had done. The soul of Anastasia turned from her with disgust.

So Tasha refused to go to the telephone, and she sat down quickly and dashed off an answer which nipped all hope of grandeur at Hesba's wedding.

"My Dear Miss Hamilton," [she wrote],

"I regret that my engagements are such that it will be impossible for me to serve at your wedding as maid of honor. I am leaving the city today for New York, to meet my father, and take a trip with him. It may be weeks before my return. My arrangements are most uncertain.

Thanking you for the honor,
Sincerely,
A. Endicott."

Tasha's arrangements were indeed most uncertain. She knew that her father was in New York, and that he was on a business trip which also included a fishing trip in Canada. Whether she could wheedle him into taking her along on any part of the trip was a question. At least it was worth trying, and seemed the easiest way out of a situation for which she had no relish.

Marie had a bad hour and a half packing, and then Tasha was off, only telling her stepmother that she was going up to see her father for a few days in New York. Lucia made no protest. She had plans herself, and was in no wise anxious to have a disapproving daughter watching her every movement. She left the house herself soon after for her favorite hotel at the shore, and so when Thurly arrived the great mansion was peopled only by hired retainers. Of course Tasha had left no message for him, because the man who answered the telephone had not thought fit to brave his young mistress' wrath to deliver it. If the gentleman came before she left, he would come, and what was to happen would happen. It was his afternoon off, and he would not have to worry about it. It was always easy enough to cast the blame on somebody else, even if he were discovered.

So, Tasha went on her way, and the little gold shoe remained at Stonington, with Marget as custodian.

To Marget Thurly said, when he handed it over with a wry smile:

"I think we'll have to adopt that shoe. There seems to be something wrong with it. I don't understand it, because I telephoned I was coming. But they tell me she is out of town again and had left no message."

Marget held the little package carefully in her hands, as if it might break, and looked down on it, thoughtfully.

About that time, Tasha, still on the train, watching the lights spring up and flee, as the train drew nearer and nearer the great city, began to face a thought that had been trying to creep up through her consciousness all the afternoon. Was it possible that the whole reason why she hated that girl who was going to marry Thurly Macdonald was because she herself was growing to care for him? She, Tasha Endicott, who might have any one of a dozen multi-millionaires! Marry a poor minister! A religionist, a fanatic, who thought of everything in terms of heaven, and had naught in common with her world?

She swung her chair around to the window, stared into the deepening dusk, and felt the hot color mounting to her temples! She, Tasha, being caught like that, in a common little romance with a man who had never even thought of her; but was engaged all the time to a commonplace, illbred girl who wore basement bargain counter clothes, looked strong minded, and hauled everybody's faults out in the open!

Well, if that was the matter she would put an end to that quicker than it took to think. She would show the man that she had no thought of him. She would never speak to him again, nor write, nor call on his mother. She had done enough to pay for his paltry trip back from the station that stormy night. He would have done it as easily for a stray cat. He had not been looking for pay. She need have no further compunctions. His kindness the night of the smash up, well, that was no more than he would have done for anyone. It was a part of his creed to be kind. And he had been unmercifully severe with her, asking her if she were drunk too! How it had cut her, when she knew she had not tasted liquor for months all on account of what he might think! Well, she was foolish! She almost felt she would go back to it. Perhaps she would order cigarettes sent up to her room when she got to the hotel! She would cut out all this nonsense and go back to life as it had come to her. Why should she reach after things that did not belong in her world? Why should she follow the dictates of a theological bully?

She stormed on madly in her soul, longing for some revenge. But somehow, behind it all, was the dread of that vision of his eyes looking at her. Or was that exorcised by the wedding invitation? Well, time would tell. She would cut loose for a while from home and all that had to do with that night of the storm, and then perhaps when Thurly and that scream of a girl were well married, and it was all over, she would be able to look back on it and laugh. She would do as she pleased through the rest of the tiresome days till her life was spent, and blown out like a candle.

Then the train shot into the tunnel under the river, and it was time to draw her coat about her and gather her magazine and bag and get out.

Tasha found her father in his hotel. He seemed almost annoyed that she had come. He was unusually busy, too busy to show her a good time, he said, but of course she might stay in the hotel a few days till she knew where she wanted to go. Why didn't she go down to the shore with Lucia? Lucia always liked to go to the shore.

But Tasha wanted to go to Canada. She wanted to fish, and to tramp in the woods, and rough it.

Mr. Endicott did not know whether he was going to be able to get away to Canada or not. There were some queer things going on in the world of finance. He did not know how long they might hold him in New York. Besides, the men with whom he intended to go, if he got off at all, were not the kind of men who would care to have a girl of Tasha's type along—at least—and the father faced her frankly, they were not the type of men that he cared to have his daughter companion with, even when he was along.

Tasha opened her eyes wide with amusement and laughed, but her father was firm, and no amount of coaxing moved him.

So Tasha settled down to amuse herself in New York, with such scraps of his attention as he could give her. She slept late in the mornings, lunched at some favorite restaurant, walked in the park for a few minutes, spent a couple of hours shopping or reading in the Library, went back and dressed for dinner. Her father usually took her somewhere in the evening when he had not some other engagement, though he sometimes found a young man among his acquaintances who was glad to take his place.

But the days went by very slowly to Tasha, out of her usual element, with only small portions of unsatisfactory points of contact with her father and nothing in which she was especially interested. The young men who called or invited her to some evening of gayety bored her. They might have interested her if her mind had not been full of an unnamed heaviness, but all things had begun to pall. She seemed to be waiting for something to happen. And when she began to analyze what it was, it narrowed down to Thurly Macdonald's wedding. She was up here in New York being bored to death till after Thurly Macdonald should have married Hesba Hamilton, *without* her for a maid of honor.

She went out one day and bought almost a whole bale of expensive embroidered linen and sent it to Hesba as a wedding gift. Table linen, bed linen, fancy linen, fine and heavy and lustrous, some of it embroidered richly and inset with hand made lace. It was ridiculous, it was unnecessary! But it eased something in her soul that yearned for action. It soothed something that hurt her almost unbearably when she thought of that linen on Thurly's table.

She reasoned with herself that it would excite comment in the Macdonald family for her, a stranger, to do so much—that perhaps they would be offended, in their simplicity. They would feel she thought they could not provide their own household outfit. But then, on the other hand of course, the honor of being asked to be part of the bridal party demanded something out of the ordinary. And anyhow, Hesba would likely enjoy it. Why should she not do a little thing for her even if she didn't like the girl Thurly was marrying. It would likely be the last thing she could do for Thurly, anyway.

So the linen went on its way, and Tasha went on hers, and the days dragged by, till one afternoon when a telegram came that drove all other thoughts out of mind and made life take on an aspect horrible and altogether new.

Chapter XX

Lucia Endicott had been secretly taking lessons in flying. Whenever her husband went away for a day or two she would slip away to the shore and fly. Oh, and there were plenty of chances when her husband was not away.

Lucia had ambition. Perhaps she cherished secretly a desire to be a lady Lindbergh of parts; or it may be she was quietly planning to slip away out of sight entirely and live a new life in a new place and fool the world out of its rightful share in her affairs.

Lucia went up in the air that afternoon with only Will Clancy along. Clancy was new at the game and known as a crazy flier. The flying instructor was away and Lucia, with the help of cash, was able to wheedle a plane out of the hanger.

So Lucia flew, and the day was glorious!

That afternoon the papers came out with the story. Those who saw the accident said that the plane took a nose dive straight to earth. They could not even tell which had been the pilot. The man was killed, and the lady was dying! The medical attendants gave no hope!

Some bystander on the field with a taste for tragedy told a reporter that the lady and the pilot had been quarreling before they went up.

The telegram reached Tasha just as she was about to lie down to rest after a morning of shopping. She had purchased a lot of trifles that she didn't need, because she had nothing else to do. The lines were bald and heartless, and did not soften the awful news:

"Mrs. Endicott fatally injured in airplane wreck. She can live but a few hours. Come at once!"

The address was a hospital at the shore near the flying field.

Tasha read the words with growing horror, clasping her hand to her throat and trying to keep her senses from reeling.

Lucia! Dying! One could not think of Lucia dying. So that was what Lucia had been doing on all those trips to the shore—Flying!

Tasha tried to think what to do. She dashed to the telephone and tried in vain to get her father. They told her at his Club that he was somewhere playing billiards but no one knew just where. She left a message for him, and dressed hastily, sobbing as she went about her room, dry hard sobs without tears. Sobs of fright and horror. Sobs of shrinking from what she knew she must do.

This was not her job, it was her father's. He ought to be here attending to everything. Lucia was his wife.

Tasha had never seen death. Lucia was not her mother, why did she have to go to her? She did not love her. She did not even like her. Yet she knew she was going to her.

She called up the office of the hotel and asked them to find out what train she could get, and send someone up for her bags. Between times she flew into some garments for the journey, scarcely able to think what was suitable. Then she tried the telephone again, frantically searching for her father. It was going to be terrible to go without Dad. Tasha had never had to do anything like this in her life before. Sickness and death, and horror had been shielded from her sight. Servants had attended to all details. She wondered why the telegram happened to come here to the hotel, and why it had not come to her father's name. Then, as if in answer to her thoughts another message was brought her, this time wired from home. It was from Marie.

"A man called on the phone and wanted your address. He said Mrs. Endicott had been hurt and wanted you at once. The address was at the shore hotel. Do you want me to do anything? Marie."

The little touch of everyday life in that word from home brought the tears to Tasha's eyes. Even Marie, asking if she could help! She began to cry softly, unaccustomed tears. She didn't know exactly what she cried for. Sympathy for Lucia in her horrible condi-

tion, or sympathy for herself all alone and going to
Lucia, not knowing just how things were. She might
wait and telephone—but—what was that Marie's telegram had said, Lucia wanted her? Lucia wanted *her!*
How strange! Lucia who had always been half jealous
of her! Lucia who had wanted to marry her off to get
her out of the way, and who had resented any voice
of warning she had ever given.

Well, she must go.

The bell boy tapped at the door and handed in a
paper with the schedule of trains, a ticket and reservation. He said the taxi was waiting.

Tasha snatched up her hand bag and followed
him to the elevator, feeling her knees shake under her.

It seemed miles to the train, yet she kept wishing
with a great shrinking that the train would be gone
when she got there. She knew herself for a coward for
the first time in her life. She began to imagine things.
Would Lucia be very horrible to look upon? Would
she be conscious? She must be or she would not have
sent for her. But maybe the report was exaggerated.
Maybe she would get well after all. Yet, an aeroplane!
It would be fearsome to fall, and crash!

She closed her eyes and tried to shut out the
dreadful thought. Oh, if she but had some strong one
to lean upon! She remembered that little old woman in
the chapel at Palm Beach, the little rusty black bonnet
shaking with emotion as she prayed, thanking God for
sending her that money for her baby. How that woman trusted in Something. If she only had something like
that to lay hold upon now! Something just to take the
tremble from her lips and the weak queer feeling from
her whole body. Some strong hand to hold hers, and
still the quaking of her heart.

The thought of Thurly Macdonald came to her
with great longing. If she only had a friend like that to
whom she could cry—who would go with her down into this horrible shadow, and keep her from going utterly to pieces. Once she would have thought of him
as a possible refuge, a helper, but how could she call
on him now, just on the eve of his marriage? He had

asked her once to promise to let him know if there was ever anything he could do for her, but she couldn't ask a bridegroom to go with her to her stepmother and watch her die. She couldn't tell him that she wanted someone near whom she could trust, like a rope to hold on to when the foundation on which she stood rocked, something sure and steadfast that would take this awful sinking feeling away! No, her pride would not let her ask for help from him now, even if there was anything reasonable he could do for her. No, this was her burden, and she must bear it somehow alone. Perhaps in some way the message would reach her father and he would manage to be there before her, riding hard in a high powered car. It was what he ought to do. But how would he even know he was needed? They had not lived together enough lately to have any feeling of family responsibility about one another. The word might not reach him until it was far too late!

Oh, if only that dear old lady were somewhere near, Mrs. Macdonald! What a tower of strength she would be. She would not be afraid of death. She would stand by, and clasp hands, and pray perhaps! If she were only near by it would not be out of place to call for her to go and stand by. But she was an old lady! Thurly would not want her troubled. She would not be able to travel so far, and anyway there would not likely be time. The telegram had made it plain that it was only a matter of hours before it would all be over.

The train dragged on its slow way and Tasha sat with her head bowed on her hand, and ached from head to foot, till it seemed that she could no longer bear it.

A young interne from the hospital met her, and tried as they drove from the station, to prepare her for what she had to meet. He said she was glad she had come, that the patient had cried for her continually, and they had hesitated to administer too strong sedatives before the family could be summoned, as she might never rally. He said Mrs. Endicott was suffering, and utterly unable to move, as the injuries were internal, but that her mind was clear now, and that she seemed to be in great mental distress. Then he made some vapid remarks about the beauty of the day, and how long a ride it was down from New York even on the fastest trains, and Tasha felt as if she would like to shout to him to keep still, and spare her from the agony of his voice. All the time she was wondering whether it was fear for herself, or fear for Lucia that gave her the most agony.

They took her straight to Lucia, and Tasha was startled anew by the ravages pain and horror had made in Lucia's face in a few brief hours. She stood back for an instant and gazed at the huddled form that had been Lucia, and in quick succession there passed before her a vision of her stepmother as she was accustomed to be, Lucia in some expensive imported sports costume walking lightly over the golf links; Lucia in cloth of gold with a great black velvet bow at one side; Lucia in frail white with a gaudy gauze poppy at her shoulder; Lucia in her riding habit ready to follow the hounds; Lucia in her vivid orange bathing suit, dropping from the diving board slim and graceful into the pool; Lucia dancing at the country club in flaming scarlet and silver. And here she lay, white and huddled, a thing all crushed and broken, and about to be snuffed out like a candle! Oh, life was a terrible thing! Why did people have to live? But the great dark eyes were upon her, with already the strange glaze of death within them. Tasha had never seen a death, but she knew instantly that that was what it must be. The thin white lips, the lips that had been wont to be so vividly scarlet, were calling her in a high weak voice that did not sound like Lucia:

"Tasha! Oh, you have come! Why have you been so long?—Tasha, *you* will get someone to help me, won't you?—You must work fast!—Oh can't you see? I haven't long—!" The breath came in weak gasps.

Tasha came near and tried to be sympathetic. She took the weak hand that pulled at the coverlet. She felt all the rancor and contempt vanish away before Lucia's great need.

"What do you want—*dear?* What can I do?" and the tears were raining down her cheeks as she said it.

"Don't waste time in crying!—That won't do any good,"—the weak querulous voice protested. "Get me somebody quick who knows about dying!—I've *got* to talk with *somebody, quick!*—I've waited years since they sent for you—Ohhh! *Hurry—won't* you?"

"But—who shall I get?" faltered Tasha, "the minister from the church where you go sometimes? He is so far away."

"No, no, don't get that infant!—He can play golf but he doesn't know anything about dying except to read the burial service, and I'm not ready for that yet. —Don't you know *any*body—Tasha—not *any*body? In the whole wide world, is there not one who knows how to die?—I had a grandmother once who wasn't afraid!—Oh, Tasha, isn't there someone?"

"Yes," said Tasha, "there is. I'll get him if I can. Where is a telephone?" she turned to the nurse. "Is there one on this floor?"

"Don't be long," wailed the sick woman, "Oh, *hurry!*"

"I will," cheered Tasha, her strong young will putting strength of hope into her voice. "Don't fret, Loo, I'll only be a minute, if I can find him at home."

It seemed an hour to her before she got the number she had called. It was a number she had memorized months ago, so she did not have to stop to look it up in the book.

As she waited sitting in the nurse's chair beside the little glass topped table in the hall, she closed her eyes and said silently to herself, "Now if there is a God, I need Him. Oh, God, if you are there, make Thurly be at home! Oh make him be—"

"Hello!" came the voice she remembered so keenly, "Hello!" and took the very prayer from her lips.

Her voice trembled with relief as she spoke:

"Oh, is that you, Mr. Macdonald? I'm so glad!

This is Anastasia Endicott. Do you remember once you told me if ever I needed you I might let you know?"

"*I do!*" came the clear ringing voice over the wire with something in it which warmed her and made her feel like crying. It was almost as if he had put his arm about her and held her up, as he had done on that night of the smash-up.

"Well, then will you come, please, quick! A terrible thing has happened! Lucia has been wrecked in an airplane and she is dying. She is wild for someone who will talk with her and tell her how to die. Can you come at once?"

"I will!" rang the voice. "Where are you? Where is she?"

She gave him the address, and made plain the necessity for haste.

"Take a taxi, or hire a fast car, anything to get here before it is too late!"

"I will be there as soon as it is humanly possible," he said, "meanwhile, tell her that Jesus Christ died to save her. Tell her to call on Him, that He will save her. Good bye. I'm coming!"

She heard the click of the receiver hung up, and drew a breath of relief. He was coming! He was coming! He had not failed her. Even though she had run away from his messages and slighted him, he had not failed her.

And God had let him be there when she needed him! That was wonderful too!

Dazedly she hung up the receiver. She must go back to Lucia! How she dreaded the white face, the staring look of the anguished eyes, the high, querulous voice. It would be an awful time to wait before he could possibly get here from the city. Would she last till he came? And how could she bear it meanwhile? What could she say to Lucia. Ah! He had told her something to say. What was it. "Tell her that Jesus Christ died to save her. Tell her to call on Him and He will save her."

Tasha went back to the room. Lucia turned her great impatient eyes on her, and Tasha shrank as she had known she would shrink from the sight of them; but she marched straight up to the bed with her quick accustomed way, and took the weak hand in hers.

"I got him," she said. "He's starting at once. He'll be here in a little while."

"Who is he?" asked Lucia despairingly. "Does he know what I need? Will he tell me."

"Yes, Loo, he's a Prince. He knows all about it. I've heard him pray and he talks as if God was right beside him."

"Oh, if he were only here now!" groaned the dying woman. "I feel so weak, as if I was slipping, slipping away! There's nothing to hold on to. Oh, if he'd only told you something to do till he gets here!"

As if the minister were a doctor who could suggest a sedative for the soul!

"He did!" said Tasha, trying to recall the exact words. "He said tell you that Jesus Christ died to save you. He said tell you to call on Him and He would save you."

Lucia looked at her for an instant as if she were turning the idea over in her mind.

"Yes, that's what they used to say, long ago, when people believed things. My grandmother talked that way. But he didn't know what a sinner I've been. I can't call on Jesus Christ. I've been wicked. Nobody knows how wicked I've been. He wouldn't have told you to tell me that if he'd known how wicked I've been."

"Never mind," said Tasha desperately, trying to think what to say, "he likely knows. I've heard him say that everyone was a sinner. I've heard that said in church this last winter. I've heard Mr. Macdonald say right in his prayer *he* was a sinner, himself!"

"Oh, yes, that way," moaned Lucia, "but not a real sinner like me!"

"Well, I'd try it," said Tasha. "He said do it, and he knows. I *know* he knows. Wait till he comes and you'll know it too. He said 'He will save you if you call'; so *call*, Lucia, *call!*"

"*You* call! Tasha," pleaded the other woman, "I can't! I don't dare!"

Tasha stood there aghast. She could not pray! Why should she pray? She was not the one who was dying! She did not need to be saved! She might be a sinner too, of course, but she was not now in such desperate situation. How could she pray for another when she did not know God herself?

And yet, Lucia was pleading with her to do it. She could not let Lucia slip out of life without at least trying to sooth her fears. Oh, if Thurly would come!

But Lucia was visibly weaker even now than when she had first come in. She could not say no to her last request. Poor broken Lucia!

How did people do when they prayed? She thought of Thurly and his mother on their knees in the little parlor at Stonington. She thought of the old woman in the rusty black bonnet at Palm Beach, down on the dusty chapel floor, with the sob in her voice; and she slid down upon the hospital floor, and closed her eyes, with Lucia's cold damp hand in hers.

"Oh, Jesus Christ! Save her!" she said, and stopped in fright at her own voice.

"Do it again, oh, do it again!" said Lucia holding Tasha's hand with a vise-like grip.

"Oh, Jesus Christ, save Lucia!" said Tasha, and said it again and yet again.

The restless eyes on the bed were watching her.

"Do you think He heard?" asked Lucia in an awed whisper.

"Why, of course!" said Tasha, trying to make her voice sound full of assurance. "Of course He did! Listen, Lucia, I met a woman last winter who told me she prayed for money when her little grandson needed an operation, and they couldn't afford, it, and *it came!* She told me it came the very next morning."

"Oh, yes, but she must have been a good woman," said Lucia. "She was not a sinner, like me."

"Well, I imagine since Mr. Macdonald says He died to save you, that there must be some way. If I were you I'd just rely on that till he comes. I don't know any more to tell you, only if I were you I'd call.

I'd do it myself if I were you. It might make some difference."

Lucia looked at her thoughtfully and then she closed her eyes, and began to murmur in a low whisper: "Jesus Christ, save me! Jesus Christ, can You save me? Do You know what a sinner I am? Will You save me?"

It was a strange awesome hour. Tasha knelt and held the cold hand, that seemed to grow colder and weaker moment by moment.

How long she knelt there she did not know, with her knees trembling and like to collapse, her back and head aching sorely, alternately praying that monotonous plea, and listening to the other woman repeat it, as if it were somehow a talisman to keep her alive until help came.

"Oh! isn't he ever coming?" murmured Lucia in an interval when she had seemed to sleep and suddenly awake. Then Tasha would murmur softly, "He's coming pretty soon. Keep on calling, Loo! It's going to be all right."

But the tears were raining down Tasha's cheeks, and her heart was almost ready to fail her. The time seemed so long, so long. Would Thurly never come?

She became aware of a stir at the door. The nurse slipped in, and the doctor. He touched Lucia's wrist lightly and looked gravely at his watch. Lucia flashed a glance at him.

"Have I time, doctor! Someone is coming! I must have time! Have I time?"

"I think so," said the doctor gravely, "you have a little time. He is here. Take it calmly, sister. Your minister has come."

Tasha looked up and there was Thurly towering above her, his grave kind eyes looking down at Lucia.

Lucia looked up as if he were someone straight from God.

Tasha arose and laid her hand on Thurly's.

"Oh, you have come at last!" she said with a sob in her voice. "Lucia, this is Mr. Macdonald!"

"Do you know God?" asked Lucia, her voice sounding weirdly strange as if she had traveled a long distance from this life, and had to call back to make herself heard.

"I do!" said Thurly Macdonald, clear and sure; and the ring of his tone made even the nurse and the doctor look up as if it had reached their hearts.

"Then I want everyone else to go out of the room while I tell you something. Hurry. I know there isn't much more time."

The doctor signed to the nurse, the nurse gave the patient a hypodermic, then they all went silently from the room and the doctor closed the door. But they did not go far away, and the nurse and doctor listened at the door for a possible recall.

What passed within that room, what confession of sin perhaps, Tasha never knew. She sat on the chair the nurse brought for her and waited, but her heart was no longer afraid. Thurly was in there making peace with God for Lucia. He had come in time, and she had done all she could.

Tasha did not know how long it was before that door was opened again. There is no means of measuring time when life and death are standing still till a soul makes peace with God.

But she became aware that the door had opened again and that the nurse was motioning her in.

Thurly stood there by the bed, with a shining in his countenance that was like a flame of triumph, and Lucia had lost the terror from her eyes.

"It is all right, now," said Thurly looking at Tasha, and speaking so that Lucia could hear him. "She wants me to tell you that it has all been made right for her, and she is not afraid any more."

"Yes," said Lucia faintly, "He died—" Her breath seemed to come faintly now and Tasha almost thought she was gone. But she roused and looked up again.

"Forgive!" she murmured and lifted her hand feebly in a little pleading motion.

"Oh, yes!" said Tasha weeping, "there is nothing to forgive—"

"Tell your father—Tash—tell him—forgive—!"

Tasha lifted her head and promised, and as she did so she perceived that her father had entered the doorway, and that he had heard. He had bowed his head suddenly as if he had received a blow; and when they both looked up again Lucia was gone!

Chapter XXI

They stood together an hour later, Thurly and Tasha, in the little hospital waiting-room, while Mr. Endicott made some arrangements for the next day.

For the moment they had the room to themselves, but there seemed suddenly a shyness upon them both.

"I can never thank you for this," said Tasha, lifting her tired face to look at him. "It seems as though I could not have got through without you. It seems as though you are always coming to help me out just when I am utterly at the limit."

"If you knew how glad I am to be able to be of assistance—" said Thurly, "and now, what can I do? Is there anything more—"

"Oh, no! Dad has come. He will look after everything now of course," said Tasha wearily. "But you— you ought to rest. You have had a hard trip. Dad will get rooms at the hotel—it's not far away—"

"No," said Thurly quickly, "I must go back to the city. That is unless there is some imperative need for me here? You see I've promised to speak to-morrow night in a place away out in Indiana and unless I leave on the midnight train to-night, I can't make it!"

"Oh, but you will be all worn out!" said Tasha appalled. "You should have told me—"

"I wouldn't have missed coming for all the preaching services in the world," said the young minister, with the joy of service in his eyes, "both for your sake, and for hers. I think she found peace. I'm sure she did."

"Oh, I'm so glad for that!" said Tasha, and the tears came to her eyes again. "She was so unhappy, and I didn't know what to do. We—we did what you told me to tell her—all the time until you came. We prayed."

"Did you?" said he, and his eyes were full of a great light like a benediction. "And the answer came I'm sure. But isn't there anything more I can do for you now, before I leave?" he glanced at his watch, "I can spare a few minutes yet and still make my train."

"Oh," said Tasha suddenly, "there's one thing I would like to ask you, if you've just a minute. I've often wondered about it. You said once I ought to be born again, and when I said I'd like to, you said it was possible, that it was up to me. Did you mean that, or were you—disgusted with me?"

"I meant it with all my soul, dear friend," said Thurly earnestly. "Jesus Christ says, 'Ye must be born again or you cannot see the kingdom of God.' It is all in the Bible. It is a birth of the Spirit, not of the flesh, but it brings you into a new life, just as fully and just as truly as your physical birth brought you into this life. Old things are passed away. You become a new person in Christ Jesus."

"But what would I have to do?"

"Nothing. It is all done for you. The moment you are willing to let the Lord Jesus come into your life and make it over you are born again. He does it for you. The Spirit comes into your life and changes it utterly. Oh, it is a wonderful change, and a wonderful thing to be born again. I wish I had time to stay and tell you all about it. But I wonder if you will let me leave my little book with you, and will you read it? See, I'll mark a few places."

He took a small limp Bible from his pocket and fluttered the leaves over, marking certain places with his pencil.

Tasha took the book gratefully.

"I will return it soon," she said. "I cannot thank you enough!"

"Don't, please," said Thurly quickly, "I would like you to keep it if you will, and read it often."

Then with a quick pressure of her hand he was

gone out into the night and she could hear the sound of his car as it shot down the drive and was lost in the darkness.

But Tasha stood there holding the little Bible in her hand.

This was the third time now, that he had come to her in distress, and helped her back to life again. And this of course was the end. He would be married in a few days, and his wife would see that he did not go around helping other young women out of difficulties. But she had this much to remember him by, and she felt strengthened by the very feel of the soft worn leather that had been carried around in his pocket and read every day.

The day after Thurly got home from his western preaching trip Hesba came home from school early and brought several packages and a hat box with her. She slid upstairs without stopping to talk, and they could hear her going about the room.

Thurly was reading the evening paper in the parlor. Marget had just come in from looking at a pan of delicious baked beans getting themselves velvet brown in the oven. She was sitting by the window darning socks. There was a savory odor from meat simmering on the back of the stove, and a baked apple dumpling stood on the shelf over the oven.

Everything in the cottage seemed right and fit, and now that Thurly was back again, Marget thought that it wasn't going to be so hard to stand Hesba for the rest of the spring till school was out. For the last week Hesba had not troubled them so much anyway. She had come in late three nights after all day away, and just in time for dinner the other three, and was altogether comporting herself like a meek and quiet person. Perhaps they could stand it, and get her away without hurting her feelings, or making any breach between the families. Marget did love to live at peace with all men—and women, so much as in her lay.

She was just thinking these thoughts when she heard Hesba coming down stairs again. Now, probably Hesba would spring something on them. She was always doing that. Marget hoped it would not be anything disagreeable, with Thurly just home again. She wanted Thurly always to have a feeling that his home was a place of peace and joy.

Hesba came down stairs slowly, not with her usual bounce and stride, and as she entered the parlor there was something in her very approach that made Marget look up.

"Why, Hesba, lassie!" said Marget, using the name she kept for very tender occasions. "Why, what have you done to yourself child?"

Hesba laughed shamedly.

"Oh, just turned foolish like the rest of the world," she said. "Been 'plaiting my hair and adorning myself.' I got a wave this afternoon, and took off my glasses. How do you like it?"

"Fine!" said Marget taking off her own and looking at the girl critically. "Why, what a bonnie lassie you are to be sure! What call had ye to hide all that beauty beneath a bushel. But won't it hurt your eyesight to take off your glasses?"

"No, I guess not. I don't really have to wear them, only for study, you know. I got in the habit of keeping them on, it seemed so much trouble to be always hunting them up. But now I guess I won't wear them any more. I went to see an oculist yesterday and he said my eyes would be all right without them now. So I've packed them away. You see—" she hesitated and two red spots became visible in her round cheeks, "you see, I've got a friend!"

"A friend?" said Marget, "that's nice. What will he be like? Or is it a lass?"

"It's a young man from my class," said Hesba straightforwardly. "He's been real attentive all winter in little ways, but I didn't have time for such things, and I wasn't sure I cared for his style. But here this vacation he just wouldn't take no for an answer, and we've kind of come to an agreement."

"An agreement?" said Marget, catching a gleam in Thurly's eye behind the evening paper. "And what sort of an agreement will it be? Has it to do with putting by your glasses and curling your hair?"

"Well, yes," said Hesba, "he doesn't like glasses nor straight hair, so I suppose I'll have to concede him that."

"And what is the wee mannie giving up, lass? It's always weel to have two sides to a bargain."

"Oh, he's given up chewing gum. He used to do it for dyspepsia you know, but it makes me wild to see him chew. And he doesn't wear red neckties any more. I think red neckties are unrefined."

The corners of Marget's mouth were twitching, but she managed a smile of appreciation.

"That's fine, so far as it goes, lass, but where does it all lead to?"

"Oh, well, we've decided to get married of course. I never thought I would give in, but he kept at me, and I see he really needs me. He's not in the least practical, though he's perfectly devoted to his work, and he needs someone to cook for him, and make him put on his overcoat when it rains, and things like that. So it's all fixed. And I came down to see if Thurly would do the ceremony for us. You see, he's got a job. He didn't expect one right away because he isn't through his course, but a friend of his is going to the foreign field and he recommended him in his place as bookkeeper in a social settlement house out in the northwest. It's a good chance and the pay is much more than most beginners get, so we thought we ought to take it. They're going to give me a job too, so it's all right if we do have to give up the rest of the term and take examinations by correspondence. We're going to be married next week, and I thought perhaps you'd let us have the wedding right here in this room. We won't make much fuss, and it would be more cheerful than going to a church we don't either of us belong to."

"Why surely, lass, surely, we'd be glad to do that, wouldn't we, Thurly? But, lass, what will your folks say? Have you told them yet? Do they know the young man? Perhaps he's not all that you think he is."

Hesba laughed.

"Oh, he's all right. The dean says he's known him for years and a steadier fellow he never saw. He's not very pushing of course, but that's why I decided to marry him. He needs me. I never really found anybody before that did need me. They all resent being helped. Yes, I wrote home yesterday that I was going to be married. They'll expect me to do my own picking and choosing. I'm that way. They won't worry, whatever I do. But we're going home that way for a wedding trip, it's only fifty miles out of the way, and we're driving of course. Edward has bought a secondhand Ford, and we expect to start right away after the ceremony. You needn't go to any trouble, Grandma, just a cup of tea and some of your nice gingerbread will be all we'll want, and when we get to a nice looking lunch place we'll stop and get a chicken dinner in the evening to celebrate. There won't be anybody we need to ask but Edward's brother, and he'll have to hurry right back to school because he's on the night shift of the elevators this week. He's working his way through school you know, and that's his job, running the elevators."

"I'm sure we'll be very glad to have him with us," said Marget simply, "and anybody else you want to ask."

"No," said Hesba, "I'm not 'specially fond of any of the rest, nor they of me. If I asked one I'd have to ask all, and we don't want to be bothered. I did ask Tasha Endicott if she would be maid of honor, but she wrote and said she had to go to New York with her father. And now I see by the papers her stepmother's dead, so it wouldn't be any use asking her again."

"You asked Miss Endicott!" exclaimed Marget in consternation, and Thurly's paper gave a quick, sharp crackle.

"Yes, I asked her last week. I sort of thought I'd like to have something pretty at the wedding, but she didn't see it that way, so of course it doesn't matter. She wrote me an awfully formal note. I suppose they get used to doing things that way. I nearly froze while I read it. But she sent me some dandy table cloths and fancy linens. I think there's enough to last a lifetime, and some of them are pretty enough to make dresses of. I shall keep them always, and I appreciate it. But I'd kind of like to have had her too. However, that's that! Thurly, will you do the ceremony?"

Thurly threw down his paper and agreed pleasantly, taking over the details and making one or two little suggestions that pleased Hesba mightily.

"You're sure you are getting the right man?" he questioned kindly as he might have done to a sister. "I wouldn't like to see you make a mistake."

"Oh, he's all right. I looked into that early in the winter before I got to going with him. He's not what I always thought I'd marry of course. Every girl has dreams. But supposing I'd married you. I don't know as there would have been anything for me to do. You're so kind of sufficient to yourself, and finished. You wouldn't need to ask me to help in anything. What good would my training have done then? There's really nothing to do for men like you but darn their socks and get dinner now and then when they're not invited somewhere else. Yes, that's what it'll come to, you'll be invited a lot. Everybody likes you. But most folks don't like me, and *he* does, so I'm just going to be contented with such things as I have and try to make a lot out of him. He's good if he isn't rich nor handsome."

Thurly and Marget with difficulty restrained their mirth. "Well, we'd like to look him over, Hesba," said Thurly unbending from the "Miss Hamilton" he had used ever since his return. "We don't want to see you make any mistakes. Why don't you bring him out and let us look him over?"

"Oh, I will if you want me to. I'll bring him out after school to-morrow for a few minutes if you're going to be at home. He isn't much to look at of course. He has light hair and I always liked brown in a man," Hesba's eyes lingered half wistfully on Thurly's crisp curls. "He has real light eyelashes too, but he's kind."

"Bring him out to dinner to-morrow, Hesba," suggested Marget, "then you three can talk over the plans. And don't you worry about the wedding breakfast. We'll have a nice wee set out, and I shall just enjoy getting it ready. If there's anything special you'd like say so, otherwise keep out and let it be a surprise."

"Well, I certainly appreciate that, Grandma. No, there's nothing I mind much about, except a wedding cake. I always did think a cake was nice for a wedding."

"We'll have a cake!" said Marget, "black with fruit and spice and all white crimps on the top. I know how to make it. I had my great grandmother's recipe, and I've always wanted a chance to use it. I haven't made one of those cakes since Thurly's cousin Elspeth Blythe was married in auld Scootland, but it turned out real bonnie then, and I'm all in a flurry to try it again."

Hesba's eyes shone.

"It'll be almost like a real wedding then," she said. "I used to wonder if I would ever have one. It's queer how I had my heart set on that cake. I never cared for most fol de rols, but I do like a rich spicy fruit cake! Say, would you like to see that present Tasha Endicott sent me? It's the real thing. You can see she didn't skimp. I suppose it's really wasteful to buy so much, and such fine stuff, but I declare I like it. I'm going to write her a letter and tell her about it. I feel as if maybe she and I'll get to be friends, even yet."

So Hesba brought down her one exquisite wedding present, and Marget handled the beautiful pieces one by one, exulting in their fineness and delicate workmanship; and even Thurly came and took up one of the embroidered pieces and gazed at the little flowers wrought so carefully. But he was only thinking how it looked like the girl, the beautiful giver.

Then Marget had to be shown the few simple things Hesba had bought for an outfit, and it was later than usual when Hesba went upstairs.

"We must show her a good time, Mother," said Thurly when she was gone. "Can't you get some flowers and candy or something? She's kind of pitiful, and not so weird without her goggles, but she's a huzzy all the same. Now what do you suppose made her invite Miss Endicott to her wedding? Do you think she really didn't know any better, or was it done to annoy us, or merely a bit of bravado?"

"Oo, mayhap a bit of the one and a bit of the

ither. But under it a' there's a wee bit of pride to have a rich lassie companion wie her. She ower conscious of her ain self-importance, I'm thinking, too, and she wad like to make the ither lassie admit she's as good as hersel'. But laddie, do ye think we should let this wedding go on withoot inquiring a bit aboot the mon? These are sair times, and I wad na hae the lassie joomp into a puckle o' trouble."

"I'll find out about him to-morrow. She need never know unless I hear something to his discredit. What did she say his name was? Edward Stebbins? But if he's the same man I saw her with in the city the other day I should say he was harmless. He looks a little like an old sheep. But if he's fallen for her, and can stick it out to be bossed as she will boss him, I should say he must be a pretty strong character. However, if she's pleased I certainly am."

Marget laughed softly, and then said, with a twinkle in her eye:

"Laddie, dinna ye think ye 'ar a bit haird on yer ain sex, soomtimes? But hark, ye, Thurly, do ye mind how soon the Lord has lifted the annoyance from our hoose, since we pit it in His hands to handle?"

"I do," said Thurly with a ring of gratitude in his voice. "I certainly do. And no harm to the other party concerned either, unless the man turns out to be a fool. I'm thinking a huzzy and a fool would make a poor combination."

Chapter XXII

The accident which caused the death of Lucia Endicott was quickly forgotten. It featured in the papers for a day or two, and then gave way to other more recent tragedies, and new feats of the air; and the toll of

death went merrily on, as society took a careless hand
in the mysteries and experiments of science.

Lucia's funeral services had been held at fashionable funeral parlors where her set usually repaired
when one of their merry company was compelled to
die. The officiating clergyman was from the fashionable church which Lucia had attended when she went
to any at all. It was a thing of solemnity, of stately
sentences, and rare music, banked in masses of expensive flowers. It was held just as soon as was at all
respectable, and was all over when Thurly came back
from his engagement to preach.

Life in the mansion on Waverly Drive went
smoothly on from day to day, just as if Lucia were
alive, only there was no Lucia and no Will Clancy
coming to call and staying to dinner. The household
reins had passed into Tasha's hands, but Tasha had
very little to do with the actual workings. The servants
were perfectly trained, and knew what was expected
of them.

Now that for a small season not much would be
expected of her in the social line on account of Lucia's
death, Tasha had much deadly leisure on her hands,
and little to occupy it.

Great restlessness took hold upon her, and sometimes she wandered from room to room in the big
house, her soul crying out and beating its wings as if
it were a bird in a cage.

She had taken to reading the little book that
Thurly had left with her. It was her companion a great
deal of the time. And as she read and studied par-
ticularly the passages which Thurly had marked for
her, a strange thing happened. A meaning sprang out
of the printed pages into her heart, a meaning that at
first reading had not seemed to be there. She was beginning to get light on some of the things she had seen
and heard in the Macdonald household, to grasp a little
thread of the meaning of life on this earth and what
it was meant to be. Not a butterfly existence, but a
sort of testing time. She was beginning to understand
that to be born again meant a surrendering to her
Maker, a severing of all connection with the old life of

the flesh, the mere physical existence, and letting a new Life come in. Gradually the meaning of it all entered into her soul, and became a new belief. She must forsake the old life with its sinfulness, and surrender to the new life as a little babe enters into the world of this life, knowing nothing, having no past contacts with a former existence, ready to make new ones in a new world to which it has been born. Why, it was all true, as Thurly Macdonald had said. One might be a new creature in Christ Jesus if one would.

Tasha went out of the house very seldom in these days. She shrank from meeting her old friends, from having them commiserate her, from having them talk about Lucia. They knew Lucia as she had been. They did not know the Lucia she had helped down through the valley of the shadow of death. They did not know how all her hardness had dropped away when she came to those last hours. They did not know that a mysterious change had passed over her with those last passing moments. They thought of her as blotted out: like a bright rocket that ascended the sky for a few brief sparkles and descended into blackness, to be no more.

Tasha used to feel that way herself about death. But now she did not want to hear others laugh and try to make her forget. She had a great loathing for all her life of the past.

Tasha's father had gone back to New York after a few restless days at home. Tasha had told him briefly of her last hours with Lucia, and he had listened gravely, had said little and gone his way. He knew she was not bereaved. He did not pretend to be greatly bereaved himself. He was quiet and respectable and conventional, but he had not been deeply stirred by his wife's tragic death for more than a day or two. It may be because his real heart had been dead years ago and had never belonged to this woman whom he had married by way of a passing amusement.

So Tasha was left alone, and she gave herself to the little book as she never would have been likely to do if she had been surrounded by friends, and the gayeties that had hitherto made up her life.

Meanwhile the cottage at Stonington was taking on a gala atmosphere. A fat pink geranium appeared in the other parlor window opposite the red one. A Boston fern, and an asparagus fern took places of honor on two little taborets. The smell of spices and citron and lemon and raisins filled the air for days while the fruit cake was in the making. Marget insisted on having the neat stair carpet taken up and turned end for end so that the worn place on the first step would be up the stair out of sight.

In all these preparations Thurly helped, cheerfully, whenever he was at home: taking down the muslin curtains from the parlor windows, putting them up again after they were washed and starched and ironed like new; dusting the globe of the ceiling electric light, to save his mother climbing on a step ladder; chopping raisins, nuts, citron and lemon peel; beating eggs, and stirring the batter with strong firm strokes in rhythm.

Hesba, goggleless, and really pretty with her straight hair waved softly about her face, went about as practically as ever.

The day before the wedding she and her Edward were in the city selecting a few things for their journey. Coming out from the store in the late afternoon they came upon Tasha Endicott who had driven down to the shopping district on an errand that she did not care to trust to anyone else.

Slipping out to her car when her errand was done, hoping to avoid meeting any of her acquaintances, she came face to face with Hesba accompanied by a meek young man bearing packages, piled high almost up to his shy gray eyes.

Tasha was about to pass with merely a nod when Hesba reached out a detaining hand.

"Oh, it's you!" she cried, "Anastasia! I'm so glad I met you. We were just talking about you. I was saying it was a pity I couldn't see you and tell you how much that linen shower meant to me. I don't expect to get any other wedding presents, and to have that one so grand, just made up for all the rest!"

"Oh, that's quite all right!" smiled Tasha, anxious

only to get away from this impossible girl who was about to marry Thurly Macdonald. She almost wished she had not sent the linen if she had to be thanked for it.

"Oh, don't go yet!" cried Hesba, as Tasha backed away, "I want to introduce you to my fiancé, Mr. Stebbins."

"I'm pleased to meet you," stammered out Hesba's Edward, with an awkward bow, and an attempt to remove his hat, which sent the packages flying in every direction, while the color mounted painfully purple in his already pink countenance.

Tasha had opportunity to recover her poise while they were picking up the packages. Mr. Stebbins was rescuing his hat which had fallen off as he stooped to get the last bundle from the gutter where a truck was about to pass over it. There was a light of eagerness in her eyes, however, as she spoke to Hesba with sudden cordiality in her tone:

"Did you say this gentleman was your fiancé?"

"Yes. Didn't I tell you his name when I wrote you? I thought I did. I intended to. Edward has wanted to meet you and thank you too for the linen. Haven't you, Edward?"

Edward ducked an embarrassed assent which bade fair to start another avalanche of bundles.

"And you can't think how sorry I was you had to refuse to be my maid of honor. Of course I understood when you had an engagement with your father and you couldn't come. But I was disappointed. You see there's going to be nobody there but Edward's brother and the Macdonalds and I kind of wanted some other girl or someone I could sort of call my own friend. Of course, though, I know you wouldn't feel like doing it now, though you have come back unexpectedly. It wouldn't look right so soon after a funeral. I understand."

Tasha caught the childish wistfulness in the other girl's eyes, the girl who had grown strangely young without her glasses, and paused. Some impulse stirred within her, an impulse she did not in the least understand.

"Why," she said thoughtfully, "why—I suppose I could. It wouldn't be at all public of course. No outsiders there. I don't know what difference it could possibly make to anybody. If you want it so much I'll come."

"Oh, would you?" exclaimed Hesba excitedly. "Say that would be just dandy!" and her face lit up with delight.

"Very well," said Tasha, "I'll come. At noon did you say? Where is it to be?"

"Oh, at the house of course. I haven't anywhere else, and Grandma is making me a wedding cake! I certainly am pleased. Thurly is going to marry us, of course. We're going to visit my home on our wedding trip and go right to his new job afterwards."

Tasha looked at the colorless young man with a wondering glance. To think of him in the light of a husband! And yet, there was kindness in the good gray eyes behind the yellow lashes, and a certain kind of shy dignity. Perhaps there might be worse lots in the world than marrying him.

"What shall I wear?" asked Tasha.

"Oh, just what you think best. Of course I suppose you'll think you ought to wear black now."

"Oh, no," said Tasha smiling. "Lucia wouldn't have wanted that. She hated mourning things. And I never could see why a color made any difference."

"Well, that's real sensible," agreed Hesba. "Say, then—wear something bright if you don't mind. It's kind of like having the sun shine on your wedding day, sort of good luck. I'll tell you what. Wear that dress you had your picture taken in down at Palm Beach. You know, the one with the rose on the shoulder. You look sweet in that. You've got it yet, haven't you?"

A wave of color went over Tasha's cheek.

"Yes, I've got it yet but—it's rather—soiled."

"Oh, that won't make any difference. Just put it on as it is. I'd like to see how it really looks."

"All right!" said Tasha. "I'll be there about eleven. Good bye," and she got into her car and drove away.

But something was singing in Tasha Endicott's

heart as she threaded her way among traffic, and planned how she would get out the little rose colored silk from its white box in her treasure chest that had been under lock and key ever since the storm.

"I'm not going to tell Thurly and Grandma she's coming," announced Hesba as they watched Tasha's car out of sight. "I'll just say I'm bringing another guest and that will do. Then I can surprise them."

"They might not like it," protested Edward.

"They'll like it all rightie!" said Hesba, taking her share of the bundles and stalking away by his side.

So she told Marget Macdonald that she was having another girl come, and Marget suspected nothing, but said it was all right of course, and the morning of the wedding day dawned.

At eleven o'clock sharp Tasha drove up to the Macdonald house and parked her car. There was a pretty color in her cheeks that was not put on, and her eyes were sparkling. This was going to be more interesting than anything she had done in a long time!

Thurly had gone out for some salted nuts for the feast, for Marget had overheard Hesba saying that people had them nowadays at all functions. Hesba had sent Edward after a bouquet for the maid of honor and one for herself. She had not intended bothering as much as that, but now that Tasha was really coming she wanted to do things right.

Marget was in the kitchen doing last things to the creamed chicken on the stove; the stuffed potatoes, the pan of puffy little white biscuits; and opening a glass of ruby jelly. The wedding cake stood on the dining-room table wreathed in myrtle from the side yard, and two tall pink candles in quaint glass candle sticks stood one on either side. Marget had been studying the magazine pictures and this was the result.

Tasha seeing no one about, came round to the side door and let herself into the dining room cautiously. She could hear Marget around the stove, and she stepped out to the kitchen, the sunshine from the window reaching sudden fingers and laying them on her cheek. She appeared to Marget like an angel.

"Well, I've come!" she announced joyously. "Can you lend me the little room off the dining room to slip into my dress. I'm to be bridesmaid and maid of honor all in one, did you know it?"

Marget turned from her cooking and her face was full of a great welcome.

"Oh, the bonnie wee lassie!" she exclaimed. "You have come to help us! What a fine, kind thing to do. Yes, go into the wee room and change your dress, and mayhap ye'll pit a wee tooch to the table. Ye ken how, finer than I."

So Tasha set the table for the wedding breakfast and then she slipped in and put on the little rose silk.

Marie had been fixing it all the evening before, cutting off the draggled draperies, fastening on a wisp more pink gauze, and sewing the rose on more firmly. Now the lovely color flowed round the girl and made her look like a flower.

She heard Thurly come into the kitchen with the nuts as she finished arranging her draperies, and casting a rosy gauze scarf about her shoulders, out she stepped in her gay attire, with one gold shoe, and one silken foot just touching the clean kitchen floor.

"I'm Cinderella," she said, "and I've only one shoe. Could you find me the other, do you think, Mr. Thurly Macdonald?"

Thurly suddenly wheeled about and faced her, his eyes full of wonder and joy.

"I can," said he. "I will."

"It's in the strong box, laddie. Ye aye ken where the key is keppit," called Marget.

Tasha leaned against the door and balanced herself on the one little tarnished gold shoe, touching just the tip of her silken stocking to the floor, and watched Marget happily.

"It's good to get back," she breathed with a happy sigh.

"And it's good to have ye back the day," said Marget beaming on her.

Then Thurly was back, and down like any gallant upon his knees putting on the little gold shoe, fastening its glittering buckle around the silken ankle.

Marget watched them furtively out of the tail of her eye and was glad, glad, glad! Hesba was being married the day and she *wasn't* marrying Thurly! Sing! Sing! Sing!

"I thought that would be about the way it would be," said a sudden sharp voice behind them, and there stood the bride, as if she had done it all, practical and plain-spoken as ever, arrayed in her sensible dark blue crêpe de chine, with a three dollar string of pearls that the groom had bought for her wedding gift.

Thurly looked up from his task, his face wreathed in smiles, and his color high. But he held on to the little foot till the slipper was fastened good and tight around the silken ankle.

Then with his brother, a mere boy, shyer than himself, the bridegroom entered the picture too, beaming over the flowers he had brought. He had got white sweet peas for the bride with a few blue forget-me-nots scattered among them, and a tight hard bunch of pink sweet peas for the attending lady. He fairly shone with pleasure in his purchase.

Tasha took the flowers, and somehow under her touch they spread themselves and became two bouquets worthy of the occasion. A little loosening here, a flower standing up there, the cord that held them cut, and a wide white ribbon produced from her belongings somewhere to tie around the bride's handful. It was a different thing altogether. Then she took her own, and transformed them, slung them over one arm as if they had been a great sheaf, and all the four stood round and laughed and looked at her.

"Come," said Thurly, letting go the little gold shoe at last and leaving it finally on the owner's foot. "Mother, aren't you ready? Take off that apron, and let's get on with this wedding. What's the use of standing around in the kitchen when there's all this grandeur in the parlor and dining room waiting for us?"

So the wedding procession formed, Thurly escorting his mother ahead, and seating her in the big chair at one side as had been arranged, the shy brother as best man following next, then Tasha, gorgeous as a flower plucked from some other world garden. With measured step in her little gold shoes she walked, her sweet peas held like a sheaf of wheat over her left arm. After her came Edward and Hesba arm in arm till they stood opposite to Thurly, with his small black book, and his fine black coat, looking as if the world had suddenly come all right for him.

Tasha listened to the solemn ceremony in Thurly's reverent tones, and wondered that in this world of disappointing people there had been yet left a man so fine as Thurly Macdonald. "Oh, Thurly, Thurly, Thurly!" her heart sang. And he was *not* marrying Hesba Hamilton after all!

But after the ceremony was over, and the groom turned and kissed his bride, Tasha caught a glimpse in those shy gray eyes that told what love might mean, even for a plain little shy commonplace man, and a round blunt little person like Hesba.

They ate the wonderful wedding breakfast, from chicken to wedding cake, all the way through, and then Mr. and Mrs. Edward Stebbins, amid a shower of good wishes, climbed into their Ford and started for their new life.

Thurly came back from bidding them farewell and, laughing, said to his mother:

"I still maintain that she's a huzzy! But perhaps that's the kind he needs."

Then he turned to Tasha, standing there in her pretty frock and her gold shoes.

"Now, Princess," said he, his eyes devouring her, "can you and I have a real talk?"

He took her over to the old couch and they sat down together.

"Now, tell me about it," he said, his eyes earnestly upon her, "you came back to us. Why did you do it, little Anastasia? Did you know what your coming would mean to me?"

Tasha was silent for a moment, letting her hands lie in the big clasp his had taken of hers. Then she lifted her eyes to his.

"I think," she said softly, "I think it's because I've been born again as you said I needed to be; and now I belong to your world!"

He gathered her close in his arms then and laid his lips against her hair. "Thank the Lord!" he breathed softly, with closed eyes. "Thank the Lord."

Marget, coming to find them, saw the lassie's face hid in her Thurly's coat, her fine gold hair against his cheek, and a little gold shoe resting confidently on the top of a big well polished black one. She trotted away with shining eyes.

"Now let the Lord be thankit!" she praised, as she put the rest of the wedding cake away in the cake box, wound the clock for the night, and did all the noisy little things she could think of to show she had no thought of such a thing as intruding into the parlor.

"Bless the bonnie lassie, she's come into her own at last!" she said aloud to the shining kitchen. "She's come back to health. She's *Anastasia!* Our little Anastasia in her fairy gold shoes."

Heartwarming Books
of
Faith and Inspiration

☐ THE GOSPEL ACCORDING TO PEANUTS
Robert L. Short   2070 ● $1.25

☐ NEW MOON RISING   Eugenia Price   2336 ● $1.50

☐ THE LATE GREAT PLANET EARTH   Hal Lindsey   2666 ● $1.75

☐ THE TRYST   Grace Livingston Hill   2705 ● $1.25

☐ MINE EYES HAVE SEEN THE GLORY   Anita Bryant   2833 ● $1.50

☐ THE GREATEST SALESMAN IN THE WORLD
Og Mandino   2930 ● $1.75

☐ I'VE GOT TO TALK TO SOMEBODY, GOD
Marjorie Holmes   2936 ● $1.75

☐ THE WOMAN AT THE WELL   Dale Evans Rogers   6436 ● $1.25

☐ LOVE AND LAUGHTER   Marjorie Holmes   7348 ● $1.25

☐ LIGHTHOUSE   Eugenia Price   7382 ● $1.25

☐ WHO AM I GOD?   Marjorie Holmes   7608 ● $1.25

☐ HOW TO TALK TO GOD WHEN YOU AREN'T
FEELING RELIGIOUS   Charles Smith   7712 ● $1.25

☐ THE TASTE OF NEW WINE   Keith Miller   7809 ● $1.25

☐ THEY CALL ME COACH   John Wooden   8146 ● $1.50

☐ DAWN OF THE MORNING   Grace Livingston Hill   8799 ● $1.25

Buy them at your local bookstore or use this handy coupon for ordering:

Bantam Books, Inc., Dept. HF, 414 East Golf Road, Des Plaines, Ill. 60016

Please send me the books I have checked above. I am enclosing $_____
(please add 35¢ to cover postage and handling). Send check or money order
—no cash or C.O.D.'s please.

Mr/Mrs/Miss_____

Address_____

City_____ State/Zip_____

HF—6/76

Please allow three weeks for delivery. This offer expires 6/77.